Something was moving, squirming, glistening black . . .

"Louise?" Dr. Litton choked as his wife's head elongated.

The bulging moved from forehead to chin and a dark shape squirmed from between her lips. It looked like a tiny black snake, licking the air. Louise's head bounced three times and the little snake seemed to right itself, planting its nose on the deck, becoming a frog's leg. Then the leg became a fat, black toad with snapping jaws and wet skin, squeezing itself out of her mouth just before the flesh of her neck split and another toad squirmed up from within, laced with tendrils of dark, fleshy slime.

"Oh, my God!" Dr. Litton gasped to see Louise's body completely disintegrate into ribbons, emitting struggling, bat-winged things that squirmed and chirped as chunks of her flesh slapped the deck and ran, rain-washed, over the side.

They'd eaten her! From the inside out!

Books by Gene Lazuta

THE SHINGLO (writing as Alex Kane)
BLOOD FLIES

BLOOD FLIES

GENE LAZUTA

CHARTER/DIAMOND BOOKS, NEW YORK

BLOOD FLIES

A Charter/Diamond Book/published by arrangement
with the author

PRINTING HISTORY
Charter/Diamond edition/August 1990

ISBN: 1-55773-374-0

Charter/Diamond Books are published by The Berkley Publishing Group,
200 Madison Avenue, New York, New York 10016.
The name ''CHARTER/DIAMOND'' and its logo are trademarks
belonging to Charter Communications, Inc.

PRINTED IN THE UNITED STATES OF AMERICA

10 9 8 7 6 5 4 3 2 1

To my younger, if not only,
brother Dan, "Mr. B-W, 1982."

PROLOGUE

July 2, 1987

10:49 A.M.

SOMEWHERE NEAR THE water, alone as the sky darkened, an old man stood firmly in the storm, hugging himself against the cold, northern air and watching the first squall of Lake Erie's new summer season churn Sharthington Bay. Overhead, lightning cracked an angular fracture that briefly defined his tangled hair and navy blue, knee-length seaman's jacket. Wind swelled the lake into foaming sheets that boiled over onto the beach, punctuating the rain's hiss with deep, mournful sighs, and sending up a frosty spray to glaze the man's eyes and melt his vision into milky streaks that he blinked away again and again.

There was a boat anchored about a quarter mile northeast of where he stood, and the man watched her with intent, excited interest as she rode the storm.

Just to the right of the boat, an island, built nearly a century before today, served as a breakwater at the mouth of the Sharthington River. The Black Tower, an eighty-foot-tall, stone-faced lighthouse, stood in featureless silhouette at the island's eastern tip, brooding, visible from just about any point on the beach, deep-rooted, and secretive.

As the old man watched, an immense, blurring cloud, darker than the storm that had turned this early morning into night, climbed up silently from the Tower's peak like smoke, lazily coagulating, stubborn against the stiff wind, bleeding down like a stain and washing over the tiny boat to extinguish its red and green running lights and blot it off the water.

At the sight, the old man smiled and withdrew from under his jacket a large, sealed jar, which had been his jealous secret for years, and which he'd hidden away from prying eyes and harsh questions until this one, priceless specimen of something that shouldn't have existed became his only companion, purpose, and obsession. It had cost him his left eye, left arm, and very nearly his life to secure, but its bloated, fragile body, bobbing amid bubbles with fogged, open eyes, an open mouth, and rough, misshapen skin, would make his dreams reality. It had been in the jar just a few hours short of forty years, and, much like the man himself, it was deformed by age and preserved by alcohol.

It was something like a toad in the jar—or at least it was about three quarters of one; the animal had lost a leg and part of its abdomen. It was very large, very fat, and very black, with swollen green eyes, white, peeling patches of blistering age in its mouth, and wings. . . .

Real wings.

From the ankle of each hind foot, to the wrist of each front claw, a thin, vein-mapped membrane stretched, forming wings that allowed the animal—when it was alive—to fly.

The needle-sharp teeth in its mouth, and the nasty, curved stingers on its tail, had allowed it to kill.

The old man glanced up, at the deep, black spot that bobbed behind rain on the water where the boat had been, and screwed the lid off the jar. Even in the wind the smell was thick and putrid. It swirled invisibly under his nose as he raised the jar to his lips, and took a tiny, careful sip.

There was magic here, magic in the jar.

His first sensation was the old alcohol's heat, grainy, prickling, and quick, spreading through him from his gut to his brain, tingling nerves in a nauseating wave and making his heart shudder. He salivated, licked back the urge to vomit, and resealed the jar before placing it down on the sand. His face was flushed, and he wiped one hand from forehead to chin, his cheek feeling hard—as if some muscle were sprained—his eyes burning.

It was happening.

He could feel it.

Blinking, he smiled wide, savoring the sensations of wind and water prickling his skin and satisfied that he had found the magic, just like the Indian said he would, if he tried hard enough, and waited long enough.

He'd found the magic.

At that moment, the *Get-A-Way*, a forty-foot, single-masted, white fiberglass sloop that slept two comfortably, and seven in a pinch, rocked on rough water and was pelted by heavy rain. Inside the cabin, Dr. Henry Litton and his wife, Louise, were sleeping—or at least Louise was sleeping. Dr. Litton was lying awake, staring at the ceiling, listening to the storm and to his boat.

During the night, he had set a second anchor off the bow to keep the *Get-A-Way* from drifting as she pivoted into the wind and denied the high waves her flanks. A small-craft advisory had sent her into the bay at two A.M., interrupting the Littons' first real vacation in fifteen years with a squall that was supposed to have come earlier, but that had started a little after seven. Now, at nearly eleven in the morning, it was as black as night outside, and the wind was strong. So far, this had turned out to be one bust of a vacation, and the storm was only the latest bump in a rough two weeks.

A rough two weeks? Dr. Litton thought as he watched a brass lantern swing overhead, throwing dancing shadows and producing tiny grinding sounds. This whole marriage has been one long, stormy cruise to someplace both Louise and I have forgotten we ever wanted to go. If it weren't for the kids, well . . .

Louise stirred and rolled over, pulling the sheet up and facing him so that her grey-brown hair lay tangled on her face.

Dr. Litton looked at her soft features, her plump shoulders, her wide mouth and high, Eastern-European cheeks.

God, I hate you, he thought, not for the first time. But I can't imagine a life without you in it. What a strange way to live. What an incredibly strange way to live for forty-four years!

He sat up.

As she rocked, the *Get-A-Way* made a million different sounds, and the doctor liked to believe that he could identify each one. But the bump he had just heard, intermingled with the rest of the creaks and groans of a straining craft, was unfamiliar, and—he didn't know why—vaguely threatening. It had come, muffled by an inch or so of teak deck, from directly over his head, and sounded like something loose, something heavy, and maybe—was it—*soft*? In weather like this, something loose could flop anywhere, tangling lines, maybe breaking windows, God knew what all.

It bumped again.

Soft?

"Nuts," Dr. Litton mumbled as he got out of bed and pulled on his yellow slicker.

Louise didn't stir; she could sleep through anything; concerts, picnics, family reunions, and, over the years, she had.

The doctor pulled the string that tightened the hood around his face and yanked out the batten that secured the main hatch. The hatch pulled from his hand, leaving him exposed to sudden blasts of icy rain that stung his face, and blurred his vision, as he climbed into the storm.

Gripping the slippery deck with his bare toes, he rolled his back against the cabin wall and faced away from the rushing air, feeling his slicker shudder and seeing, silhouetted against the sparkling lights of shore, the Black Tower, wavering insubstantial in the gloom and howl. Around him, the *Get-A-Way* was all but invisible; the sky and water met in one wash of darkness, and the boat's lines sang a metallic chant overhead. Carefully, he withdrew a flashlight from his slicker's pocket and snapped it on.

There was movement—large, fluid, animal movement, surrounding him, seeking shadow more quickly than his eyes could follow. As he swung the beam through the wind, making raindrops sparkle twenty at a time in a fleeting ball that hung before the flashlight like a tiny moon, he ran one hand over his face, pushing moisture from his eyes and blinking.

Nothing.

He could have sworn . . . they were as big as cats . . . black . . . hundreds, maybe thousands . . . on the deck . . . scuttling away from the light, scuttling back, into darkness, into the water. . . .

Impossible.

He grabbed a line, swung his weight forward, kept his knees bent, and began working his way aft, absorbing the angry swells with his legs.

Lightning cracked and the doctor froze, momentarily disoriented by the sheer quantity of light and awaiting the thunder's inevitable roar. When the roar came, the lake trembled and the wind picked up, producing a ghostly whine that drifted across the *Get-A-Way*'s bow like a wounded bird.

Dr. Litton's head snapped around and his flashlight beam searched the gloom. Something was moving on either side of the cabin, squirming, glistening black behind sheets of silver streaks, like tentacles from the depths, climbing up, into the windows that he had left open, just a crack, to let in the night air but hold out the rain.

The ghost whined again and the doctor knew that it wasn't the wind.

"Louise!" he shouted, his mouth filling with water as rain slapped his face and eyes. He couldn't move, couldn't make his legs remain firm as . . .

"Louise!"

Atop the cabin, just aft of the mast, was a hatch, three feet by two, hinged forward so that it opened fully to lie flat on the cabin roof. Louise, shadow-cut and shimmering in the flashlight's ray, her long hair soaked and wild, was climbing through that little opening, her arms working frantically for purchase on the slick deck, her beige, lace-frilled nightgown wet and hanging so that one of her breasts was revealed briefly before her head flopped forward and her hair washed everywhere.

"Louise?" Dr. Litton shouted again as he tried to make his fingers let go of the line he held.

His resolve was punctured as a flash of lightning defined the way Louise's body stiffened and rose with a jerk.

"Henry!" she screamed, her face turning automatically in the direction of his flashlight and then down, as if she intended to look right through the cabin's roof. "No, not there! Don't touch me there! Henry!"

As if someone large and determined were forcing her up into the storm, she spasmed, her head flopping as her arms dangled and her torso bent forward. Her head, just her head, was bouncing now, up and down on the cabin roof, producing a staccato rhythm of hollow pops that made the doctor wince. And then her face snapped up again, her mouth agape and her hair peeling in strings over her eyes.

Were those eyes open? Did they see her husband as he slid and fell, his legs pumping on the deck as he struggled to keep the flashlight focused while he groped for a line to hold? Did they see anything at all as bulges under her flesh puffed out her cheeks and strained the tender fibers holding those eyes in place?

"Louise?" Dr. Litton choked as his wife's head elongated. He wasn't trying to approach her anymore.

The bulging moved from her forehead to her chin and a dark shape squirmed out from between her lips. In the flashlight's bouncing beam, it looked like a tiny black snake, licking the air. As the doctor inched back, closer to the rudder, Louise's head bounced twice, three times, and the little snake seemed to right itself, planting its nose on the deck and becoming a frog's leg. Then, horribly, the leg became a fat, black toad with snapping jaws and wet skin, squeezing itself out of her mouth just before the flesh of her neck split and another toad squirmed up from within, laced with tendrils of dark, fleshy slime.

"Oh, my God!" Dr. Litton gasped as he stumbled back again, slipped, caught himself, and turned in time to see Louise's body completely disintegrate into ribbons, emitting struggling, bat-winged things that squirmed and chirped as chunks of her flesh slapped the deck and ran, rain-washed, over the side.

They'd eaten her! From the inside out! They'd crawled in through those little cracks that he'd left in the cabin's windows and they'd eaten his wife before his very eyes!

Something dark and fast flew past his ear.

SSSSSSsssssss!

He gasped and spun, raising the flashlight, crooking one arm across his face, and cowering.

SSSSSSsssssss!

"No! Leave me alone!" he screamed, swinging the flashlight like a club, stumbling, trying to find a clear path amid quivering lines that stretched from the deck into the wind and rain overhead.

SSSSSSsssssss!

"Help!"

The lake was absolutely dark over the *Get-A-Way*'s edge. Thunder roared. The boat rocked. Toads hopped close, brushing his bare feet with their wings, hissing. The doctor looked back one time, briefly, to where the runny mass that had been his wife of forty-four years hung atop the cabin, crossed himself, held his breath, and leapt into the safety of the waiting waves.

He was so close to shore that he knew he'd make it in all right, even without a life jacket.

He was wrong.

The last image to be imprinted on his mind was the glowing circle of murky, bubbling water where he was to land. Illuminated by his flashlight, that circle was surrounded by a bumpy mass of floating, waiting eyes.

Under the Black Tower, there was a stone-block room, with a fifty-foot ceiling, a pool of water half the length of the dirt floor, and a huge, oak-beam door that locked from the outside.

The chamber was ill-lit but not entirely dark. Two kerosene lanterns, suspended, one on either side of the exit, flickered bravely while vainly confronting dampness and chill. The room had been gouged into the very base of Black Island, at the bottom of the lake, completely underwater, and there was a hole in the center of the ceiling, three feet in diameter, matching the holes that bordered the perimeter of the room just where the walls and ceiling met.

As silent bubbles broke the surface of the pool, circular

ripples groped their way to the water's edge. The bubbles
drew the dark surface into a brief swelling that bulged, broke,
and finally slid apart, revealing the first of the struggling
toads, pulling and flapping at Dr. Litton's dead body.

The corpse, open eyes caked with black, lake-bottom grit,
mouth and nose spewing water, arms flopping in unnaturally
limber ways, was covered with pieces of aquatic plants and
with mud. When the body was fully on dry ground, the toads
hopped and croaked, faster, louder, until their grunts and
burps came so quickly that they blended into a deep rumble
and, then, a buzzing roar that vibrated the air and bounced
off the rock, finding its way into the tunnels along the ceiling's edge.

After a moment, the song was answered from within the
gloomy openings, first by a similar, though more tentative,
buzz, then the new singers appeared. Catching the oily yellow
kerosene light, moist, amber-colored eyes glistened in each
tunnel's mouth as thousands of the things hung back in the
shadows, burping, buzzing, viewing the kill but not daring
to move into the light.

Along one wall, near the door, five layers of sagging
wooden shelves reached from floor to ceiling. They had once
been used to store boxes of notes, some equipment, preserved specimens in jars, and bound volumes of theories and
observations. These things were now scattered on the ground,
trampled.

The shelves were empty now, except for two, which held
the body of a man, Clay Mallard, a fifty-year-old Sharthington resident who had rowed *Leviathan*, his little boat, out to
Black Island the previous morning to fish and drink beer, and
a nineteen-year-old, out-of-town girl named Bonnie, who had
gone swimming three nights back and who hadn't returned.
In both cases, there'd been quite a bit of screaming, but eventually they'd been taken through the same underwater passage
as had the doctor. Now they rested on the shelves farthest
from the door, naked and bloated, a greenish hue covering
their skin, their throats swollen with pockets of gelatinous,
white eggs.

With a great snap and grunt, the leader bull grabbed at Dr.

Litton's shirt, and, with the aid of the rest of the hunters, began dragging the body toward the wall. As the secret creatures watched from above, the doctor was positioned amid the bone chips and fossilized remains of the animals, men, women, and children who had gone before. Under the lanterns' dancing shadows, the doctor's body was manipulated into place, his head tilted back, his mouth forced open, and his face covered by a fat female, who positioned herself to add another pocket of eggs to this newest part of the nest.

The old man's head swam and pounded, his mouth felt dry and his throat was tight as he flexed his right hand under his nose, focused, and came slowly back to himself from his vision of the kill. It was like a dream, almost: details in his skull and memories in his bones.

He was facing the Tower and breathing hard, because of what he had just seen, and simply because he had seen it.

The legends were true.

They were true!

Forty years he'd waited for this day! Forty years he'd waited for the time to be right, for the Shawnita to be ready—strong and developed, amassed in a killing swarm that could be led by someone who knew how.

Forty years!

"Hello, Joshua," a voice said, threading itself through the slicing wind and finding the old man's attention.

Joshua turned his head, squinted, and tried to organize the images and sensations he'd experienced in the past few hours, and the past few moments in particular.

"Joshua?" a voice said again, closer.

"Who?" the old man began, his voice a tiny gasp as the form of a man, taller than he and much younger, wearing a baseball cap that, even in the gloom, showed CAT in bright yellow letters, took shape from the rain.

"You? No!" Joshua said, his concern immediately focusing on the jar, which lay in the wet sand, half-hidden and looking like trash. He thought of that jar, of everything he had gone through to keep its secret, trembled, pressed his teeth together, and hissed, "Fuck you, Boyle!" before turning and starting into a stumbling run down the beach.

"Come on, Josh!" Ronnie Boyle, who had parked his Chevy van almost a mile up the road so that no one would recognize it near the scene of a crime, called with a grin as he broke into an easy, long-legged stride. "Ain't you glad to see me?"

Joshua didn't look back, but ran unevenly along the water's edge, his seaman's jacket flapping, his right arm stiffly protruding for balance.

As Boyle followed, wet sand sucked at his shoes, making his legs feel heavy and his steps short. He moved carefully in the gloom, not pushing himself, taking it slow, knowing that Joshua didn't have anywhere to go. With his predatory gaze intent on the old man's hobbling figure, and his fists clenched hard at his sides, he was anticipating the thrill of committing his very first murder.

PART ONE

Cold . . . Rages

One

July 2, 1987

8:05 A.M.

"ACCIDENTS HAPPEN. PEOPLE trip. They fall down stairs sometimes," said the cop with the perfect tan and tobacco-stained teeth just before he and his partner threw Pete down a flight of battered, linoleum-covered steps. The linoleum was burnt orange, with white swirls, and the steps had metal runners on their edges.

Pete made a terrible racket as he fell, his elbows and hands slamming the walls as he tried to grab something, anything, the runners cutting his arms, one knee, and the back of his head. His head bled so much that, by the time he was locked in his cell, his tee shirt and jeans were thickly blood speck-led, starting with a soaked ring around his neck and spread-ing to dots on his white running shoes.

By morning, the bleeding had stopped, but the cell floor was a mess.

At about four A.M., he had vomited into a seatless toilet; by four-thirty, he had been convinced that he had a concus-sion; at five, he had changed his mind; by six, he wasn't sure.

A cop brought him cold coffee and a doughnut at seven.

"Hey, hell's angel. Breakfast."

Pete dropped the doughnut in the toilet but drank the cof-fee.

Outside, beneath a dark morning sky of swollen clouds and misty rain, three policemen were throwing a canvas tarp over a rowboat called *Leviathan*. The boat had been brought in earlier, and the police were placing it on the grass behind the station, just in front of Pete's basement-level window.

Their uniforms were strange: powder-blue short-sleeve shirts, white Bermuda shorts, powder-blue knee socks, and white shoes. Except for the heel-shaped patches on their shoulders that read, SHARTHINGTON OHIO POLICE, and their guns, they looked like porters on a cruise ship.

"What happened to you?" the guy in the next cell asked when he awoke.

Pete ignored him.

When he had first been thrown into his cell, the other man had watched blearily with an uncomprehending half-smile. Sharthington was a lakefront town and, as such, had more than its share of drunks who came to drive their boats into things.

"Don't I get a phone call?" Pete shouted through the window.

"Don't fuck around," the man in the next cell suggested amiably.

Pete faced him and frowned.

The man sat down and ate his doughnut.

"Christ!" Pete said, dropping himself on his cot and looking through the open door that led out of the tank and into a darkened hallway.

That hall, like a deep, lightless tunnel, seemed invitingly familiar, and Pete's large, inquisitive, green eyes settled on it without blinking.

His eyes had always been his most prominent feature, next to his hair, which was sandy brown—almost blond in the summer—and shoulder length. His mother said that his eyes were like a dog's—not like a little dog's, all curiosity motivated by fear; and not like a friendly dog's, affectionately waiting for a treat; but like a big dog's, interested, unafraid, and maybe just a bit too honest. Flashing with whatever emotion he felt automatically, they displayed his deepest secrets to whomever took the time to look, spoke more eloquently in silence than he could ever hope to speak with words, and made it impossible for him to lie. They were an honest man's eyes; eyes that seemed to bring out the best in women, and the worst in men; they were the eyes of a poet, perched precariously over a scientist's face, and, now, they were locked on the hallway, as memories came.

Maybe it was the bump on his head, or the bleeding, but for an instant the hall resembled a part of the dream that had brought him a quarter of the way across the country, and smack into trouble with the Sharthington Police.

The first time he had had the dream was the night of his twenty-sixth birthday party. He was drunk, and exhausted, and when the nightmare came he bolted upright in bed, and then took an Alka-Seltzer.

That was two weeks and two days ago.

"Two weeks and two days?" he mumbled, rubbing the knot on the back of his head and feeling a rough, torn patch of flesh with ragged edges that were sickeningly numb.

"Two weeks and two days ago I was twenty six; add two and six, you get eight, which is two fours; four is two plus two."

He smiled humorlessly and stiffly bent his swollen elbow, feeling something like sand grinding in the joint.

"And now I've got two broken bones. It's got to be an omen."

He had had the dream again the night after his party, and again the next, and every night since. He wasn't the kind of person who would allow a dream to bother him. And he especially wasn't the kind of man who could be driven away from his home, his family, and his third year of graduate school by a nightmare—and, even as he was allowing the dream to make him do all those things, he joked, shook his head, and laughed. Eventually, and to his own wonder, the dream had demonstrated an incredible power over him, which he found amusing, and irresistible.

He didn't know exactly what kind of creature he was in his nightmare because he could never see all of himself, but whatever he was, he had a lot of arms and legs, with long, delicate pink fingers and deep, rippling folds in his flesh. He was very big, and he was buried in dark, warm earth, where he was happy.

Suddenly a shovel blade started cutting earth over him with

abrupt plunges slicing mud and terrible clanks of breaking rock. Confined in his grave, he tried to block the blade with his puffy, soft hands, throwing them up to guard his face reflexively without stopping to think that they were no match for steel.

The shovel came down again, and again, and . . .

He screamed, plunging his injured hand into his mouth and tasting blood, a lot of blood, bubbling down his throat and surging in rhythm with his pounding heart. His fingers were wet stumps on his tongue, and sharp, sensitive slivers of broken bone scraped his teeth.

But still the shovel came!

Cutting off his fingers wasn't enough.

Whoever was up there, whoever wanted to dig him up, slammed the blade down again and Pete grimaced, pulling his injured hand free and listening as grit ground between his teeth. Rolling himself over, he began tunneling away, but his back was held exposed by the hard clay and he screamed as the shovel slashed a bloody smile into his flesh. At that same instant, the ground beneath him gave way and he fell, spinning in dark air and landing in warm, muddy water.

Above him, the shovel pocked and probed, its filthy blade licking the mud as he turned to find an incredible light glowing somewhere down the tunnel very far from where he lay. The light—his savior—was calling to him, begging him to follow, filling him with a terrible sense of impending doom and telling him, in some intimate, urgent way, that he could prevent something bad from happening if he would only come, right away.

He tried to move and . . .

That was it.

He'd awaken each morning with a sticky, uncomfortable feeling deep in his chest that he needed to do something, needed to follow the light, but that he didn't know how, where, or why. He'd mope around, staring into space and recalling the sensations of warmth, pain, and longing from the previous evening, anticipating the night, and dreading the dream.

At the end of the first week, he was haggard, irritable, and frightened. At the end of the second week, he knew that he had to go west. He didn't know why, but he could feel the call of the horizon, taking it to mean that he needed a vacation. After packing up his saddlebags, he set out from New York on his motorcycle, denying to himself why he had done it, and amused by his own impulsiveness. At dinner time on his second day away from home, he saw a sign on the freeway that said, WELCOME TO SHARTHINGTON, YOUR SUMMER TOWN. Sharthington was a place he had visited once or twice, years ago, but had since forgotten. Seeing that sign, though, he somehow felt as if he had arrived.

Arrived?

Arrived where?

Sharthington, Ohio?

No one ever arrived in Sharthington, he thought from his cot; arriving implied the attainment of a goal, and he couldn't imagine anyone purposefully setting out for *Your Summer Town*. You didn't arrive in Sharthington; you wound up there.

The place was a crumbling mess that had hit hard times when the Kannon Fishing Company, which Pete's father owned, pulled out, leaving half the population unemployed. Almost everybody else worked out of town and lived in the Lagoons, where they docked their boats and parked their BMWs, and gathered the resentment of the people who couldn't get past the security guards to the beach.

He'd spent one night in town, and been arrested.

If they'd left my saddlebag alone, they wouldn't have had a reason to lock me up, he thought, running his tongue over his teeth in search of any that might be loose.

Hell, I didn't even hit the kid, although in another minute or two I might have killed him.

Killed him!

Me?!

Amazing.

The kid, Ronnie Boyle, was probably nineteen, starvation thin, with beef-jerky biceps that stuck out of a sleeveless black tee shirt. An orange baseball cap with the word CAT written across the front covered his curly black hair, and his face was so acne scarred, and so sunburned, that it looked like alligator hide. He had worked his way through the combination weekend/holiday crowd—the Fourth of July was coming up— over to where Pete sat admiring Lori, the barmaid, and had taken a seat on Pete's right side.

Lori had medium-short blond hair, big blue eyes, a gentle pout to her full lips, and a practiced ''ain't interested'' look. The sparkling butterfly decal on the front of her yellow tee shirt was elongated by her generous figure, and when she moved Pete was enchanted.

Like all the guys in town, Ronnie Boyle was in love with her.

Pete had spent the day lying in the sun on the Black Beach, which was named after his great grandfather, William Noah Blackwell, and which was where he'd slept the previous evening. He'd come into town looking for a place to eat, and, on Center Street, had heard loud, country music pouring through two open barn doors under a red, white and blue neon sign that read, BILLY'S COLD RAGES. It had said Cold Beverages, but part of it was broken.

At midnight, after he'd been drinking for nearly two hours, the band took a break and an old man stumbled into Ronnie Boyle, almost knocking him off his bar stool.

And the trouble began.

''God damn it!'' Boyle said, shoving back at the old man and straightening himself. Suddenly, there were three more young men grinning and clutching cigarettes nearby.

The old man had been tall once, but he was stooped now, and the left sleeve of his dark blue, knee-length seaman's jacket was empty. When Boyle pushed him, he flinched, as if he had expected worse, but his face came up to confront the boy with a look of absolute hatred.

''Pardon,'' he said coldly, and Boyle hesitated.

Pete turned and saw the old man's face at the same time that the Michelob sign behind the bar flashed red.

His long white hair stood up, as if electrified, suddenly bleeding pink under the light and framing his features with an animated tangle that squirmed at the slightest breeze. He was sunburned—like everyone else in town—so that when the pink light hit him he washed an eerie pale. Unlike Boyle, he needed a shave, and when he spoke the left side of his mouth remained partially closed, which made Pete think that he must have had a stroke. His left eye was blind, gleaming dully when he paused before focusing his attention on Lori as if Boyle had ceased to exist.

"Got something for back o' the bar," he said, producing from under his jacket a battered ship's lantern, which he gingerly set down directly in front of Pete, who apparently did not exist either.

Behind the bar, mixed with the dozens of liquor bottles, was a jumbled display of nautical mementoes, each bearing the name of the regular who had donated it and the date it had been given up, marked in ink somewhere on the object's surface. There were ship's clocks, dead eyes, broken planks, fishing nets, and cork floats. And, suspended in mid-leap over the cash register was a gold, six-foot, carved wooden greyhound that, according to the legend scrawled on its belly, was all that was ever found of a ship that had gone down during the great Fourth of July storm of '69.

The lantern was red.

"You know I can't trade, Josh," Lori said, at the same time drawing a glass of beer for which the old man made no move to pay.

"Pardon ain't good enough," Boyle said, and his friends grinned harder.

"It's off the *Emma*," the old man said, reaching for his beer.

"I said that pardon ain't good enough," Boyle said, sliding off his stool.

Lori had lifted the lantern and was holding it up, as one of the boys standing behind the old man poked him in the ribs and said, "Pardon, Josh."

Joshua, who had been lifting his glass to his lips, flinched, jerking around and knocking Boyle's Miller bottle from his hand. It crashed to the floor with dreadful finality.

The three boys giggled.

The old man looked at the golden puddle at his feet.

"Now, Ronnie . . ." Lori began.

"You owe me a beer," Boyle said, unmistakably uninterested in the drink.

"Here," Lori said, drawing a draft and placing it on the bar.

"Got no money," the old man mumbled.

"You owe me a beer, Joshua," Boyle said into the hush.

When Pete slapped a twenty down on the bar, he thought he was putting an end to the whole problem. But he wasn't.

Boyle snatched up the lantern and jangled it on its handle, saying, "This is worth a beer."

"Damn it, Ronnie!" Lori shouted, heading around to the front of the bar.

"It's off the *Emma*!" the old man added, his face twisting into an angry knot.

"Hey!" Pete said, sliding off his stool and sending it clattering to the floor.

"What do you think?" Boyle asked one of the grinning boys as he pitched the lantern to him.

"Looks like a trade," the boy said, rolling the lantern in his hands.

"Leave it be!" Joshua shouted helplessly.

The boy with the lantern was already hurrying down the bar, and the three others were laughing and moving to follow. Joshua stumbled and was knocked into the bar railing by Boyle as he trotted toward the door. He flailed for a moment, and Pete realized that his left arm was not in its sleeve because it was paralyzed.

Someone was laughing. Then someone cheered. And then everyone was laughing and cheering.

Pete emerged into the parking lot and found that darkness lay overhead like a roof supported by the flood lights perched atop four poles, one at each corner of the lot. White haze bathed Joshua as he stumbled and swayed, his good arm grabbing for the lantern and clawing the air as one of the boys waved it within his reach and pulled it away again.

"Come on, Josh!" one boy said.

They had formed a circle.

"You ain't trying!" Ronnie Boyle said, his face glowing

under the floods and his teeth flashing as he plucked the lantern from the air and pitched it away.

"You can do better than that!"

The old man remained silent, lunging for the lamp each time one of the boys would toss it, and then following it again as it took flight. His hair blew wildly and his long navy coat flapped about his knees, tangling between his legs and making him stumble, only to tangle again after he had released himself.

"Come on, Josh! It's right here!"

There were people behind Pete now, but they only added their own insults, creating a din that encouraged the boys to move faster.

"Stop it!" Lori screamed as the old man stumbled and landed on his side.

Rolling to his knees, he lunged after the lantern as it passed, and landed on his chin in the gravel.

Pete was running.

He headed for his huge Harley-Davidson—a 1947 museum piece, painted black and modified with a lot of new chrome— parked at the lot's edge, under one of the corner lamps, jumped into the saddle, fired the engine, and spun the tire. Throwing dust and grass in a wicked spray, he leaned hard into a tight circle and pulled the throttle as the front wheel lifted and the threads on the back tire dug in and rocketed him forward. In a second, he was level and picking up speed, directly at the circle of motion under the hazy parking lot lights.

The boys spread into a wider circle, breathing hard, one still laughing but the others wide-eyed and holding their sides as Pete roared into their midst and stopped the bike with a screech and a cloud of dust. He lifted a three-foot length of heavy chain and held it in his fist, using his other hand to gun the engine, which sent a black wave of smoke into the crowd huddled in Rage's doorway.

"Give it to him!" he shouted, his voice quivering.

The bike lurched forward two feet and sat trembling.

A siren wafted from the darkness, lights began flashing, and the crowd made a disappointed rumble.

Pete ignored the lights, and the siren, and the people, concentrating instead on the pimpled boy whose cap had CAT written across the front. He made the bike jump again and fingered the chain.

"Last time. Give it to him!"

Joshua was kneeling in the gravel, bleeding from a rough patch on his chin, his hair falling over his face and his coat gray with dust.

As a policeman stepped into the circle of light, the boy said, "Sure. Why didn't you just ask nice to start with?"

He pitched the lantern at the old man and it landed on the rocks with a tinkling glitter. The globe smashed and spread itself over the gravel, the wire handle twisted and popped, the lantern rolled a foot and stopped, gleaming in shards amid the stones.

Joshua looked at it, but didn't move.

"All right, mister. Put the chain down," a policeman said, reaching for his gun.

Lori was standing under a naked light in Rages's entrance, surrounded by an undulating blob of flitting black bugs. Even from where he stood, Pete could see that she was crying.

"Drop it!" a close voice said as Pete's eyes locked with hers.

The motorcycle's engine died, someone yanked the chain from his hand, and someone else pulled him off the bike. The next thing he knew, he was in the back of a cruiser, with a man in the passenger's seat reading him his rights and a cop on the driver's side offering addendums like, "Yeah, the right to remain silent, or lose your teeth."

And Lori stood, looking right at him the whole time, even after everyone else had gone back inside.

"I never even touched him," Pete finally said, prompting the cop behind the steering wheel to silently lift his right arm and dangle the plastic bag of pot that had been hidden in the Harley's saddlebag.

"Oh, shit," Pete whispered, falling back on the seat and closing his eyes as the car started to move.

They took him to the station, searched him, took his picture, his fingerprints, his wallet and wristwatch, asked him questions, and traded jokes between themselves.

NAME:	BLACKWELL, PETER WILLIAM
DATE OF BIRTH:	JUNE 16, 1961
HEIGHT:	6 FEET, 1 INCH
WEIGHT:	198 POUNDS
HAIR:	SANDY BROWN, SHOULDER LENGTH

"Mr. Blackwell, you're being charged with public intoxication, disorderly conduct, intent to commit assault with a deadly weapon, and possession of an illegal substance," said the cop with the perfect tan, who had driven the cruiser, when the preliminaries were finished.

Then he explained how much he hated out-of-towners who thought they could just roll in and do whatever they wanted all fucking summer long, and then he seemed to get really angry, and then he and his squirrely little partner—who Pete thought should be playing the banjo on the back of a pickup truck somewhere—threw him down the stairs and left him in his cell to "Sober up."

Now, he was sober, and maybe scared.

"Hey, how about my one phone call?" he shouted out the window at the men who had tied Leviathan down. "Hey."

"What'd you do to my floor?" someone asked.

"I'm supposed to get a phone call," Pete said when he turned to find the same tanned cop standing close to the bars of his cell. The anger that had been building while he was alone had now been deflated.

"Come here," the cop ordered, curling his index finger under his nose several times but keeping his eyes on the bloody concrete.

Pete swallowed, glanced at his feet, and stepped forward.

"Closer," the cop smiled.

Pete took another step and the policeman lunged, shooting

his hands through the chipped yellow bars and grabbing the front of Pete's stained tee shirt.

"Now," he said through a teeth-grinding grin as he leaned back and slammed Pete into the bars once before his other hand slapped down to the young man's groin and squeezed.

Pressed flat against steel, his face turned to the left and his eyes shut as pain climbed up from between his legs, Pete was silent.

"I don't like you!" the cop shouted, his mouth so close that the words hurt. "Understand?"

Pete tried to speak, but couldn't.

The policeman squeezed harder and slammed him into the steel with a sharp clang.

"Understand?"

Pete nodded a little.

"You better disappear when they let you go," the cop continued. "When you walk out of here I want you to ride your fucking motorcycle out of my fucking town!"

Pete opened his eyes carefully, but before he could speak the policeman pushed him so that he stumbled and fell. When he landed, the area of his left kidney hit the toilet.

The cop slid the cell door open and placed his hands on his hips, saying, "Remember, no matter what anyone tells you, when they let you go, keep going! Now, Mr. Kyrik wants to see you."

Pete got up stiffly.

Kyrik was the man he had been wanting to call all along.

Blackwell? Lori thought, feeling the tingle of caffeine jitters—too much coffee—on the back of her neck and suppressing a yawn—no sleep—as the bright yellow center stripes on Route 11 flashed under the hood of her car. A Blackwell in Sharthington? I'll be damned!

It was going on eight A.M. and she'd been driving more or less nonstop since closing time at Rages, which was supposed to be two, but which was usually closer to three-thirty or four. (At two, Frank, Rages's new owner, would shut down the beer taps and set-up bottles of Seagrams along the bar. If a cop should wander in after hours, it was understood that any-

one handy was supposed to grab a bottle and hold it, as if
they'd brought it in themselves.)

Along the roadside, scrawny trees tangled in a formless,
grey mass under thick clouds, brooding in the dark and
smothering the sun, which, Lori knew, was up there somewhere. With large intermittent drops that hit the windshield
hard and climbed the glass in long, convoluted feelers, it was
starting to rain.

"What a fucking day," she said aloud, turning up the radio
when Bruce Springsteen started singing—she liked Bruce a
lot, which would have shocked her mom even more than hearing her swear—and, yawning outright, she drifted over to the
right lane as the *Your Summer Town* sign flashed headlight-
silver to her left.

Lori Sterling was the twenty-five-year-old daughter of an
auto worker who'd died when the school bus in which he and
his family were riding one Sunday was hit by a train at an
unmarked crossing, sending a quarter of the Grand Valley
United Church of Christ's congregation straight to heaven and
providing the impetus for the erection of a pair of black and
white automatic gates that everyone had to drive around to
beat the trains. Her mom still carried the scars, but Lori,
who was three at the time, had no memory of the event at
all, nor of her older brother, Danny, who died with his dad.
She had no memory of it, but the accident left her changed;
it left her tough.

At home, she was known as the girl who had out-toughed
a train.

When she was twenty-three, over her mother's strenuous
objections, Lori had moved to Sharthington, using as her reason a desire to get a better job than the one she'd held at
Lawson's, without expressing verbally her belief that, because it was so small, Lakeland Grand, the town where she'd
lived out the whole of her life so far, was strangling her.

But, after two years away from home, she was just about
ready to move again, because Sharthington made her feel so
weird, so strangely stiff—as if something bad-tempered and
large had been watching her, wherever she was, whatever she
was doing, since her first day there. And, seeing the way

those people in Rages had laughed when that asshole, Ronnie Boyle, went after a poor, crippled old drunk . . . well, that was the last straw.

For her, Sharthington was history.

She'd worked out the rest of the night, demanded what money she had coming, and quit, on the spot, infuriating Frank . . .

"Who gives a shit?"

. . . and cutting off her only source of income . . .

"Big deal!"

. . . leaving her broke, except for the eighty-eight bucks Frank had grudgingly forked over—less the two-fifty he'd deducted for all the potato chips she ate—and with an apartment full of second-hand furniture and a red 1976 Chevy Monza with a hole in the floor on the driver's side so big that she'd stuffed a two-by-four under her seat so that she wouldn't fall through it.

And now she was on her way to the police station, feeling ragged and riding the high of a caffeine buzz, to help out a complete stranger named Peter Blackwell because he'd stepped in and gotten involved in a bad situation simply because it was the right thing to do.

And because he reminded her of Robin Hood. All he needed, she thought with a smile, was a moustache and green panty hose.

At the corner of Center and Ridge, a yellow light blinked solo in the dark.

"Blackwell?" she said, rolling the word over her tongue slowly. "What the hell is a Blackwell doing around here?"

As Pete walked up the same stairs he had fallen down just a few hours before, thunder shook the pale-blue walls, and Lenny Kennedy, the tanned cop—nice name, Pete thought when he noticed the ID badge on the man's breast pocket—grabbed him by the arm and hustled him into the lobby toward a door that read, LIEUTENANT D. DANKO on its frosted glass. Outside, wind was bending trees and spraying rain into sheets that splattered windows like slaps. Lightning flashed and the lights in the station flickered.

Lieutenant Danko's door opened.

Thunder roared.

Randolph Kyrik appeared from the dark office, his white shirt, pants, and shoes precisely defined by the hard white light in the hall, making him look almost luminous. He was an old man, seventy, maybe seventy-five, with spindly arms and large, vein-mapped hands that he moved slowly, like flippers. His white hair was cropped short, except for his eyebrows, which were bushy and unkempt. His face was smooth. From the top of his forehead to the bottom of his chin he didn't have a single wrinkle—not one. His neck was pouchy and loose, but his face was smooth.

Pete stopped dead, expecting Kennedy to push him. But the officer had disappeared.

Lightning flashed again.

Kyrik shook his head and said sadly, "Son, I hope what they've been telling me is a mistake."

He hasn't changed, Pete thought, licking his lips and becoming suddenly self-conscious. He hasn't changed a goddamned bit in, what, thirteen years?

"It's no mistake, Mr. Kyrik," a voice from behind the old man said as a dark form took shape in the office gloom, blossoming into a hugely fat man in a policeman's uniform. "He's in a lot of trouble."

"Oh, come on. How much trouble can I be in?" Pete asked, aiming his question at Lieutenant Danko and his face at Kyrik, who had been one of his father's business partners, years ago, and who still scared the hell out of him, God only knew why.

He remembered the old man on holidays, sitting at a table amid a group of grey suits who had come to eat turkey or open presents because Pete's father, James Blackwell, their boss, had told them to. As a child, Pete thought Kyrik looked like a spider, and now, as an adult, he still thought so.

"There wasn't even an ounce in that bag," he added as the old man arranged himself in the seat behind Danko's bleached-oak desk.

The air around Danko smelled like coffee, Kyrik smelled like dust, and the office smelled like dead fish. A window was open and the rain pounded an aluminum awning, producing a sound like sand sifting through a screen. In a corner to Pete's left, shaded by gloom—everything in the ill-lit office looked grey—a man sat silently. Kyrik was Pete's height, and thin, threatening because of his age and the intensity of his sharp, brown eyes; Danko was shorter, with an immense belly that made him look about as threatening as Oliver Hardy; the man in the corner was as big as a bear, and Pete was glad that he didn't rise when the others entered the room.

"The substance found in your luggage has been misplaced," Kyrik said, waving his hand slowly.

"Then there shouldn't be a problem," Pete said, smiling inwardly. "I never even touched the guy."

"What guy?" Danko asked.

"That redneck in the bar."

"Where did you sleep the night before last, Mr. Blackwell?" Danko asked, his voice tight.

Kyrik was watching Pete's face, and his stare made Pete feel dirty.

"On the beach."

"Black beach?"

"It's family property."

"Black Beach, across the bay from the lighthouse?"

"Yeah."

Kyrik was frowning.

"What's he talking about?" Pete asked, suddenly getting the feeling that he and the policeman were discussing two entirely different things.

"A man named Clayton Mallard was found on Black Beach this morning," Kyrik answered, laying his big hands flat on the desk top and settling a gaze on Pete's face that made the younger man feel as if he were being evaluated before purchase. "He'd been beaten."

"He was bloodier than you," Danko added.

"Kennedy did this to me," Pete snapped at the fat lieutenant. "The guy's name is Kennedy! He threw me down the stairs!"

Lifting a pink sheet from the desk, Danko said flatly, "According to the record, you arrived at Rages around midnight, covered with blood. You demanded to be served, but the owner refused because you were already visibly intoxicated. When you became belligerent you were escorted from the bar by Ronald Boyle, a local man, whom you threatened with a deadly object.''

"That's not true!" Pete shouted.

"It was a chain," Danko smiled.

"That's the official version," Kyrik said.

"But that's not what happened!"

"And this morning we found a dead body, and a boat called *Leviathan*, on the same beach where you spent the night, presumably drunk," Danko said.

"How did you get hurt?" Kyrik asked.

"I told you!"

"I want the truth."

"I told you the truth!"

"Prove it," Danko said, still smiling. There was a piece of something wet and colorless stuck in his teeth.

"Those people in the bar, they'll tell you . . ." Pete began, his voice trailing off as Kyrik shook his head grimly.

"Everyone we talked to confirmed the official version of last night's events," Danko said, placing the paper back down on a blotter.

I'll bet they did, Pete thought, glancing from the policeman's eyes, to Kyrik's, and back. "So, what happens now?" he asked whomever wanted to answer.

"That depends on you," Danko said easily. "If it were up to me, you'd stay locked up until I could draw up a murder charge. But Mr. Kyrik seems to think that there's been some mistake, and his judgment means a lot to me. So, I'm willing to turn you loose, for now, provided you agree not to leave Sharthington until I say so."

Behind Pete, the bear-man was moving; he could hear the vinyl cushion on his chair inhaling as he rose.

"And what happens if I don't agree?" Pete asked suddenly, a hot feeling rushing up his spine and darkening his face as rough hands grabbed his shoulders. "This is crap! You can't just jerk me around like this!"

"Show the young man where he can claim his property,

Mr. Cornichuk,'' Kyrik said as Pete was lifted from the floor and hustled into the bright hallway.

"Yeah, and a telephone!" he shouted into the dark rectangle of the office door. "I know about ten dozen lawyers who would kill for a piece of this! If I didn't already own this town, I'd sue the shit out of you, and everybody in it!"

The hallway was hushed and peppered with people, who looked shocked as the big man dragged Pete toward the door and heaved him through it. Pete landed with a splash in the parking lot mud, sliding on his hands and knees and scrambling for balance. Raising himself up, he found unfocused, streaked faces peering at him through the station's windows and Cornichuk, pointing his finger and saying, "Remember, no matter what anyone tells you, don't leave town!"

Then the door slammed, and the big man was gone. A brown envelope containing Pete's wallet and watch was lying in the mud.

Lori was standing under an awning, holding her hands together protectively and clutching something to her breast. She looked first at him, then at the people in the windows, and then back again. There was fear in her eyes.

"What kind of place is this?" Pete shouted at her, slapping his hand down and sending a muddy spray in a five-foot circle. His anger had blossomed into rage—intolerable, complete, and without an object—and was aimed at the girl only because she was convenient, only because she was there. She couldn't know that, of course, but Pete didn't have any alternatives; he was a stranger, a foreigner almost, and, though he would use his money to correct these injustices as soon as he could get to a phone, he could do nothing to satisfy his need for control *now*, other than using this beautiful girl as a sounding board.

"What kind of nut farm are you people running here?" he hollered, climbing to his feet as his attention was drawn by the Black Tower, rising over the police station's roof and fuzzy in the mist.

"There!" he shouted. "The Tower! The fucking Tower!"

He raised his arm and pointed furiously, as if a demonstrative act would clarify his cryptic words.

"It's why I'm here! It's why I had to come. . . ."

"What happened to you?" Lori asked, her voice sounding trivial, far away, and small.

Pete paused, confused to silence by the shock apparent in the girl's eyes.

"Who hurt you?" she asked, stepping closer, her blond hair running in wet streaks over her forehead and her brassiere intimately defined beneath her soaked tee shirt.

"Kennedy," Pete said, almost as a whisper. "He's a cop."

At the sound of the name, Lori grabbed his arm, dragged him to where she had parked her car, and pushed him into the passenger's seat. Slamming the door, she took her place behind the wheel, turned the ignition key, and slung gravel out of the parking lot. With her eyebrows knotted and her knuckles white, she hissed, "He's an animal."

The windshield wipers clattered and squeaked as her tires hit concrete pavement with a boom.

"That whole bunch in there . . . it's a snake pit if you're from out of town," she added with a tone that hinted at personal experience. "You're lucky they didn't kill you!"

"They wouldn't kill *me*," Pete said softly, lying back heavily in his seat with his head rocking and his hand over his eyes. He was breathing hard and his heart pounded in his ears.

"Yeah, right. Superman," she said, taking a turn tightly and knocking him against his door so that he had to scramble to stay upright. "I'll bet you've got a concussion."

On the misty glass, Pete's muddy hands left distorted, leaking shapes that resembled deformed animals.

"A concussion?" he said, blinking as the car bounced passed a green Route 11 sign. "No. I . . ." He paused, turned, examined Lori's profile as she studied the road ahead, and asked, "What did you just say?"

"I said that you've probably got a concussion."

"No, before that."

"I asked who hurt you."

"Didn't I look like this the last time you saw me?" he asked, reaching out and grabbing her arm excitedly.

A flash of something that might have been pain crossed

over her eyes as she glanced down to where his fingers were pressing the blood from her flesh in white, crescent moons. "Of course not," she answered, an edge to her voice.

"I wasn't bloody?"

"No."

"No bruises?"

"No."

"Where've you been since I got arrested?"

Yanking her arm from his grip, she searched his eyes briefly, as if for something she suspected was there but had not yet actually seen, and dropped the package she'd hidden in her fist into his lap.

"They told me on the phone that your bail was five hundred dollars," she said, pasting her attention on the melting road and stiffening her spine. "I drove all night, to Lakeland Grand and back."

Pete looked at the roll of twenty-dollar bills, wrapped in a plastic sandwich bag and stained pink by the running red band laced across Jackson's moist face.

"I borrowed it from my mother," Lori added before pressing her lips together so hard that they went pale.

"Then you haven't talked to a cop about last night?" Pete asked, inadvertently wondering if the rain had washed her makeup off, or if she didn't wear any.

"No," she answered.

Pete laid his head back on the seat gently, closing his eyes and relaxing for the first time since he'd been locked in the back of Kennedy's cruiser.

"Well," he said, his voice soft and his smile genuine. "At least there's one innocent left in the wilderness."

Lori frowned, turned her headlights on, squeezed the steering wheel, and nudged her left foot close to the .38 caliber policeman's special she'd kept in the pouch on her driver's side door since she was sixteen years old.

Two

KYRIK SAT BEHIND Danko's desk in a dark, empty office, trembling. He was watching his hands—his huge, age-spotted hands—which were lying flat on the blotter, covering something small, furry, and alive. When he lifted his right hand, a shadow, just a glimpse, shot out and squeezed back under his left. When he lifted his left, the shadow squeezed back under his right. When the door opened, he didn't look up.

"That kid's a real asshole," Cornichuk said, closing the door behind himself and stopping in his tracks.

The big man was clean shaven, his dirty-blond hair was cut short, military style, and he wore a white dress shirt, dark blue suit pants, and black, wing-tipped shoes. His thick neck, broad shoulders, and muscular arms strained the fabric of his clothing, making him look as if he were packed too tightly and might pop a button or split a seam with one wrong move.

"How bad is it?" he asked, covering the length of the office in three steps.

Kyrik lifted his bloodshot eyes and watched Cornichuk close the blinds and snap on the desk lamp. He also saw the walls behind the big man quiver, as if made of rubber, and dark, fuzzy things scurry behind pictures and into that weird, angular space where the ceiling and walls met.

But what disturbed him most was the glittering ring of color that tunneled his vision as if he were looking through a window that had been frosted for Christmas, except that this frosting was vibrant in hues of red, the darkness of which, he had come to understand, indicated how close he was to unconsciousness.

"It isn't too bad," he said, finally, his lips dry, his tongue sluggish, and his vision framed in gentle pink, which was a good sign. "A little optical distortion, paranoia. It's been worse."

Cornichuk withdrew from his pocket two glass vials about the size of shotgun shells and stood them up on the desk as he bent over the blotter and said, "Just in case."

"Thank you, Corky," Kyrik said weakly, leaning back in his chair and feeling sweat run down the center of his chest. Cornichuk was the one man he felt he could really trust, and, somehow, his simple presence had a calming effect on him. Maybe it was because of Cornichuk's past—about which only Kyrik knew—or maybe it was because of the depth of the violence of which Cornichuk was capable. But, being in control of such power, which Kyrik was, by being in control of Cornichuk, made the old man feel good, and, sighing, he added, "I just got upset and the adrenaline activated my blood. It'll pass. It always passes."

"One of these days *you're* going to pass," Cornichuk said harshly, which was his way of expressing genuine emotion.

"No cyanide," Kyrik ordered.

"Just in case," the big man repeated stubbornly as he straightened up.

"Is Blackwell gone?"

"Yeah. And you were right. It's the Tower he's after. He said so after I flipped him out."

"He called home yesterday to let everyone know where he was, and then his father called me," Kyrik mumbled, re-membering the concern in James Blackwell's voice.

"He says he dreamt it," Blackwell had explained, calling him Mr. Kyrik, just as he did while he was the old man's employer. Kyrik called him James, but James liked to be formal.

"He tried to make a joke of it when he called, but his mother and I are worried sick. He's in Sharthington and he wants to see the inside of the Tower—if you can believe it!

Keep an eye on him for us, will you please, Mr. Kyrik. There'll be compensation, of course.''

Of course, Kyrik thought, saying to Cornichuk, "He was a pest child, and now he's a pest adult.''

"After the treatment Kennedy gave him, he'll break his neck to get back to New York,'' Cornichuk said, taking a seat in front of the desk.

Kyrik said nothing because his hand was convinced that it felt hair growing between its fingers, which his brain was vociferously denying while his eyes were checking things out, just to be sure.

He glanced at his hand.

No hair.

He smiled, which Cornichuk seemed to interpret as a cue, saying, "But, to be certain he doesn't interfere, he could always have an accident: hit-and-run, no witnesses, probably never find the responsible party, country roads, him on a motorcycle.''

"That won't be necessary,'' Kyrik said, almost regretfully. "I think we 'hicks' have frightened him enough so that he'll stay out of the way for at least a day or two. After that, he won't matter.''

"What about Mallard?'' Cornichuk asked as Lieutenant Danko stepped into the room and closed the door.

"What about him?'' he asked casually, pouring himself a cup of coffee from a pot near the window.

"What if his body turns up?'' Cornichuk asked, addressing Kyrik.

"It won't,'' Danko answered, taking a seat on the couch and pulling out a pack of cigarettes. "A patrol boat found *Leviathan* tied up on the Island before sun-up this morning. He's out there, and he ain't coming back.''

"How can you be so sure?'' Cornichuk asked.

"You wanna go out and have a look?'' Danko snapped in return.

Kyrik watched the two men eyeing each other, almost certain that he could see their mutual dislike hanging in the air between them as his visual border darkened from pink to a kind of orange he'd come to associate almost exclusively with the fat Lieutenant. He knew Cornichuk could break Danko's neck with his bare hands, and he knew that Danko could blow the big man away with his revolver before Cornichuk could get out of his chair. But he also knew that either might be fatal for *him*. The more excited he got, the more the poison in his bloodstream became toxic.

So, to break the tension, he said, "It doesn't matter where Mallard's body is. All that matters is the Flies."

Pushing himself to his feet, he felt the floor sway beneath him when he turned and pulled open the blind.

Outside, the storm had reached its blackest pitch, obliterating his otherwise uninterrupted view of the Tower, and making him think that there wouldn't be another boat within five miles of the Island.

Through the storm, he couldn't see the *Get-A-Way*, bobbing on her anchor.

"Gentlemen," he said, his face so close to the window that his lips brushed the screen. "In twelve hours or so, we're going to be the exclusive distributors of the world's deadliest poison. Absolutely nothing is worth more money than death distilled to its purest essence."

He turned so abruptly that Cornichuk and Danko jumped up from their seats. His face was drawn, shadow-cut and pale, but his eyes burned with an intensity inconsistent with his frail demeanor. He wanted to say something appropriate, something that would place a perspective on the importance of this moment, which would be the first in the final few hours leading to what he and Cornichuk, and later Danko, had been planning for years.

"Just a few more hours," he said, his concentration wavering.

Inside his skull, he felt himself turning the wrong way at the end of a corridor and heading down a stairwell into a pool of light. . . .

A pool of red light!

"Just a few more hours," he said again, and Danko shot Cornichuk a sidewards glance that Kyrik did not miss.

The muscles around the old man's mouth suddenly froze,

contorting his face into a frightful grimace, which he quickly turned his head to the wall to hide.

"Just a few more goddamn hours!" he shouted, waving Cornichuk and Danko away.

Danko left, as he always did, since he had no stomach for what was to come, but Cornichuk stood silently by with the glass vials in his hand.

To Kyrik's horror, there was a fire swelling up from his belly. When Cornichuk had entered the room, Kyrik had believed that he could keep it under control, that thing he saw as a bloody-red snake, coiled in his guts. But, soon, he knew, it would be wrapped around his throat.

Cornichuk was reaching out, with long, twisting arms . . . long, twisting, snake-red arms . . . reaching for him as the room tilted to one side and . . .

He awoke on the couch, under irregular knobs of ceiling plaster slithering sinuously around the big man's caring face. From his neck down he was sore, but it would pass.

It always passed.

"It's eating me alive," he whispered, and Cornichuk held his hand. "It'll make us rich, but it's eating me from the inside out."

Cornichuk nodded and Kyrik noticed the bloody patch of torn skin under the big man's right eye for the first time. He'd gone violent again, so violent that he'd injured a man twice his size, and half his age.

"I'm sorry, Corky," he said as the awful pressure of unconsciousness settled over his eyes. He was always weak after an attack, and he'd probably sleep for three or four hours. But before he did finally slip into the darkness inside his skull, he motioned for Cornichuk to bend close, and, when the big man's ear was all he could see through his nearly closed eyes, he whispered, "It's time to kill Danko. Do it for me, Corky. Please."

Three

I DON'T KNOW why, but Kyrik wants me out, Pete thought as he cocked one arm over his head and squirmed in the tiny bucket seat of Lori's Monza, pulling off his bloody tee shirt and trying to wiggle into a clean dress shirt at the same time. There was steam on the inside of the windshield, and Lori's window was open a little, despite the rain.

There's got to be something going on in Sharthington, he reasoned, rolling up his shirt and dropping it on the floor behind Lori's seat as he began peeling off his jeans. And somehow, I ended up right in the middle of it. That's why he cooked up this shit: he couldn't keep me locked up, so he's trying to scare me into running away. What could he have going that's so important? And what's it got to do with me?

Lori, her hair wet against her skull and frizzled dry at the ends, turned off the main road and onto a narrow path that wound toward the lake.

Pete looked at her and realized that he didn't even know her last name. She'd borrowed money for his bail, picked him up from jail, driven him to Rages—where he moved his motorcycle out of the rain, picked up some clean clothes, and also some money, to replace what had been taken from his wallet while he was in his cell—to a K-Mart, where he sent her in with a fist full of bills and a shopping list, and, finally, to the beach just west of town.

She'd done all that, and he hadn't even bothered to ask her name.

Peter Blackwell, he thought, turning and seeing his own face reflected on his dark window as slithering branches and fleshy swellings of mist insinuated themselves into his features. Sometimes, you're one cold son of a bitch. The least you could do is thank her.

And he was about to.

But, before he could speak, lightning cracked and he gasped, drawing his face back from the window and leaning his weight away from the precipitous gorge that suddenly yawned below him.

They were on a bumpy path at least a hundred feet over a feeble stretch of pale beach. To the north, the lake foamed and spit, and, to the south, a shear rock wall jutted up, trapping the milky sand and littering it with chunks of black stone. It was along the lip of that wall that Lori was directing the Monza, quickly, in the dark, on wet pavement, with wind buffeting the tiny, almond-shaped car and no guardrail to guide her.

But it wasn't vertigo that shook him; it was the sight of the Black Tower, thrusting itself mysteriously up from the island his great-grandfather had built a century ago, featureless in swirling waves of rain . . . watching him—like the eyes of a portrait that follow you around a room—the damned Tower was perpetually watching him.

He felt it:

On the beach where he slept his first night in town . . .

Watching.

In his cell while those cops in their stupid uniforms tied *Leviathan* down . . .

Watching.

In the parking lot after Cornichuk heaved him into the mud . . .

Watching.

And now . . .

Watching, watching, watching!

Pete was huge, he remembered dreamily, with long, delicate pink fingers and folds in his flesh. He was so big that he couldn't see all of his own body, and he was safe, happy, and warm.

But someone was trying to dig him up! Someone wanted to expose him from where he'd been buried for . . .

"A long time?" he whispered.

"We're here," Lori said and the car jerked, settling into a wisp of steam.

"Buried for a hundred years?" he said, even more softly.

"Hey, we're here."

Pete blinked and looked over the Monza's hood.

At the bottom of the hill that began where the road ended, a small, white house sat surrounded by pieces of broken snow fence and high, pressing drifts of sand. Between the car and the house stretched a treated-wood-plank ramp that looked something like a ski slope, suspended on posts over weeds and beach, ending at a concrete slab close to the water. The ramp was wet and looked very slippery.

"You're sure you want to do this?" Lori asked, turning to face him in her seat.

"What other choice do I have?" Pete answered, his eyes still on the beach as he noted that, other than its location, there was nothing unusual about Joshua's house. He didn't know why, but he'd expected something, well, different from what he'd found. "He's the only one left in town who might testify that I wasn't bloody when I walked into the bar last night. Unless the cops got to him too."

Lori frowned.

Immediately after she picked him up, Pete had expressed his gratitude for what she'd done for him by saying that she could testify in court against Mr. Kyrik and the Sharthington Police Department in his favor. And, after saying that she had the opportunity to publicly contradict the sworn testimony of everybody else who'd seen the fight at Rages and put herself on the line for a total stranger who'd be leaving town the first chance he got, he was genuinely surprised when she responded with You must be nuts!

"Randolph Kyrik runs this place," she said as Pete turned to face her, his eyes sparkling green from the dashboard lights. "And Danko and Kennedy do what he tells them to. If Mr.

Kyrik says you were drunk and bloody, I'm sorry, but you were drunk and bloody; yes sir, no shit, now and forever, amen. I mean, what other choice have I got? I have to live here, and they can be very unpleasant when they put their minds to it.''

You're beautiful, I don't even know you, but I think I could love you—I *know* I want to *make* love to you—and I'm sorry I ever even suggested it, Pete thought, running his eyes over Lori's face and allowing his thoughts to drift to her soft shoulders and gentle lips. He'd never met a woman who attracted him so quickly, and so completely, as she did, and he wanted so badly to tell her, over dinner, someplace nice, someplace with a view, and candlelight, and soft music, and expensive food that would impress her and flatter her and make her smile. . . .

But that was the rich kid in him coming out: even in the face of real problems—he knew he shouldn't have brought that dope along—his first impulse was to worry about the girls, knowing, deep in the pit of his brain, that no matter how badly he screwed himself up, good old dad and his money were back there somewhere, ready to pull him out whenever he called.

He'd never really grown up, he realized, not for the first time. He'd never grown up because he didn't have to. Dad, in the person of his real father, and Dad, in the image of the company—Blackwell International Enterprises Inc., two zillion feet tall and half again as wide—were always there, holding his hand, protecting him with a fortress made of cash bricks and keeping him a boy—unintentionally, but for sure.

''Thank you for borrowing that money from your mother,'' he said apologetically, remembering that he'd thought, Big deal, five hundred bucks, when she first told him what she'd done, and realizing now that, Hey, five hundred bucks to a girl who works in a joint like Rages is *a lot of money*.

Lori moved the gear shift to park.

''I was wondering how long it would take you to say that.''

''Why'd you do it?''

''Why'd *you* do it?'' she asked in return, and Pete wasn't sure he understood her question.

His confusion must have shown on his face because Lori said, "I mean, why'd you help the old man?"

"I don't know," he answered, and it was the truth. "I've never done anything like that before in my life. It was almost like a dream, or a movie."

"A movie?" Lori said after a pause, pointing to the bay and adding, "You own that, don't you?"

"The Tower?"

She nodded.

"I suppose so," Pete said.

"And the beach, and the fishing company—well, the empty buildings now—and most of the land in the Lagoons?"

Pete said nothing.

"I brought you here because you helped Joshua when he needed it. He's a drunk, and he's probably a little nuts, but he's been wandering around town since I can remember, and he's never hurt anybody. He didn't deserve what he was getting from Boyle, so I'm paying you back for sticking yourself in just because it was right.

"I'm paying you back, but, I'm curious too," she said, turning and looking into the storm. "When I was young, I used to dream about just being allowed to play on Black Beach. Since it's fenced off, it was naturally the one place every kid wanted to go. But Mr. Kyrik made sure everybody stayed off. What's it like to own something like that?"

"I don't really own anything," Pete said softly. "My family does, but not me personally."

"Nobody in Sharthington's got anything," she said as soon as he finished, as if she'd anticipated the answer and had planned a rebuttal. "Since the fishing company went bust, nobody even knows somebody who's got something."

"I'm not sure I'm following you."

Lori faced him.

"Around here, there are some folks who'd say that the Blackwell family caused them their hard times when they closed Kannon down. Around here, there're some folks who'd dislike you instantly because of your name."

"I didn't do anything," Pete said, shaking his head. "I just got here."

"It doesn't matter," she responded. "I'm saying this as a warning. You didn't get hassled back at the jail house because you had a little grass in a bag, or because you ride a motorcycle and wear your hair like you've seen *Easy Rider* one too many times. You got hassled because of the name on your driver's license."

"You don't think Joshua's going to talk to me, is that what you're saying?"

Lori shrugged. "We'll soon find out."

"I'm in my underwear!" Pete said abruptly, throwing his door open and jumping into the rain, leaving Lori smiling under the coach light and a little buzzer snarling in the dashboard.

Hopping on one foot, he tried to slip on his clean jeans as Joshua, who had just stepped off his front porch, raised his good arm to protect his face, and started climbing up the ramp toward them.

"Let me do the talking," Lori said as she stepped to the front of the car and into the glowing headlights. The white beams, fuzzy wet and sliced into six individual blades around her legs, faded somewhere high over the lake. "Sometimes Josh gets a little spooky around strangers, and he'll probably be especially spooky around you. He lost his pension when Kannon closed down, and I don't think he's had an income since. He's dirt poor, and, if he finds out who you are, he ain't gonna like it one bit. So don't say anything. Just listen."

"Do you dislike me because I'm a Blackwell?" Pete asked quickly.

Lori didn't answer.

Doing up his fly and pulling his long hair out of his eyes, Pete moved his gaze from the girl's harshly lit figure, to where Joshua rose up from below like a bent, gnarled gargoyle. The sight took Pete's breath, and suddenly he felt that same quivering wash of unease he'd experienced after seeing Kyrik, for the first time in so many years, holding out his hands in Danko's office. The two men, Kyrik and Joshua, so different in appearance, produced the same, queasy lump of moist terror in his stomach that chilled his senses and reduced him to childish, cowardly hesitation.

"Hi, Josh," Lori said with mock cheerfulness, but the old man ignored her as he stepped up, his face finding the blue edge of a headlight beam and bursting into shimmering, dramatic detail.

His skin was coarse, puzzle-cracked with thousands of wrinkles, and as pale as milk. On his chin, a greenish-dark patch of scab hung where he had landed in the gravel, and his left eye was black, its pupil frozen and fully dilated to erase the iris amid a web of broken capillaries. But, unlike his left, his right eye sparkled with close attention and deep, intricate intelligence.

"You're a Blackwell!" he barked, lifting his arm and levelling a sharp spiky finger at Pete's face. "I ain't never seen one for real, but I seen pictures, and you're one for sure!"

And then he moved, with a wet swish of his navy jacket's heavy material. In an instant he was embracing Pete in a hug of surprising strength as he said, "I'm so glad to see ya, boy. I knew you'd come! I just knew you'd answer the Call!"

Over Joshua's bent head, Pete found that, instead of a look of amusement, Lori's expression betrayed confusion, and, perhaps, a little fear.

Approaching Joshua's house was an object lesson in perspective's ability to distort reality. From atop the hill, the structure had seemed secure, if not actually inviting. But, as he descended the ramp, his feet sliding on the slick wood and his attention focused over the load of boxes and bags he carried, Pete watched the house transform itself into a ramshackle hulk, its walls chipped and running with streaks of rust from twisted gutters, its cracked windows hazed with grime, its foundation split and hazardous. Each step revealed some new detail, which ultimately showed a dwelling much closer to the one he had expected the old man to call home.

And, inside, it was worse.

The bare walls were teased by one electric bulb hanging from the ceiling into producing grotesque marionettes of shadow as the three people moved. A rumpled bed squatted against the far wall, a broken-down writing desk hid under a window, and two mismatched kitchen chairs sat aimlessly to one side of the door. There was no other furniture, but there was the smell—the awful, fishy smell that was worse than simple age, and certainly not produced by anything human.

Something had died in this room.

Setting the packages on the concrete floor and thinking, How could anyone live in a place like this? Pete straightened stiffly, feeling the sore spot where his kidney had struck the jail's toilet. Lori was behind him, placing her bundles near the rest and stepping so close that he felt the heat of her skin right through the cold glaze of rain that frosted the hair on his arm—the hair that was standing straight up, bristling like a pig's.

Discreetly, she grabbed his hand, and held it against her hip.

"What did you mean?" Pete summoned the nerve to ask as Joshua circled the pile of packages, peering into the tops of bags but not touching anything. "About answering the call . . . what did you mean by that?"

"What's all this?" the old man asked in return, and Lori stepped forward.

"It's for you," she said, tearing open bags and laying items out for Joshua to see. There were blankets, medicines, cartons of cigarettes, and secret things yet to be revealed. She paused, displaying a brand-new, dark-blue, knee-length seaman's jacket.

"We thought it might make you feel better after last night," Pete offered as explanation.

Joshua looked at Lori, then at the jacket, and then at Pete, who was standing directly under the ceiling light so that the pallor of his mud-splattered skin was sharply contrasted with the vitality of his new, clean clothes.

"I'm no bum," the old man responded gruffly.

"Try it on," Lori said, holding the new jacket at arm's length.

Joshua leaned back, hugging his arm across his chest as his expression suddenly turned fearful.

"If I thought you were a bum, I wouldn't be asking you to help me," Pete said, his attention on the lump under Joshua's coat—the lump that was way too big to be just a hidden, paralyzed arm. "And that's really why I'm here, because I need your help."

Joshua picked up a pack of cigarettes, and, in a brief display of dexterity, tore it open with his teeth, saying, "I know why you're here, Blackwell. I know all about you. I know what's in your flesh, I know what's in your bones, and I know what'll be in the grass growing on your grave. So don't bullshit me."

Breaking off the Camel's filter, he touched the flame of one of his new lighters to the hairy end of the fractured cigarette, adding, "I've been waiting a hell of a long time for you to come."

"I'm not bullshitting," Pete said as smoke made his eyes itch. He'd always hated the smell of smoke, ever since he was a kid. "I'm in trouble, and you and Lori are the only people in town who can help me out."

"Liar!" Joshua shouted, shooting out his hand and grabbing Pete's face, a thumb on one cheek, four fingers on the other, squeezing his lips into a pucker as he spit, "Why'd you *really* come?"

Pete tore the old man's hand away with a broad sweep of his arm that sent him staggering back three steps, directly into the writing desk, which produced an empty, rattling thud as it bumped the wall.

"I don't know!" he said, his voice quivering as his objective self—the self that was watching this whole macabre display from the shadows behind his eyes—was shaken by the naked honesty of his statement.

He didn't know why he was here. He didn't know why he was in Sharthington, or in trouble, or in a horrible, crazy old man's house that smelled like smoke, and death.

"Bullshit!" Joshua shouted back.

Pete blinked, and then whispered, "I had to come."

Honesty again.

Joshua was nodding, his eye squeezed into a narrow, crafty squint.

"I had a dream," Pete mumbled, looking up at Lori, who was standing next to a window with the Tower visible through the storm behind her.

"Not a dream," Joshua grinned, stepping toward his bed. "It's the Call! You came because They called you. They called you, because They're afraid!"

Lori moved up and broke Pete's fist by gently slipping her hand into it. Her eyes were silently eloquent, speaking of an urgent desire to get the hell out of the mistake they had both obviously made by coming here in the first place.

Pete looked deeply into those eyes for a moment, briefly lost in clear, icy blue. . . .

And suddenly, Joshua was close again, screaming, "There! There's why you came!"

Pete snapped his head around and found hideous green eyes, open, staring . . .

So, so close.

Bubbles, swimming behind dirty, oily glass . . .

So, so close.

A wormy, swollen tail, bobbing like sin . . .

"Jesus!" he said, lifting his hand with a jerk.

"There's why you're here!" Joshua laughed, throwing his head back and waving the jar under Pete's nose. "Look at it! It's why you came! They called you! They did! The Flies! The Blood Flies! *They* called, and *you* answered!"

There was something dark dripping from under Joshua's jacket that, even through his shock, Pete couldn't miss. It was thick, green and greasy, forming a puddle around the old man's muddy boots from which rose the smell—that goddamned, putrid, fishy smell of decay that hung in every corner of Joshua's house, in every fiber of his clothing, and in every breath he exhaled. It swelled suddenly up from the floor in a wave that was overwhelming, and unbearable, making Pete think that, no, something hadn't *died* in this room— whatever that something was, it hadn't *died*, it was still *dying*, and it had been for a very, very long time.

"What's wrong with you?" he asked, his voice weak and his eyes staring alternately at the jar, and the horrible, slimy puddle under Joshua's shoes. "What the hell kind of place is this?"

"I know 'bout you," Joshua said, brandishing the jar as his hair fell over his face and his blind eye pointed itself slightly more to one side than his other. He took a deep breath and curled his lip into something that might have been a smile, but wasn't, as he added, "And you should know 'bout me."

Pete squeezed Lori's hand and together they watched Joshua's shuffling feet smear dark, juicy patterns on the concrete as he advanced, unsteadily, his coat hanging limp and his expression indecently expectant. The air reeked of decay, rain drummed the roof, and humidity buttered his skin as Pete shook his head and said, "Tell you what: you just enjoy that stuff we brought, and we'll take off, okay?"

"You're afraid!" Joshua announced in a voice filled with wonder. "You're afraid of what your great-grandfather gave his life to find!"

The jar was close to Pete's face again as the old man shouted, "It's your legacy, Blackwell! Don't be afraid. It can't bite no more!"

Suddenly, a chill washed through him, freezing Pete's attention and prickling his flesh.

The jar was glowing!

Just inches from his face, it was glowing, producing a sickly light that tinted Joshua's twisted fingers and bathed the room in an aquatic, liquid blue. And, behind the jar, Joshua's eyes pulsated with that same vital color, beckoning Pete closer and inviting him to share the secret that burned blue inside an old, old man, who should have been standing in the mouth of the freak tent at some carnival. . . .

That was it! That was the image that had been gnawing at Pete's senses since he first saw that sign, WELCOME TO SHARTHINGTON, YOUR SUMMER TOWN.

Sharthington was a carnival: things in it looked real, but appearances were deliberately deceiving. Kyrik looked like any other retired businessman in expensive clothes, but the police, who looked friendly and helpful, were really his private thugs. The boats and buildings all created the illusion of normality, when underneath there was desperation and dirt. It was all a show, and Joshua, disguised as the town drunk, was the Freak Master, keeper of Sharthington's secrets, which, in the unearthly shimmer of some invisible spotlight, he was now displaying.

"Hurry, hurry, hurry!" Pete's imaginary Freak Master called in circus tones. "Step right up and see the unreal, the unnatural, the un-possible, sealed inside a jar. It's wicked, it's dangerous, and it's diseased! But it can't hurt you, ladies and gentlemen. It can't hurt you from behind its glass."

That was a lie, Pete thought. Simply knowing it existed hurt him. It was hurting him now.

"You can feel it," Joshua said.

"What is it?" Pete whispered.

"Sit down," Joshua ordered and Pete found the command irresistible.

Pulling up a chair, he complied, with Lori furtively following his lead.

Joshua placed the jar gently down on the writing desk so that its light silhouetted his tangled body as he snapped the filter off another cigarette, and said, "The jar's real. It's no joke, and it ain't the only one. A thousand years ago they was the Shawnita to the Indians. The settlers knew 'em, but didn't. And, after your great-grandfather built this here town, they was called Black's Sons. But the name that stuck is Blood Flies—I don't know why."

He paused to light his cigarette, and then said, "You're one of Black's Sons, and me too. Forty years ago to the day, that's what they made me, and that's how I knew you'd be called here. I've heard the Call going out for two weeks now, and I knew you'd have no choice but to come."

"Two weeks?" Pete frowned, thinking, Two weeks and two days ago I turned twenty-six.

Joshua sat down on his bed. From where he had been standing to where he had seated himself, there was a dribbled black flourish of glistening spots. While he spoke, the puddle beneath his feet grew as more liquid seeped down his leg.

"Kyrik doesn't know it, but every time he kills one of the Flies, the rest of the group can feel it," he said, using his cigarette as a pointer. "Killing one has the same effect on the group as if I'd cut off one of your fingers. That's how much they feel it. *They're* afraid of him . . . so *you're* afraid of him too.''

"How do you know I'm afraid?''

Joshua pointed to his temple and winked, '' 'Cause I know they've touched your mind.''

"That doesn't make sense.''

"Once you see how simple it all is, it'll make good sense. It's all happening 'cause Kyrik plans to dig up the Flies from where they've lived under the Tower for a hundred years. I been watching him going back and forth to the Island, thinking he's so smart, that everybody else is too stupid to see what he's up to. But I know all about it, and I know why the Blood Flies finally called a Blackwell back to Sharthington after almost a hundred years! They called you to stop Kyrik from digging up the caves!''

Pete's thoughts were a jumble. He saw his delicate, pink fingers flying in the bloody mud of his dreamy grave. . . .

Killing one has the same effect on the group as if I'd cut off one of your fingers.

He saw himself buried deep underground, where he was safe, and warm. . . .

They've lived under the Tower for a hundred years.

He saw the shovel, probing over where he lay in a tunnel filled with a beautiful, blue light. . . .

Kyrik plans to dig up the Flies.

I've heard the Call going out for two weeks now.

They've touched your mind.

It makes good sense.

Pete glanced at Lori, who returned his puzzled gaze with one of impatience, which wasn't surprising. She didn't realize that Joshua had just cut open Pete's chest and sealed his heart in another, different jar. She didn't know that the old man's crazy talk was sounding less and less crazy—or did it just sound less crazy to Pete? That was an uncomfortable distinction that he chose to ignore. And she couldn't understand that, no matter how much he wanted to, Pete couldn't leave until he had heard every last whacked-out detail, starting with . . .

"Clay Mallard," he said, bunching his hands into one big fist on his lap. "Who the hell is Clay Mallard?"

The question seemed to amuse the old man, prodding from his chest a rattling grunt that evolved into an ugly laugh.

"Clay was one of the stubbornest men God ever rolled of spit and mud," he said, half-choking on convulsions of joy and smoke as a particularly large drop of mucus hung at the end of a thick, green line before joining the stain between his legs. "That fat-ass Danko spent most of his time chasin' him off the Island. Didn't do no good though. Clay kept rowin' *Leviathan* up there to fish, and, last night, he got what was comin' to him. I seen it happen."

Pete opened his mouth to ask another question, but Joshua dropped his cigarette—which fizzled in the dark—and raised his hand abruptly, saying, with authoritative finality, "You shut up and I'll tell you a story I thought I'd never tell another soul. But, by your birth, I figure it's your right to hear it. It's a story that goes back over a hundred years; it's my story, and it's yours. And it starts like this . . ."

Joshua paused and fished a half-empty bottle of bourbon from amid the sheets on his bed and lit yet another cigarette before saying, "Once upon a time . . ."

He exhaled a lungful of smoke.

"Once upon a time, old Noah Blackwell came along and built Sharthington on this nice, natural bay with its own river that nobody else seemed to want. That was in 1872. He was twenty-two years old, fresh over from England, and holding a bunch of money from his father's estate, since Blackwell's been a rich family since God was a boy. He settled here, at the mouth of the river that the Indians, who'd been gone for more than a hundred years even then, called Shawnati."

As the old man spoke, Pete tried to keep his expression even, but the smell leaking from beneath Joshua's coat was turning his stomach and making his head feel light. He squeezed Lori's hand and she scooted her chair closer.

Joshua took a long swallow of bourbon, grimaced, and said, "Now, you'd think a smart fella like Noah Blackwell would say to himself, 'Hmm, mighty funny, this place being deserted when there's other towns all around. Maybe I better stay shy of something I don't know nothing about, 'cause there might be things going on here that I don't see.' You'd think he'd say something like that.''

He shook his grizzled head, as if, even now, over a hundred years after the fact, he still couldn't believe Noah Blackwell's poor judgment.

''But he was one of them real Americans: see a chance and take it. So, he bought up the Lagoons, built the Island, and started the fishing company. In twenty years, Sharthington was on the map, Kannon ran itself, and folks thought the man was a real goddamn genius. But, when things go good, there ain't nothing for a genius to do. So, to keep busy, old Noah mixed the mess we got going today.''

Joshua paused abruptly and the unexpected silence snapped Pete's attention back from where he'd been mentally correlating what he knew of his family's history with what he'd heard so far.

''You listen to me,'' Joshua said, lifting a warning finger. ''This is where your great-grandfather changed what was natural. The things the Indians called Shawnita were solitary, and rare. They was as old as the land, and lived under rocks in the lake, hunting bugs and fish, killing rats and gulls when they got half a chance, and generally doing what they did best, which was keeping to themselves. They was poisonous as hell, and just looking at one could kill ya, but the medicine men used to catch 'em for ceremonies 'cause, to the Indians, they was magic. That's how Noah heard about 'em, and he got so interested that he set up a laboratory under the Tower, and nobody ever saw him again.

Joshua's voice had dropped to little more than a whisper as he leaned forward, studying Pete with his sparkling eye.

''God didn't intend for 'em to have it as soft as Noah made it. They bred and bred and . . . well, what they was when they was only a few wasn't nothing like what they became when they got thick in the caves Noah dug under the Island. Them caves was deep, and the Flies lived there for ten years before they finally turned on him. They been living there ever since—growing, digging new tunnels, stretching out and changing into what they always coulda been, but what it took Noah Blackwell to make 'em.''

"Which is?'' Pete asked, surprised at how soft his own voice came when he spoke, and also surprised at how deeply Joshua's story moved him.

"Death,'' Joshua replied, raising his fist and holding it up, producing a twisted shadow over his face, inside of which his eye gleamed a watery, iridescent blue. "Pure death, dripping poison, with a common mind—like ants—thinking as one squirming evil. It's a beast out there, one huge, hungry animal, with a million pairs of eyes, and a hundred million teeth. And, soon, It's gonna reproduce!''

Joshua was trembling, his hand clawing at his moist trousers and his eye sizzling hot inside a patchwork of animate flesh.

"It needs our skulls!'' he announced in a frightful half-laugh. "It lays Its eggs in your mouth, and the first thing It tastes in life is your brain. Bugs do that a lot, lay eggs on a food source. Like maggots.''

Lori gasped—an unwilling, unintentional expulsion of disgust that sucked her hand to her mouth and Pete's attention to her wide, frightened eyes.

"What are we talking about?'' she asked, standing, addressing Pete, and pointing to where Joshua sat like a troll wrapped in threat. "Why are we listening to this crap?''

Suddenly, a moist, heavy slurp—like a huge tongue moving over dry lips—came from where Joshua was huddled on his bed, and Lori gasped again. The sound was liquid, reptilian, and so weirdly appropriate, given his surroundings, that it produced an unpleasant, intimate sensation in Pete's bowels that lifted him from his chair and propelled him to Lori's side, where, for the first time, he noticed that she was holding a gun.

The sound slapped again, and Pete jerked to face Joshua, and . . . he saw it—briefly, and yet so clearly that his senses froze and his mouth dropped open—*something was moving under Joshua's coat!*

As another muffled hiss escaped from beneath that horrible blue fabric, the jacket's sides parted slightly at the center of the old man's chest and Pete saw something quick, fleshy and pink, bulging for the length of one racing heartbeat before Joshua glanced down, covered the opening with his hand, and lifted his head to say, "Sometimes, your mouth ain't the only place they lay their eggs."

"Jesus Christ," Lori whispered, raising the gun.

She saw it too! Pete thought, as blue light suddenly surged bright, erasing shadow as if it were radiating from the very walls of the cabin and not the single source of the jar on the desk at all.

"It's true," Joshua said, as something substantial and dark fell from between his legs, landing with a slap on the floor.

Pete refused to look at whatever was laying in the shadow, preferring ignorance and wishing that Lori would hand him her gun—he wasn't sure why.

"Forty years ago tonight," Joshua said in a voice suddenly rich with reverberations, as if his throat were changing shape, becoming at once deeper and less flexible, "I went out on the lake with my best friend. He was like my brother. Right out there . . ."

He pointed to the window but neither Lori nor Pete followed his gesture.

"It was on the *Emma B.*, forty years ago today. . . ."

And Joshua's story was told.

"She ran aground sometime in the early thirties, the *Emma* did. She was a ninety-foot, humpback, mid-deck loader that hauled fish for Kannon and got so close in during a storm one night that she ended up with her tit in a wringer and her nose in the sand just north of the Island. She's been there ever since 'cause nobody bothered to drag her off the rocks: just left her to rust, old as she was, probably not worth fixing.

" 'We could see 'em move from the bridge o' the *Emma*,' he says to me one night, over to Rages. 'We could row out and hide in the pilot house and, when they fly, we could see 'em!'

"That was the best friend I ever had in all this world said that. The name most folks knew him by was Charlie Wolf, and he was half-Indian, and half-crazy. He never told nobody but me his whole name 'cause the Indians 'round here believe that if a man knows the whole of your name, he can use it to make magic on ya. But Charlie trusted me, so when he said that he'd been waiting ever since he was a kid to see the Flies move, and that it was something his father had told him he'd seen when he was a boy, I was honored that he'd ask me along. I was honored, and, because he believed, I believed.

" 'We gotta be real careful,' Charlie says, screwing up that wrinkled face of his. 'I wanna live to tell my boy that his old man saw the Dark Cloud.'

"Dark Cloud's what the Indians call what happens the night the oldest Flies swarm and head for open ocean. Happens every forty years on the exact same night and it's a secret the Indians keep—like a religion almost. Because it doesn't take but two minutes to happen, ain't nobody that doesn't know when to wait ever seen it. And the Flies get mighty irritable on the night of the move, so any little variation close to the Tower can set off a killing swarm that'll leave nothing living in its path. We decided on the *Emma* 'cause she was just a hundred yards from the Island, and we could hide on her without being seen.

"That night was still and warm, with a sky so clear that the moon was only about eight feet high, glowing bright on silver water. We headed out in a dingy at about eleven-thirty, Charlie telling stories, me rowing, and us both drinking Scotch from a bottle.

" 'The great old chiefs used to fly with the Shawnita,' Charlie says, just as the *Emma* came dark and clear ahead 'bout two hundred yards. The way her masts and antennas prickled up off her deck, she looked like she'd been rolled over a couple of times since running aground, and hadn't sat peaceful at all.

" 'They said that whoever partakes of Shawnita takes part in the flight of Shawnita, and that, by eating one, the chiefs could become one, for a while.'

"Charlie was always saying shit like that.

" 'They'd go flying with the Cloud,' he said, 'and when they came back, they was changed in how they acted, and how they thought. They was stronger, deadlier warriors, brilliant like animals, and touched by Shawnita for the rest of their lives. They became the tribe's greatest leaders because of it, and they became the tribe's greatest killers.'

"I was only half-listening 'cause I'd heard all of Charlie's stories before and 'cause we were pulling up close to the *Emma*'s starboard side, where there was a ladder made of rungs leading up to deck. We was both drunk, so it was a little tricky climbing, but we did, without neither of us falling once.

"Now, remember, this is in 1947, and the *Emma*'d been sitting still for going on fifteen years already. Her skin was slick with green slime, and rusted brown beneath—she crackled under your feet where she was steel and groaned where she was wood plank and rot. All her windows were busted out, and scattered all around was what was left of her railings, twisted into knots by the ice that locked her up every winter, bashing her plates into dented sheets and scraping whatever it could off her bones.

"We stood, me holding a kerosene lantern, Charlie holding a double-barreled shotgun and a bottle of Scotch, both of us shaking our heads, knowing there wasn't nothing but us aboard, and feeling like the *Emma* knew we was there, and didn't care for it.

"The pilot house door broke right off its hinges when we forced it, and, from inside, we saw the Tower, directly to port, clear in the moonlight and black against the glimmers of town.

" 'There's bat shit on the floor,' Charlie says, and I nodded, telling him, 'Good thing we came after dark. If bats woulda flew outta here when we came through that door, there'd be shit someplace else but on the floor.'

"He laughed and found a couple of old bent-up tube chairs propped close to the window, opened up the Scotch, and said, 'My father once told me that our tribe's greatest chief is yet to come. Someday, nobody knows when, a leader's going to partake of Shawnita, and Shawnita will see his strength and follow him into battle to take back the Indians' home. And here's to him. . . . He stopped to take a mean pull on the Scotch before handing me the bottle. 'The Tower's going to be the castle of the new chief—as if he'd want it. . . .' ''

"And, then, Charlie's voice just kind of dropped off, like he'd walked into a room and shut the door. Looking out to the Tower like he was, his eyes got as big as silver dollars, his face went lean and he froze, half-bent over, just getting ready to sit down as he whispered, 'There!'

"I almost shit.

"I mean, even after saying that I believed because he believed, I didn't really expect to see no magic lizards come flying out of that old lighthouse. I expected to sit up most of the night, out on the water with my Indian, talking nonsense and drinking good booze 'til we both got heep drunk, plenty fucked-up.

"But Charlie's face was as pale as the moon's, and he was trembling. I forced myself to look where his eyes was pointing, and fuck if it weren't the Dark Cloud, just like he'd said it'd be, boiling up from the tip of the Tower, a little at first, but then heavier, like a stain in the air, quiet, swirling like smoke in the night and blotting out the moon as Charlie raised his hands over his head, mumbling a few Indian words, turned to me, and says, 'We're gonna die.'

"The lantern was sitting right in the window like a beacon.

" 'Holy shit!' I said, lunging for it but knowing it was already too late. When I looked up, the Dark Cloud was gone.

"Charlie picked up his gun, cocked both hammers, and said, 'We'll fight. We ain't got a prayer, but we'll fight.'

" 'Fuck that!' I told him, grabbing at his shoulders and trying to pull him toward the hatchway. 'Let's get outta here!'

" 'Too late. Too late,' he kept mumbling, shaking his head and staring out at the Tower like some kinda zombie as I beat at him, feeling the fear rising in my guts and realizing that I was all of a sudden sober.

" 'Too late. Too late.'

"And then it sounded like somebody threw a rock in the water up close to the *Emma*. Just a little pop, but enough to break out the gooseflesh on my spine and stop my heart.

" 'You hear?' Charlie says.

"I nodded, and we both leaned to the window, peeling the reflected moons off the water and trying to see under the surface, down, to what we knew was there: a dark blur of thousands of Blood Flies, their wings stretched in the cold black, their little green eyes watching the pilothouse where we was huddled close, clutching between us a shotgun and a bottle of Scotch, holding our breaths and hoping, without any real hope, that they'd flown their last flight without seeing our lantern.

"I screamed when the first one shot past the window; and then I squeezed Charlie in a bear hug that he broke by lifting his double-barreled and pointing it at my chest. With his eyes blind with fear, he let go both barrels and blew the window frames into thousands of little pieces just as I dove out of the way. Behind me, the air exploded with flapping wings, and, in that same instant, that horrible, high-pitched buzz the Flies make when they're mad filled my head, and the next thing I knew . . .

"I was down on my hands and knees in bat shit and broken glass.

"Charlie was screaming.

"And the Shawnita came!"

Joshua paused, climbed to his feet, and turned to face the desk with an intense gaze that announced his complete involvement in memory. Lifting the jar and holding it over his head so that its blue light bathed his face, he looked up and said, "In life they ain't quiet like this. You almost never see one good 'cause they're so fast, quick, and sure. All you ever see is where they was a second ago, and then they're gone. I found this one later, out on the deck, right where Charlie had shot it from the air."

The specimen rocked inside its cell, suspended in shimmering alcohol and hynotizing Pete in his chair. He could see quite clearly now the semicircle of white, puckered meat over the Fly's hip where it had lost its leg, and from that wound the gashed, swollen remains of crudely embalmed internal organs protruded, making him realize that, like some immense species of hideous lightning bug, the Fly was glowing from within.

And so was Joshua: when the old man spoke, his crooked teeth were silhouetted by the light bleeding up his throat.

"Charlie staggered to the door and hung in it for a time as he fumbled in his pockets for more shells," he said, his voice a gurgling wave of passion and distorted, inhuman timbers.

"And, outside, the Flies pounded the air and buzzed through the windows. In just a second Charlie's hands was out of his pockets and up over his head. He was covered, just covered, head to foot, with Flies that was snapping at him with their teeth, and slashing at him with their tails.

"They coulda killed him right out, poisoned him dead, but they musta been pretty sore at us busting up their migration 'cause they tore him to pieces right in front o' my face. In just a coupla seconds he was everywhere, on the walls, the ceiling, all over the room. His head was lying close to me, just his head, with two Flies on it: one halfway up in the neck, with its hind legs a-squirming to push itself in farther, and the other holding onto his hair, sliding its tail into one o' his eyes and feeling around in there like it was looking for something."

Joshua stopped, licking his lips, and placed the jar back down on the desk.

"God, I was scared.

"And then things fell quiet . . .

"Awful quiet.

"I looked 'round and they was sticking to the walls and ceiling, three deep on the floor, pointing their faces at me, looking, watching, crawling over each other in a big mess and breathing so hard that their throats were swelling, up and down . . . up and down. . . ."

The old man went into a bent-kneed crouch, swept his hand slowly around himself to define a perimeter, and froze for a dramatic silence.

"There was a two-foot circle 'round me that was clean," he said finally, his voice low, and rough. "But outside o' that, all there was was eyes, just eyes, and tails, and dark in the window—dark, like they'd swallowed up the moon.

"I was dripping sweat," he whispered, scorching the air with his staring eye. "But I didn't move a muscle.

"A Fly snapped past my face.

"And I closed my eyes.

"A hiss came hot by my ear.

"But I stayed still.

"Something shuffled around my legs.

"I wouldn't look.

" 'Don't be afraid,' somebody says.

"And I opened one eye.

"Ain't nobody there, and the Flies had stopped moving. The lantern was still flickering up in the instrument console and shadows fell, but nothing solid in the room was moving.

" 'They won't hurt you,' somebody says, real soft, and I let go a tear 'cause I recognize who it was. I don't want to admit it, and I don't want to know it, but there it was, a voice I knew so well. . . .

"It was me! I was talking, out loud, to myself, going crazy, right there, with the Flies waiting to tear me to shreds like they did my sweet old Charlie. . . .

" 'It won't hurt,' my voice says, as the biggest, fattest, meanest looking toad I'd ever seen plops right down on my hand and starts climbing up my arm.

" 'You're the legendary chief,' I said to myself, real loud, feeling the wet weight of that dark, squirmy black thing working its way over and holding onto my shirt, which was hanging open. 'You'll lead the Shawnita to glory on the day of the next Dark Cloud. Until then, you'll carry the Mark!'

"I'm on my hands and knees, remember. On my fucking hands and knees!

" 'You're one of us!'

"The Flies all buzzed and croaked together.

" 'You'll feel no pain!'

"I tried to shake my head, but couldn't! I couldn't move!

" 'You'll carry the Mark!'

"I'm crying like a baby.

" 'Now!'

"No!"

Joshua screamed, flinching his arm up and holding it across

his chest with his head hung down and his hair falling over his face as he whimpered and trembled in the center of the cabin floor, a bent, quivering sculpture of silent agony.

Lifting his head, he pulled his hand slowly away and looked at his chest, saying, "It cut its stingers in what seemed two feet. Hissing and snapping at my face, the thing was holding on and pumping its tail, squirming so that my chest burned and my spine went to butter and I could see the ridges on its tail, bulging out my flesh and moving around.

"The room was swimming and my eyes felt like they was gonna bust like grapes, and all the while that ugly thing tore at me, making me bleed and . . .

"Then I couldn't see out of my eye no more!" he said, touching his cheek gently. "My arm . . ." he added with growing alarm. "Was tingling like it was asleep. I could still move it, but it felt funny."

He turned and held his face up with an expression of genuine wonder as if he were looking at something large and beautiful.

"And then, the sun," he said, awe crowning his performance as sincere. "The next thing I knew, there was daylight. I was alive! My arm was tingling and my eye was dark, but goddamn it I was alive!"

He turned and leveled a silent look of expectation through a shimmering haze of blue cigarette smoke and swirling dust.

"And the spot on my chest where the Fly had planted its seed was nothing but a blue welt, like a bruise, closed up and healed, right then, the next morning, where I woke up alone on the bridge of the *Emma*. Alive!"

Pete blinked.

Lori tugged at his arm, prompting him toward the door.

Joshua squinted, and then screamed, *"It's true, damn you! It fucking happened! I'm the king of the legends! I'm the chosen one! And I told you because you helped me in the bar. And now we're even!"*

The hysteria in the old man's voice was so complete, so panicked and near to frenzy, that it terrified Pete into doing something he'd never done before. Unconsciously, and by re-flex, he placed his body in front of Lori's, as if to shield her from the heat radiating from Joshua's bulging, trembling eye.

The power of the old man's attention was so focused, so physically urgent, that it seemed to pass through Pete like microwaves, raising his body's temperature and tingling his skin. Maybe it was simple adrenaline, engorging his muscles in preparation for flight, or maybe it was some mystical, extraordinary premonition, but, in that instant, Pete realized that everything Joshua had said had actually been directed at Lori, and that Pete had simply been the excuse the old man had used for saying it.

"You don't believe me?!" Joshua roared.

Pete pressed back, pushing Lori toward the exit and inadvertently slamming her into the door, where she immediately started rattling the handle.

"You don't believe that I'll fly?!" Joshua bellowed, throwing back his head and raising his good arm to claw at the ceiling. "That I'll be lifted up to glory in a majestic arch of pure power? That I'll fall from the heavens and smother Sharthington and everyone in it? That I'll destroy Kyrik and his plans to sell poison for gold? That's what he wants to do, you know: he wants to sell the Flies! He wants to sell their poison!"

The cabin door burst open and Pete felt Lori disappear in a rush of cool, fresh, lung-cleansing air as he too staggered back, away from the horrible blue light and into the rain.

"*Run!*" Joshua's voice resounded, pursuing them in a vibrating blister of blue that swelled out from the door and entered the darkness without its body. "*Run, both of you! Run, or die! Leave Sharthington! Leave now! Run! Run! Run for your lives!*"

Pete slid on the slick wood of the plank deck, landing with a hollow thud and scrambling for purchase as Lori's desperate hands found his shirt and dragged him five yards before he regained his feet and took her arm. Together, they clambered up the ramp, heaving huge breaths of steam and clutching at each other like children until they reached the top of the hill and collapsed into the car, slamming the doors and locking them in unison.

Below, bleeding liquid through the sheets of rain that melted the Monza's windshield into layers, Joshua's cabin was a black box punched through by two shimmering blue windows.

Pete's shoulders quivered as he gripped the armrest, staring down at Joshua's silhouette dancing within a blue rectangle, waving its arm and moving frantically back and forth. He swallowed back a gasp, sighed, and forced himself to hold his breath for a moment before finally saying, "Gets a little spooky?"

Lori, mimicking his movements from the driver's seat almost exactly, closed her eyes, and smiled, weakly, as she nodded and said, "Yeah . . . he does get a little spooky around strangers sometimes. You're lucky I came along to put him at ease."

And then, in a rush of release and unfulfilled threat, Pete and Lori laughed: hard, together, and as if something really were funny.

Four

"LET ME EXPLAIN . . ." Kyrik had said in the restaurant that evening two years ago, after feeding Lieutenant Danko a sumptuous meal and getting him half-drunk on some wine with an unpronounceable name and unbelievable price tag.

At that time, Lieutenant Danko was still Mr. Danko, owner of Danko Security Services, Inc., Vermilion, Ohio, which was in the process of going belly up because the guards kept stealing from their clients and their clients all knew it. Given his financial position, or lack thereof, he tended to notice little details, such as the fact that the wine he was drinking cost more per bottle than he had made in the past week, but still tasted like chilled piss.

"It's a business arrangement," the old man added later, lighting a cigar and instructing Cornichuk, who stood like Kyrik's shadow, to open the curtain on the big sliding doors in his expensive—Jesus, did it look expensive—living room, offering a panoramic view of the lake as it sparkled passively under the early evening sun a hundred feet below the suspended patio. "It's a very profitable business arrangement."

Profitable?

Bingo!

He'd liked that word. "Profitable," he thought, bouncing his cruiser through the puddles of the narrow maze of mud that wound between broken-down trailers in Vista View, Sharthington's formerly popular tourist park, and presently crumbling shantytown. Through the sweeps of his window wipers, he was looking for the trailer with Ronnie Boyle's name on its mailbox, and remembering. . . .

Profitable was a good word, and Danko liked hearing it; he was fully expecting Kyrik to hire his company to keep an eye on something of his that was valuable—why else would the richest old poop around invite him out to dinner? So, when the old man asked him if he'd like to become the new Chief Lieutenant of Sharthington's police force, he would have jumped at the chance—Yes sir, Mr. Kyrik; who do I have to kill?—even without the baby.

Especially without the baby.

"Mr. Cornichuk, if you please," Kyrik said, and the big man left the room.

While he was gone, Kyrik explained the amazing, and ridiculous, reason that he'd offered Danko his new job.

"You're untrustworthy, devious, and completely unprincipled," he said, blowing smoke rings from deep in his leather chair. "Your company's reputation has reached all the way to Sharthington: extortion, thievery, trafficking in stolen property. Normally, these qualifications would hinder your chances at securing a position as a police officer. But, in this case, those, shall we say, character traits could come in quite handy. And, you're greedy. I like that. It's an ideal motivator. Have you ever heard of the Blood Flies?"

Sure, Danko shrugged. Anybody who grew up on Lake Erie's northwestern coast had heard of the Blood Flies. They were one of the Lake-Nasties in Grandma's bedtime stories, one of the Boogies in Grandpa's come-sit-on-my-knee-and-I'll-make-sure-you-sleep-with-your-lights-on-'til-you're-twelve-years-old spookers that seemed so silly, so childish . . . at least until it got dark. Sure, he'd heard of them. So what?

"Did you know that they live right over there?" Kyrik asked, pointing with his cigar at the Black Tower, which was visible on the horizon from where Danko sat.

"I beg your pardon?" the fat man said, politely.

Nobody believed in the Blood Flies. Sure, people reported

seeing one every now and then—or at least they reported seeing something, dark and fast, flying out over the water, late at night, way the hell out, far from land. But nobody really *believed* in them. Did they?

"They're real," Kyrik said.

Oh, shit! Danko thought.

"They live right over there. And I want you to make sure that nobody bothers them," Kyrik added. "That's why I'd like to make you my new Lieutenant."

Danko was certain that, if he opened his mouth, he'd say the wrong thing, and he didn't want to blow his shot at a full-time paycheck. He didn't know if Kyrik was serious, testing him, joking, or crazy. But, in just a few minutes, he'd decide on crazy.

"Ah, Mrs. Ellington," the old man said, rising from his chair with a cheery grin as Cornichuk returned, accompanied by a young, red-haired woman wearing jeans and a tee shirt and holding a baby.

"Mrs. Ellington works for me a couple of days a week, Mr. Danko," Kyrik said. "Don't you, my dear?"

The woman's face was strangely limp as her eyes moved slowly to find Danko's as he rose from the couch. She nodded, stood still, and waited. Danko smiled at her, wondering why her child didn't move.

Speaking loudly, Kyrik said, "She works for me because she wants her infant son to have everything a child could possibly require. There's no love in this world like that between a mother and her child. You do love your son, don't you, Mrs. Ellington?"

The woman nodded.

"Of course you do. And, if anything were to happen to your beautiful baby, that would be a tragedy, wouldn't it?"

She nodded again.

Kyrik smiled and said, "Mr. Cornichuk."

Cornichuk took the child from its mother's unprotesting arms.

"For the rest of our lesson, it'll be necessary for us to retire to the balcony," Kyrik said, holding out his hand for Danko to pass.

On the planking, the group's steps echoed loudly as the evening sun dipped lower on the lake and a breeze sucked the white draperies around the jam, fluttering them without sound.

Danko watched Mrs. Ellington's impassive face, and then moved his gaze to Kyrik, looking for some warmth in the old man's eyes, but finding none.

"At the risk of sounding redundant, let me ask again," Kyrik said in flat tones. "Do you love your son, Mrs. Ellington?"

The woman nodded.

"He's a beautiful boy, isn't he?"

She nodded again.

"He's bright and cute and he makes all the sacrifices of being a parent worthwhile, doesn't he?"

She nodded, the hint of a smile playing on the corners of her mouth.

Water splashed sharp rocks one hundred feet below as sea birds climbed the swirling breeze.

"On lovely, summer evenings like this, isn't strolling along the beach with your son in your arms wonderful? Isn't it going to be nice when he's a bit older, and can walk, clumsily, so that you have to help, catching him when he falls, feeling his tiny hands reaching for the protection of the most important person in his world? Won't it make you feel fulfilled, knowing that you gave him life?"

Mrs. Ellington's eyes grew slightly moist as she smiled a deep grin of love and pride.

"But," Kyrik said, his voice suddenly growing cold. "He is a big responsibility. If it weren't for him, you wouldn't need to work so hard, cleaning up other people's slop, demeaning yourself for a few dollars so that he can cry and crap and make you lose sleep—make you feel so old when you're really so young. If it weren't for him, you'd be like other women your age, and life would be so much easier."

Mrs. Ellington's eyes narrowed, and she looked at her child as if she were no longer sure how she felt about him.

"A woman as lovely as yourself shouldn't be chained to a

baby," Kyrik said, his face hard. "Mr. Cornichuk, would you please free this fine lady from her servitude?"

The big man wrapped one huge fist around the infant's feet and dangled him, headfirst, over the railing.

"No! Are you people crazy?" Danko yelled, pushing his way past the woman and placing his hands on Cornichuk's arm.

The big man returned the child to its mother, who accepted her son lazily, and without comment, as if nothing out of the ordinary had happened.

"That should be enough," Kyrik said. "You may go, Mrs. Ellington."

"Thank you, Mr. Kyrik," she said softly, before turning to leave the room without another glance at the man who had just offered to kill her son.

"How about a drink?" Kyrik asked, and Danko nodded, allowing himself to be led into the house. He swallowed most of what Kyrik gave him before tasting Vodka.

"What the hell was that all about?" he asked finally, and Kyrik placed his big hands flat on the top of a black, marble bar.

"That, Mr. Danko, was all about what I want you to protect," he said evenly. "The Flies produce a venom, which Mr. Cornichuk and I have been collecting. It's unique in all this world; it's worth more money than you can even imagine; and only Mr. Cornichuk and myself know about it."

He refilled Danko's glass and stepped around the bar, taking a seat in his recliner again.

"When injected directly into the bloodstream," he said, examining the end of his cigar, which had gone cold, "the venom simply kills. I won't bore you with too many chemical details, but, after injection, the magnesium level of a subject's blood increases dramatically, and all that new magnesium replaces calcium in the muscles, paralyzing the heart. It's quick, almost painless, and the way in which the Flies go about killing their food."

He lit his cigar and Danko downed his second drink, thinking, he's serious! He means it!

"But if the venom should be ingested—as in Mrs. Ellington's case—or if it should be introduced into a person in very minute quantities, the magnesium is digested slowly, and therefore neutralized, allowing the other agents in the poison to produce the wonderful side effect you just witnessed.

"These other agents are fat soluble, meaning that they're stored in fatty tissues, mainly the reproductive organs and the brain. They're very potent, mind-altering chemicals that do their work without making a person feel drugged in any way. You don't even know it's working on you, until it's too late. . . .

"But I didn't give the baby any drugs!" he suddenly snapped, his eyes swimming and his hand rigidly pointing his smoking cigar at the ceiling. "His mother was pregnant when I first put the venom in her food, so he was born with some very interesting birth defects. It wouldn't have made much difference it we'd killed him or not; he'll be dead in a few weeks anyway. But I'm not the sort of man who'd poison a baby."

Danko blinked, very slowly.

"Being fat soluble," Kyrik went on casually, "the drug stays in the system, and, as exposures continue, its level increases, producing, in women, because of their hormonal structure, a state of mental suggestibility similar to that of hypnosis, in which she can function but not initiate any independent thought."

Danko glanced at Cornichuk, the brooding, silent robot standing in the corner, and shuddered.

"But, in men," Kyrik smiled, "adrenaline and testosterone will react with our poison, producing violent fits during which a subject will kill—others, or even himself—which is what happened to Mrs. Ellington's poor husband. So, a subject's brain can be completely ruined and he will never even feel it, while his wife remains behind as a mindless slave."

Danko shook his head, saying, "And where do I come in?"

"The Flies live in the Island," Kyrik said, his eyes sparkling with excitement. "And soon they'll be swarming for a migration to the sea. When they do, we'll be able to harvest our poison. Between now and the time of the move, your job will be to see to it that they aren't disturbed in any way."

"How much?" Danko whispered.

"A lot," Kyrik smiled.

"How much is a lot?"

"As much as mighty men might be willing to spend on something that could kill or enslave a population—mighty men here, and abroad."

"Holy shit," Danko said as a smile began to spread over his face.

"In a way," Kyrik responded solemnly.

"With a little imagination, the potential's fantastic. When's this migration going to happen?"

Kyrik stood up.

"That's none of your concern," he said, his face darkening. "You'll be our third partner, entrusted with using the resources of the Sharthington Police Department to protect the Tower. You may have to be somewhat devious to perform your duties, but that's why I chose you. Nobody is to go near the Island, but, at the same time, it mustn't look as if you're going out of your way to keep people clear. No one must suspect that there's anything special about the Tower: that's your concern, your only concern. Other details remain with me—as insurance. Not even Mr. Cornichuk knows everything about our dangerous little friends. That way, everyone remains at least marginally honest, out of necessity. Agreed?"

"Sure," Danko said.

And why the hell not? The salary was fabulous, the potential for wealth unlimited, and the alternative unappealing. . . .

"If you had refused," Kyrik confided later, "Mr. Cornichuk would have broken your neck."

Big surprise.

Great minds think alike.

At least they did until one of them got soaked in poison and started acting weird, Danko thought, turning the cruiser's engine off and killing his headlights. Over the two years that he'd been Kyrik's Lieutenant, the old man's mental capacity had deteriorated alarmingly. Danko had done his job, which was really very simple since nobody but Clay Mallard wanted to go out to the Island anyway, and now Kyrik said that the time had come, the Flies would be ready for the move sometime today.

Terrific.

But you'd think that, after all the planning and risks, Kyrik would be more careful—especially now, of all times. His behavior was becoming more erratic, especially when he got tense. When he got tense, he got goofy.

Danko didn't think the old man was in control any more, so he'd come to Vista View, where a smart-assed punk named Ronnie Boyle lived in a rented trailer, out of which he sold dope and, occasionally, his girl friend, because, in Danko's mind, Peter Blackwell was too dangerous to leave unattended.

Ducking his head down while pulling his hat low over his eyes, the fat man skipped up the two concrete blocks that served as steps to trailer number 117's front door. Standing close, but still in the rain, he pounded on the trailer's side, hard, until the door opened and Boyle's face appeared behind the screen, grinning, silent, and wearing his cap with the word CAT written across the front in big yellow letters.

"Move it, asshole," Danko said, pulling open the screen.

Boyle stepped back, his eyes intent on Danko's face, his smile so firm that it appeared painted on.

The trailer was humid and warm, and a bristle of sweat popped out on the Lieutenant's forehead almost instantly as he stomped water from his shoes next to an open, wooden door.

Boyle's girl friend, a thin, twenty-year-old redhead with a tattoo, was sitting on a battered sofa with her eyes locked on Danko's face. As the Lieutenant moved his attention from Boyle to the girl, and back, he realized that something in this room was making him terribly nervous.

"What's the matter with you two?" he asked harshly, taking off his hat and shaking it dry. "Why are you looking at me like that? You stoned?"

He looked at Boyle again, who's face was a mask of evil

amusement and anticipation, and then at the girl, who just sat there, watching him, her legs curled under her like a cat's, a bloody hand over her mouth, and tears rolling down her cheeks.

Blood?

Tears?

Someone had just finished slapping her around!

Danko's eyes went wide and his spine stiffened as he caught sight of himself in the large, oval mirror over the couch. There he was, dripping wet in his powder-blue uniform, standing next to an open, wooden door, on the other side of which lurked a huge, dangerous shape.

Boyle, still grinning, stepped back quickly as Danko drew his gun in a smooth sweep. The boy would have died on the spot had Danko's aim not been ruined when the door slammed into his left shoulder, knocking him into a TV cart and revealing Cornichuk—the shape in the mirror—as he lunged from his hiding place with his huge hands aimed at the Lieutenant's throat.

Concussion shook the room as Danko's 44 magnum exploded, blowing a hole in the wall just inches over the terrified girl's head and sending her screaming from the couch toward the bedroom door.

Cornichuk's hands found the fat under Danko's chin.

Boyle was standing, slightly hunched in a corner, watching and grinning behind a thin veil of swirling gunsmoke as Danko saw little points of bright light envelope the room when Cornichuk squeezed.

He'll break my neck! he thought, trying to struggle, but unable to move. He's so fucking big! So fucking strong!

Cornichuk was working one of his hands to the right side of Danko's head when Danko aimed his gun at the bridge of the big man's nose. . . .

A sound like thunder tore through Danko's ears and, suddenly, he saw the other side of the room. He'd been looking right at Cornichuk's face, just about to squeeze the trigger when a crack exploded under his chin and he was looking at the other side of the goddamned room.

His gun was on the floor because his fingers wouldn't hold on to it any more.

Boyle looked amazed, his girl friend screamed, and Cornichuk hissed, "Did you see? Did you?"

Danko couldn't even move his eyes. He wanted to look at Cornichuk's face, but he couldn't move his eyes as the big man repositioned his hands so that one was on each side of the Lieutenant's flopping head.

"Now, do like I told you, or you're next!" Cornichuk said as he leaned back and . . .

. . . a terrible, scraping sound like a series of knuckles popping, ground with stomach turning finality and . . .

. . . briefly, very briefly, Danko was looking at Boyle again.

Five

"JESUS C. AND Mary!" Ronnie Boyle hissed as he slid down the hill near Joshua's house. "What shit!"

The hill was steep, and wet sand ran in oozing arteries between clumps of twisted weed, cracked root, and sharp rock, making his descent clumsy and uncomfortable. He'd parked his Chevy van almost a mile up the road so that no one would recognize it near the scene of a crime, and had chosen to approach the cabin from the west, along the ridge, avoiding the ramp, and he hoped, the accidental sight of strangers. The lights from town disappeared the instant he dropped over the crest of the hill, and it got really dark.

"Kill him," Cornichuk had said. "Kill the old man and be sure you leave his body out where it'll be found."

Cornichuk's orders carried a considerable amount of impact for two reasons—one, he was the man who'd paid Boyle five hundred dollars for starting the fight at Rages and involving Pete, and Joshua, who'd been convenient, and, two, when Cornichuk had said them, he was standing in the middle of Boyle's living room, holding the body of Lieutenant Danko up off the floor by the front of the fat man's uniform. A person tended to pay attention when a man who'd just committed murder with his bare hands spoke.

The cabin's windows were glowing a television blue, Boyle noticed, finally reaching the beach and crouching as he ran, bent-kneed, toward it. There was a red Monza parked up on the ridge, its nose protruding over the pavement and its head-lights dark. As he got closer, he spotted three silhouettes inside the cabin, and he knew Cornichuk had been right:

"Blackwell and the girl are going to head straight for the old man's place to try and talk him into backing their version of what happened last night."

He'd have to wait until they were gone.

Which wasn't long.

Just as he found a chunk of driftwood to sit on, the cabin's front door flew open and a man and woman stumbled out, scrambling over one another and tearing up the ramp toward the car. Boyle lay down flat in a puddle behind the driftwood log, watching them run, and hearing eerie, insane screaming emanating from within the cabin that reminded him of wind, and steam, and, inexplicably, animals—big, angry animals.

The weird sounds went on for a long time, and the blue light in the cabin seemed to burn brighter, until it became a white pulse that faded only when the cries settled and the wind carried them away.

After the Monza drove off, the cabin's door opened again, and Joshua stepped into the storm, looking out toward the lake and pulling up his collar as he closed the door, and started walking directly toward the spot where Boyle lay hidden. Ten feet from the log, he paused, glanced over his shoulder, and then moved to the very edge of the lake, where he stood, quietly staring out into the howling storm.

Boyle squinted, trying to see what was so interesting out by the Island, but finding only the tiny white speck of a boat, bobbing on her anchor, flickering red and green running lights, and disappearing under a dark cloud that seemed to fall from the sky.

And then Joshua moaned, startling Boyle into freezing where he crouched, one hand on the log, the other on his knee as he lifted himself to his feet. Joshua had just taken a drink from a large, glass jar and was reeling, as if from a blow, making low, harsh moans that were a mix of pain and pleasure and rolling his head as if his neck were broken.

A light—maybe a flashlight—was bobbing out on the boat. It was just a speck, but its movement caught Boyle's attention for an instant before Joshua screamed, *"Shawnita! Shawnita shea negarik!"*

The little light jumped off the side of the boat and Joshua threw back his head, laughing into the storm, *"Negarik negee shawnita!"*

Boyle ran his hand over his face to peel away the glaze of sand that had formed there as raindrops splashed around him. He was feeling uneasy, and frightened, which was terribly unusual for him.

It wasn't what the old man said—garbled into nonsense by the wind—but how he'd said it that chilled Boyle's blood and made him afraid. It was the loud, piercing tone of voice Joshua used to lift his cries over the rumbling storm; it was the feeling of impending contact his tone communicated, as if the old man believed that there was something out there, in the cold dark, listening, perhaps preparing an answer. Talking to invisible things in the air—at least in Boyle's estimation—indicated that the old man was crazy, and Boyle's mother had once told him that crazy men were stronger than normal people, and that listening to them could make another person crazy too.

Joshua fell silent, his arm dangling limp at his side, his head tracing a rough circle in the air, his hair soaked tight against his skull as he swayed on the sand.

"Kill the old man so that I've got a body to hang on that Blackwell kid and instead of five hundred, I'll give you five thousand," Cornichuk had said, dropping Danko's limp corpse on the floor with a flat, heavy thud.

Five thousand dollars!

"I once heard that a crazy man down near Lakeland Grand tore his wife's tongue out with pliers," Boyle's mother had told him when he was any-age-under-six, for no particular reason, on some dateless, years-ago occasion that had faded in every detail except for that one, indelible revelation.

"When the cops went to arrest him, he broke out the back of the police car by smashing his hand right through the window and unlocking the door. They found blood all over the car, and a trail running off into the woods, but they never did find him, alive or dead, and nobody's seen him since. But every year, 'round Halloween, a woman dies near where he used to live; and the bodies never have no tongues.''

Five thousand dollars!

Joshua lifted his hand to his head, staggering a little and looking around as if he weren't sure where he was.

Five fucking thousand fucking dollars!

When Cornichuk broke Danko's neck it had sounded like someone tearing the drumstick off a thirty-pound turkey.

''Do like I told you, or you're next!''

''Promise your ma that you'll never listen to a crazy man. Promise me!''

Boyle stood up, dripping wet and darkened by running patches of sand and mud, clenching and unclenching his fists, his eyes gleaming under his brow as he stepped forward and said, ''Hello, Josh.''

The old man didn't seem to hear.

''Joshua?'' Boyle said, louder.

''Who?'' the old man began, turning and rubbing his eye. ''You? No!''

Boyle took his hat off and smiled wide. There was fear in Joshua's voice and that made the young man feel better. If he was afraid, that meant that he knew what was going on, and that meant that he wasn't crazy. Boyle would have hated killing a crazy person.

''Fuck you, Boyle!'' Joshua suddenly cried, nearly falling in a quick, stumbling flourish and starting down the beach.

''Come on, Josh! Ain't you glad to see me?'' Boyle said, easing into a long-legged stride before Joshua could get ten yards. He was surprised that the old man was heading away from the house, but grateful since he'd be easier to catch in the open.

He let Joshua run for two or three minutes, giving him time to clear the cabin so that his body would be visible from the road, and to get him winded before the inevitable, though surely brief, struggle to come. Another twenty yards passed before he gave a quick kick, sprinted up and caught Joshua by the scruff of the neck, pushing him so that his forward motion sent him sprawling headfirst into the water, where he struggled, his arms and legs squirming as he tried to right himself before Boyle kicked him in the ribs and lifted him, wheezing and fighting, only to hurl him down on the stones.

The quickest way to do this, Boyle thought, would be to plant one knee between Joshua's shoulder blades and hold him face down . . .

. . . and then Boyle's eyes bulged and his teeth came together, slicing his tongue as his mouth filled with blood and his fingers flexed spasmodically on his belly, where Joshua had planted something hard, and cold, and sharp, and deep.

He tried to pull away, to step back from whatever it was Joshua had done to him when the old man, kneeling now, let out a grunt and yanked his arm up with all his weight, slashing the seven-inch fishing knife he always kept in his belt up, slicing flesh and catching bone with a snap. The knife pulled from the old man's hand, ruining his balance so that he reeled back and flopped into the water.

"Oh, God!" Boyle hissed, knock-kneed and staggering, groping with his trembling hands at the numb, steaming place under his bloody shirt where parts of himself he'd never seen, should never have seen, oozed from the horrible gash raked from his right testicle to his ribs. There was surprisingly little pain, just an unbelievable sensation of displacement and panic as his brain registered that he was about to die.

His legs folded up.

He was warm, and wet—up to his elbows and down to his knees; he was cold and wet and his face felt hot; and then he was cold, and then hot, and then something slid beneath his belt and . . .

"Oh, Jesus!"

Joshua was standing over him.

It must have been the blood—all that blood, rushing out, swirling in the stinging murk of lake water and sand in his eyes—because it couldn't be real, he knew, it couldn't be, shouldn't be real. . . .

"Promise your ma that you'll never listen to a crazy man. Promise me."

"Shawnita! Shawnita shea negarik!"

He'd heard the crazy man's words.

"Promise me!"

"I'm sorry, ma," he whispered, his face touching the cool water and a muscle in his leg twitching into a steady, lonely tremor that he had the strength neither to stop nor to continue for long.

It couldn't be real. . . .

Joshua stood with his coat hanging open and the Black Tower dark behind him, staring at Boyle, smiling at him, speaking to him in a voice carried away by the wind and blurred by the rushing of ebbing blood. The coat hung open, and beneath its dark blue folds was an abomination the likes of which Boyle could never have imagined.

It was wet, running with streaks of dark moisture over a convoluted mass of bulbous growths. Emergent, yet-to-firm bones folded in a kind of fishy, spinal pattern along something that resembled an arm, but that was now an ophidian, fetal length of pink, vein-mapped flesh. And a white, translucent membrane that was crusted with what must have been the dark remains of Joshua's decaying skin, quivered over this secret, burgeoning horror, as the pouch seemed to struggle for its own independent breath.

It can't really be there! Boyle thought as water entered his mouth. It can't really be.

Somewhere, nestled deep in the mass of pink and white tissue, there were two sharp, folded lengths of cartilage, as big as butcher knives, like stingers. . . .

It can't be glowing blue. . . .

And lengths of cordlike flesh, that squirmed . . .

It can't be real. . . .

And long tears where the sack was splitting open, and moving . . .

It can't be. . . .

It can't. . . .

PART TWO

The Black Tower

One

"ARE YOU SURE he's not there? Could you check again, please?" Pete said into the receiver as sunlight sparkled on dry, streaked glass and ants swarmed around an empty milk-shake cup on the phone booth's floor. He moved his face into the shadow of one of Ronald McDonald's golden arches and closed his eyes against the throb of his aching head. And, in that instant of personal solitude, his dream flashed before him, all of it, at once, a single image of probing shovels, bloody mud, severed fingers, and dark tunnels.

With a quick jerk of his head, he opened his eyes, banishing the vision and finding, across the restaurant's steaming parking lot, the very tip of the Tower, poking up over the tangled horizon of TV aerials and slick roof tiles, black, and unnatural.

It was real, he decided, the dream.

It was as real as Joshua's cabin filled with eerie, blue light—where the hell had that light come from?—and as real as Kyrik's groundless accusations of murder. It was as real as Lori's willingness to join a perfect stranger in his senseless troubles, and, most importantly, it was as real as Pete's very presence in town.

Here he was, standing in a phone booth, in Sharthington, Ohio, talking to an undertaker about a man he had never met, in the clean, storm-washed sunshine of a beautiful July afternoon, while, just a couple of miles away, a building—a lousy pile of rock—was calling him. . . .

Calling him!

He could feel it, tingling every nerve in his body!

And he couldn't even remember exactly how the hell he had gotten here; when he was really honest with himself, he couldn't recall one precious thing about the trip that had brought him to Sharthington from New York.

It was as if he'd just gone to bed drunk on the night of his birthday party—the party his parents paid for, the party with two hundred guests—and had awakened to a head-pounding hangover, his mind filled with the burned-out, afterimages of a really intense stupor and his entire being reacting to something strong, and dangerous, out there, in the Tower, coming to him in waves of welcome that passed through the ground like tentacles, bleeding up through the corrugated steel floor under his shoes, turning his stomach inside out, and settling like an infection in his groin.

Either it was real, or he was losing his mind.

And he sincerely didn't want to believe that he was irrational. Not yet, anyway.

"Listen, pal," a voice that had been sickeningly pleasant just a few seconds before said into his ear, dropping a register in pitch, and an attitude in tone. "This is a funeral home, not a shoe store. He ain't here. Now get off my back!"

A loud click broke the connection, and Pete blinked, stared at the dead receiver, and hung up, muttering, "Crabs," as he turned, paused, and forced a smile.

Lori was sitting on the hood of her car, her face profiled against the vivid blue sky, surrounded by a dozen or so sea gulls that hovered and squawked, swooping down and riding the newly warm air to pluck French fries from her outstretched hand.

She's beautiful, he thought. Positively stunning.

With her lovely, tanned legs revealed by the cut-off jeans she'd put on in the McDonald's ladies' room, and her yellow tee shirt knotted casually under her bust, she looked at ease, and sensual—the kind of girl who looked right with her shoes off, the kind of girl Pete had never known. He was familiar with the dress-code crowd, the girls with money, the girls who kept their shoes on even when they were too stoned to find their feet.

She glanced his way as he stepped from the phone booth, the sun sparkling her golden hair as she asked, "Did you find him?"

"No," he said, leaning on the Monza's fender and shaking his head. "Nobody at the county morgue's ever heard of him, and the guy at the funeral home says that not only isn't he there but the whole place is empty right now. Either Mallard's body walked to the next town for burial, or Kyrik was lying."

"About what?"

"About Mallard having been found dead, I suppose," Pete said, helping himself to one of her French fries. "Or about him having died at all."

"Did you call Mallard's house?"

"No answer."

"Well, there's only one thing left to do," she said, jumping down and brushing salt from her lap. "Let's go ask Kyrik why he lied."

Pete didn't move. The idea was so appallingly simple, and yet so absurd, that he was left temporarily speechless.

"You're a Blackwell," Lori said, opening the driver's-side door as disappointed gulls fluttered overhead. "And you've got a zillion dollars behind you. Why let Kyrik push you around?"

Pete watched her slam the door and decided that she deserved an answer.

"Because," he said, using a tone of voice that he meant to sound serious, "between this thing with Mallard and what happened with Joshua before, I'm beginning to think that I'm in way over my head. This whole thing: the town, and Kyrik, and Joshua, and, well, even you in a way . . . everything . . . I don't know. . . . I just get the feeling that something's coming. Something big. And I guess I'm spooked because I'm so small. I really am."

"So, you believed in Joshua's magic frogs and devil boats?" Lori asked, starting the car and snapping her safety belt.

"He had *something* in that jar," Pete said, climbing into the passenger's side with a frown. "And, whatever it was, it was glowing. . . ."

"But you're not the least bit curious about what it was, right?"

Pete paused.

"If there's one thing in this whole world that I am, it's curious," he said, solemnly. "I always have been. I can't pass up a puzzle, or a mystery, I can't leave a dark spot alone until I find out what's inside, and I can't stand the temptation to stick my nose where it probably shouldn't be.

"When I was a kid, my grandmother gave me one of those wooden dolls that they make in Russia—the ones that you open to find another one inside. . . . You know the ones?"

Lori nodded.

"Well, I opened mine until I got to the last one, the smallest doll, and, when I found that it wouldn't open, I got a saw, and cut it in half, just to see . . . just to be absolutely sure that there wasn't something else, deeper inside, that I might miss if I wasn't careful."

He turned to her, and his face was absolutely firm.

"I'm almost pathologically curious; at least that's what my professors say, anyway. But that's why I do so well in school. I'm going to be Dr. Blackwell pretty soon, the first full-fledged Ph.D. our family's ever had. That's how curious I am.

"But as much as I'd like to find out what was in Joshua's jar, and why Kyrik's acting like he is, I can't ask you to put yourself at risk anymore. You've already done more than anyone else would in your position, and I really don't want anything to happen to you."

"You just worry about you, and I'll be fine," Lori said with a smile as the car lurched toward the street. "Before you came along, nothing interesting ever happened to me, and I've lived in this lousy town for almost two years now. But in the past twenty-four hours I may have actually seen a Blood Fly!—that's like seeing the Easter Bunny, for Christ's sake—I've met a Blackwell—which is like meeting the Easter Bunny's uncle—and now I'm going to meet Randolph Kyrik!

I can't stop yet; there's too much that I've always wanted to see around here, and, because of you, I'll have my chance. I should probably be scared. I mean, exposing your childhood memories to the light of adulthood and everything . . . I don't know. I guess I should be scared. But I'm not, really."

Not yet, Pete thought, seeing Joshua's eyes burning in his mind as the Monza headed for Route 11.

You're not scared . . . yet.

"Maybe he went to lunch," Pete said, pushing the doorbell again and noticing that his watch read one o'clock.

Taking a step back, he placed his hands on his hips and ran his eyes over the front of Kyrik's tall, white, immaculate mansion. Its high peaked roof, intricate green gingerbread, and dark windows were clean and startling against the featureless mirror of the lake behind. Just forty-five minutes ago, Erie had been a monster of churning waves, and now she was calm, smooth, and bright. He'd never seen such an abrupt change, or such brightness—it was as if the sun were melting down and coating the water, making it sharp, intense, and almost painful to look at.

"I still can't believe I'm standing here," Lori said at his back. "Ever since I was a little girl, this house has been like a fairy castle. My mother used to tell me that the man who owned Sharthington lived here."

Pete frowned, thinking that she wasn't too far off.

"We'd come into town on Sunday to see a movie," she continued, strolling along the flowers bordering the porch. "And then we'd ride around, eating ice cream and looking at houses like the movie hadn't ended, like we'd climbed into it for a while. We'd ride along, pretending we were characters on a screen, trying to find the house where we belonged, the house that was just right for two beautiful ladies like us. We always looked at this one last, because this was the one we both always thought was right."

A movie? Pete thought as Lori changed direction and walked back past him to climb the six stone steps to the porch.

While he tried to understand why her image of Sharthington as a movie set unsettled him so much, she examined the white, wrought iron lawn furniture arranged in front of the picture window, running her hands along the finely formed, metal embellishments that twisted themselves into an ivy pattern, and saying, "Nobody's used these chairs in years. Except for the people we'd see cutting grass or trimming bushes, there was never any sign of life around here."

Suddenly, she swung the chair up and sent it crashing through the window, leaving a huge, jagged hole through which a cool, air-conditioned breeze escaped from the dark.

"What the hell's wrong with you?" Pete shouted, bouncing around on the lawn like a clown and glancing around to see if they had been observed from the road. "Jesus! What if they come back?"

"Don't sweat it," she assured him, smiling and crouching as she climbed into the house. In a moment, the front door opened and she said, "Ain't you ever done anything wrong?"

"Not like this," he answered from the lawn. "What if we get caught?"

"Come on," Lori said sternly, motioning with her hand and stepping back, into the darkness of the foyer. "It's a movie. Nothing bad happens in the movies."

Pete forced his feet to move, following her through the dark hole in the screen that was Kyrik's front door, and into the next scene, which was the old man's living room. She took his hand and led him past where the lawn chair lay on its side in a nest of broken glass.

"Look," she said at the back of the house, pointing to a window overlooking the lake.

Pete strained his eyes, seeing a large, white power boat about a quarter-mile out, gliding slowly away from shore and toward the Black Tower.

"Kyrik?" he asked.

"Kyrik," she nodded. "I noticed it while we were still out front. Nobody owns that kind of a boat around here except for the old man, and, since his boat's out there, I'd assume that he is too, with Cornichuk standing one pace back and to the left, as usual. He says you killed somebody. You say you didn't. I just thought that taking a look around in here might help you figure out why he's trying to get you in trouble. And besides, I've always wanted to see what it looks like in here anyway, and this might be my last chance.''

''But what about burglar alarms?''

Lori paused and knotted her eyebrows.

''Shit,'' Pete said, and quickly they looked over the front door and window for wires or cameras, finding none, which they thought was a little strange, but lucky.

''Okay,'' Pete said when their search was through. He was standing near the black marble bar and facing the window over the lake. ''Since we're here, we may as well see what we can find. You take this floor, and I'll take upstairs.''

''What are we looking for?'' Lori asked, stepping toward the kitchen.

''I don't know,'' Pete answered, heading for the stairs.

He was gone in a moment, and then Lori heard his soft, careful tread on the floorboards above as he began searching the upstairs hall.

He was such a strange man, she thought, opening a door off the living room and stepping through. He was brave—like the way he jumped right in at Rages and stood up to Ronnie Boyle—and, yet, he was childishly unsure of himself—like his fear of Kyrik, which she thought overblown and unfounded. She liked him a lot, but she wasn't sure why.

She paused.

The room in which she stood was empty. Not a stick of furniture or a scrap of carpet.

Easing herself back, she closed the door and headed down the hall to the next, thinking that, outwardly, with his long hair and jeans, Pete looked pretty much like any of the other guys who might walk into her life. But, underneath, she sensed a gentleness and capacity for affection that was unique in her experience.

Behind the next door, she found another empty room.

''What the hell?'' she said, feeling suddenly uneasy and pulling the door shut. ''I know somebody lives here.''

In her newfound concern, she forgot about Pete for a time, and worked her way around the first floor, opening doors and

growing more confused by the minute. Soon, she was standing in the living room again, with her back to the patio,
running her eyes over the hall and shaking her head.

Other than the living room, not one room on the first floor
had been occupied. Behind every door she opened, she found
the exact same things: dust, grime, cobwebs, and the heavy,
unhealthy smell of dry rot. The place looked as if it had been
abandoned for years—except for the living room, which was
clean, fresh-smelling, and elegant.

The whole house was like an elaborate prop, she thought,
remembering her comment about nothing bad ever happening
in the movies.

"Who says?" she whispered.

From the outside, Kyrik's home looked like the perfect
retreat for a retired man of wealth, while inside . . .

There were old newspapers on the floor, for Christ's sake!
She'd looked at one brittle, yellowing page in a room with a
fireplace facing the lake, and it was dated 1967.

1967!

Twenty years!

Stepping to the front door, she looked the place over.

From where she was standing, she had a view of a perfectly
normal house, nothing amiss. A visitor, moving—as she was
now—from the foyer to the living room, wouldn't be able to
tell that most of the house was empty without actually setting
out on a search.

Why, a person could spend an entire evening talking and
visiting in absolute ignorance, only to go away thinking that
Randolph Kyrik's home was comfortably decorated with a
tasteful mix of modern and antique furnishings and saying,
sincerely, "I'd love to see what he's done with the rest of the
place."

"Wouldn't you be surprised?" Lori said, almost smiling.

The only room on the first floor that she hadn't seen was
the kitchen, and, stiffening up her spine, she walked over to
it, and pushed open the swinging door.

She found a tiny kitchen set, with two chairs, and a table,
a sink full of dirty dishes, empty TV dinner trays smeared
with lumps of hard, brown food piled in a mound on the

counter, grocery bags full of garbage, stacked, one atop another almost halfway up one wall, and movement amid the clutter that she knew meant bugs: roaches probably, and flies. There were a lot of flies.

With a jolt, she realized that the fairy castle of her childhood, the perfect movie house for two ladies as lovely as her mother and she were on those long-ago Sunday afternoons of ice cream and film fantasy, had a dirty little troll living in it. A weird, dirty little troll of a man who spent his whole life trying to convince everyone that he was something that he most certainly was not, which was *normal*.

"This place is nothing but a squirrel cage," she said, glancing through the greasy window and making sure that the squirrel's boat was still in sight.

Turning her attention back to the kitchen, her eyes fell on a door to the left of the refrigerator. Instinctively, she knew the door led down, to the basement. It was painted yellow, like the rest of the woodwork in the room, and it was locked from the kitchen side.

Who locks their cellar? she thought, snapping the tab and turning the knob. When the door opened, she found the stairs flimsy, old, and dark.

God, she hated the dark.

Light switch . . . light switch . . .

Okay.

It was on the wall to her right, and when she snapped it on, the stairs didn't look so bad any more. Just plain old wood-plank cellar steps, between plain old cinder-block walls, like a plain old mine shaft into a plain old pit.

"Why me?" she said, the urge to close the door strong in her, but the urge to dig deeper, to see what was at the heart of her ruined dream house, overpowering caution.

Carefully, she began her descent.

Twenty, thirty, fifty steps?

That couldn't be right. . . .

Running her hand along one rough wall, she reached step number sixty-six, the last, and found a small room, perfectly square, with two concrete-block walls, and another door, a big one, with large, black bolts and heavy bands of dark steel running across it, again locked, with light bleeding beneath, straight ahead.

A large key hung on a peg to her left, and she lifted it, noticing that there was a policeman's nightstick leaning in the corner nearby. Picking it up, she wondered why it was there, bounced it in her hand, and decided to keep it. She had a gun in her pocket, but, for some reason, the stick felt comforting, and she patted it against her thigh as she slipped the key into the lock and swung the great, old door open, surprised at its weight, and glad that it didn't squeak on its hinges.

Inside, she found a series of overhead lights, glowing single-file along the ceiling of a long, cool, fly-filled room. The bulbs were dim, producing intricate shadows on either side and a dingy path down the room's center. The air smelled of urine and sweat, hanging thick over two rows of stables, or pens, built along both walls, with three-foot-high, wooden gates and reinforced chicken-wire enclosures.

Fingering the club nervously and taking a deep breath, she stepped through the light and peered into the shadowy series of cages to her right, wondering what kind of animals Kyrik kept in such a place, and feeling a prickle of unease on her skin. Something formless and vaguely familiar was huddled against the wall, featureless in the corner's shadows, crouching in the straw. Whatever it was, it was big, motionless, and silent.

Pigs? she thought, moving her face closer to the wire and lifting her hand to shade her eyes.

It's a big pig. . . .

"Jesus!" she whispered as the shadowy lump assumed a familiar form in her mind. "It can't be . . ."

But it was. A woman, a young woman, maybe Lori's age, maybe younger, squatting, her head pressed into the angular space where wall met wall, her knees drawn up to her chin and her face hidden by colorless, tangled hair, beneath which black, buzzing spots crawled undisturbed. She didn't move or speak, didn't acknowledge Lori's presence in any way; but she was watching, warily, defensively, like an animal might watch a visitor at the zoo.

Lori was trembling.

Why didn't she speak, the woman in the cage, the woman who wore nothing but a visage of defense and terror? Why couldn't Lori find her own voice as she stepped on, to find another girl, locked tight in the next pen, and the next, and the next, twenty women, maybe more, various ages, various sizes, but identical in condition and solitude? What queer, violent emotions were building in her chest, vibrating her arms and legs in a quivering dance of fear and outrage as she completed her circuit of the cages and stopped at the center of the room, raising her eyes to the ceiling and her voice to the sky that she knew was blue and clear, up there, somewhere, over this evil cell of secret abuse, as she screamed, "What have you done?!"

Her words seemed to echo endlessly between her ears, finding terrible loneliness in her mind.

"Damn you, Kyrik! Damn you to hell, you bastard!" she screamed, first words, and then guttural, choking sobs of pure emotion as she buried her face in her hands, the nightstick clattering to the concrete at her feet, the clarity of what she stood amid washing through her senses, freezing her heart and cracking her precarious composure.

They were mindless, the women watching her from their cells. Void, staring with empty eyes and distorted looks of confusion and deluded misunderstanding. They were naked, bruised, smeared with straw and dirt and their own filth that was piled like horse droppings around them. Their faces were swollen, distended and rough, bulging with black welts and running sores the likes of which Lori had never seen, the cause of which she could only imagine as . . .

The nightstick!

She stared down at the chipped, crippling rod at her feet, hating it, despising it, seeing it whistling into the flesh and bone of a cowering body—her cowering body! What Kyrik had done, he'd done to her, to all women, any woman, any human being, because to do this thing, people, in his mind, could only be objects to be used, manipulated, tortured for . . .

What?

What did this mean?

"Son of a bitch!" she shouted, kicking at the stick and sending it babbling across the floor, where it came to rest against a door she had not yet noticed.

She drew her gun and cocked its hammer.

Kyrik wasn't here, which she suddenly regretted. Evil had blossomed a face in her mind: a single, human face of smooth, flawless skin, and demented, focused intent. Kyrik wasn't here, but if anyone he employed should be hiding behind that door, he would die.

She could do it, she decided.

She'd carried her gun as a protection against rape, against the Ronnie Boyles of the world, against the destructive, harmful capacity of the men she'd seen strutting and swearing and posing at Rages, drunk on the alcohol she poured.

She could kill, she now knew.

Maybe she hadn't been sure before—she'd always wondered if the gun were not simply a talisman against the monstrous side her mind found in others—but now, she could, and she would, for what she'd seen, and for what she'd discovered in Kyrik's hidden soul.

But as prepared as she believed she was, what she found in the room behind the door shocked her beyond words, beyond terror, beyond even a scream.

"My God!" Pete exclaimed, rising from his seat behind Kyrik's desk.

The office was plush, private, and expensively furnished in the same delicate, tasteful manner as Pete's father's office in New York. Deep, dark-brown carpet supported heavy, Victorian furniture and offered a gentle base color for the rich mahogany paneling and thick, velour draperies. But, in contrast to the security and impregnable sophistication the decor implied, the desk, floor, and every other available surface was covered with notes, pads, books and pages, scattered—blown, it seemed—around the room, as if by a whirlwind of anger, or excitement.

Pete had discovered the office first, and had settled imme-

diately behind the desk, reading and digesting what he found
in quick bursts of comprehension, and interest.

And now . . .

"Lori!" he shouted, heading for the door. "Jesus! Lori!"

"Pete!" she responded, nearly knocking him over as she
stumbled into the room.

"You won't believe what I found!" he shouted.

"The basement!" she sobbed. "Down there! My God!"

They stared deeply into each other's eyes for a moment
before the impact of the emotion they seemingly shared overwhelmed them both, driving them into one another, where
they suddenly entwined, hungrily, their arms reaching out
and drawing what warmth and support they could find, meld-
ing them, briefly, into one single, shuddering expression of
terror and need.

Pete, his face buried in her hair, his eyes closed and his
arms aching with his desire to protect her, and to be protected
by her, spoke first, saying, "It's worse than I thought."

Which was not what he meant to say, and certainly not
what he should have said—it was too dramatic, too blunt, and
too hopeless.

Lori was nodding, and, he noticed for the first time, crying, softly, and without sound.

He pushed her away gently, holding her shoulders and
looking into her wide, red-rimmed eyes.

"What happened? Are you all right!" he asked, the fear
rising in his stomach that she may have been physically
harmed. After what he had found, he knew that there was
simply no telling what this house could contain.

And he'd sent her into the basement!

He'd told her to go!

"Down there," she said, her voice strangely flat, and unnaturally weak. "Bodies . . . cut . . . hanging on hooks and
floating in barrels. Women . . ." she stopped, stared, continued. "In cages, like animals . . . babies, pinned open on
tables, under lights, with cameras!"

She closed her eyes and squeezed her lips together tightly
for a second, during which Pete tried to pull her back to him.
But, suddenly, she was free, her feet planted on the carpet

and her back rigid as she threw her hand out accusingly and screamed, "What have you done?"

"Me?" he responded.

"Yes, you!" she cried. "You brought him here! You paid him to come, gave him our town, and then went away so that he could do as he pleased with us! You! Blackwell! You!"

His family *had* sent Kyrik to run Kannon in Sharthington, but did that really make *him* responsible?

"You did it!" Lori said again, staring at him and seething in her place.

Pete shook his head.

"He's got them in cages," she added. "And he chopped them to pieces on a steel table."

"No, he didn't," Pete said softly. "Cornichuk did. He's a vivisectionist."

"A what?" she asked, incredulous.

"He dissects living animals. That's why Kyrik hired him."

"You knew about this?" Lori asked, her cheeks flushing from pale to pink.

"I know now," Pete said, pointing at the pile of books scattered on the desk. "He spelled it out."

"He admits it?"

"He's very specific. He has to be."

"Has to be what?"

"Specific. He's dealing with an almost unbelievable amount of money. The people buying his product want concrete, verifiable proof that they're getting their money's worth. That's the reason for the cages, and the women, and everything else. All you found is Kyrik's research and development department."

"All I found . . . ."

"There's more," Pete interrupted, stepping around the desk.

Lori frowned.

"There's so much that it's almost impossible to believe," Pete said, sitting down. "But it must be true. I mean, my God, it all fits."

Lori stepped up and slammed her hands down on the desk, saying, "What about those women downstairs?"

Pete looked up and tried very hard to make his voice sound reasonable, despite the impact he knew his words would produce.

"They may as well be dead," he said. "Their minds have been so severely altered that they can't think for themselves at all. They're zombies."

"You're serious?" Lori asked, her voice softening.

Pete nodded once, grimly.

"But how?"

"It's all tied in with the Flies," Pete said, lifting a blue notebook. "What Joshua said about my great-grandfather was true, for the most part. He really did discover some kind of animal out in the lake, and he did spend the rest of his life studying it, until he disappeared. Apparently, Kyrik found his notes and journals, and believed what was written there, because, for the past twenty years or so, he's been getting ready for tonight."

Lori sat down in a chair by the desk, her face pale again, her eyes watching Pete's face carefully.

"Joshua was right," he said, opening the blue book and pointing to something at which neither he nor Lori looked.

"The Flies do migrate every forty years. Kyrik was planning to move into the Tower and live there, like Noah Blackwell had. But during the renovation process he ran across the notes and records Noah left in the basement. He read them, found out about the migrations, and the poison the Flies produce, and saw dollar signs. I know his type, and I can tell you, without a doubt, that what he saw were gargantuan dollar signs. Since then, he's been recording evidence that the poison is just as deadly as he thinks it is, and just as dangerous as a drug."

"He drugged those women?" Lori asked, sitting forward in her chair.

"Systematically," Pete said. "And he hired Cornichuk to cut them up and record the changes in their metabolisms and anatomy caused by the drug. The dissected bodies are his database, the evidence he uses when presenting his sales pitch."

"But who would buy such a thing?"

"The government, for one," Pete said, digging through the stack and producing a draft copy of a sales agreement between Kyrik and a dummy corporation, cross referenced in the blue book as a front for the defense department. "And every other government Kyrik contacted. He's been running a kind of auction, providing different countries and companies with tantalizing footage of those women, and quite a few who've died with their husbands along the way, changing from human beings into deformed vegetables after controlled exposure to his toxin. And that's why he had Danko threaten me, so that I'd leave on my own without poking around or calling my family. He's been doing everything exactly the right way."

"The right way?" Lori cried.

Pete lifted his hand appeasingly.

"If you look at it from his point of view, sure. He's been cultivating a number of accounts, and creating a competitive atmosphere to drive up the price."

"He's been using those women as guinea pigs," Lori said sternly. "And you're sitting here and analyzing it?"

"That's what I know how to do," Pete said, his eyes fixed on Lori's face and his expression open and hopeful. "Before I came to Sharthington and became a criminal, I was a graduate student, hiding in a lab and growing bugs in Petri dishes on my way to a Ph.D. in molecular biology. It turns out I've followed in my great-grandfather's footsteps a lot more closely than I ever realized. I analyze, that's what I do—I study, and I learn. And we're lucky I do, because, if I didn't, I don't know what could have happened. We've got to stop him. . . ."

"Because of some goofy poison?" Lori interrupted. "With all the nuclear bombs and nerve gases in this world, how bad can one more poison be?"

Pete was nodding.

"You're right. It's a terrible thing, but it's just terrible, not mind boggling, like the part of my great-grandfather's notes that Kyrik's apparently chosen to ignore."

"What are you talking about now?" Lori asked suspiciously.

Pete picked up an obviously old volume and set it before her. It was flaking with age and peeling, and when he opened it she saw that the yellowing pages were filled with a tight, hand-scrawled script that she could hardly make out.

"It's my great-grandfather's summation, dated July 2, 1907, the year he disappeared."

Lori squinted her eyes, and then sat up, saying, "It's Greek to me."

"But not to me," Pete said, handing her a new piece of paper upon which he'd written something.

Lori examined it and shrugged.

"It says, 'My name's Peter Blackwell, and I love you, Lori,'" Pete said.

Lori blinked, swallowed, and said, "It looks just like the handwriting in the book, like your great-grandfather's handwriting. It's the same."

"Identical," Pete nodded. "And very spooky."

He noticed how she ignored his statement of affection, and chose to overlook it for the time being.

"Anyway," he said, laying the paper down and picking up the book again, "in the summation, he describes briefly what led up to his final experiment. And it's a lot more frightening than anything Kyrik's doing today."

He turned the page and pointed to a pen-and-ink drawing of something worm-like and dark, with tiny, vein-webbed wings near the center of its body and ridges from nose to tail.

"It looks like a leach with wings," she said.

Pete nodded.

"Exactly. This is what a Blood Fly looked like in 1879, when my great-grandfather first caught one."

He turned the page and displayed another drawing.

"Joshua had something like that in his jar!" Lori exclaimed.

Pete nodded again.

"Sometime between 1879 and 1907, my great-grandfather physically altered this animal, literally created a new species. And the scary part is that he didn't have the slightest idea of what the fuck he was doing!"

"I don't understand," Lori said, still examining the second picture. "It looks like he crossbred a frog with a leach."

Pete's eyebrows lifted a little, and he smiled.

"That's just what he did," he said.

Lori shook her head, saying, "That's impossible."

"It certainly is," Pete nodded. "But my great-grandfather did it! I don't know how—he says he explains it in his journal, but I haven't gotten that far yet. But, however he did it, he did, and the resulting implications are terrifying."

"So," Lori said quickly, "if this other thing's so amazing, why'd Kyrik pick the poison to monkey with?"

"Because he's a salesman!" Pete said, standing and lifting his index finger for emphasis. "The implications of changing life are staggering, but they aren't concrete. Kyrik went for the big bucks, the clear product, that handful of something to sell: poison!

"Everybody understands death, and he found it: death, purified to a liquid. He went for the big sale, like a trophy. Before he dies, he wants to sell something bigger than anyone's ever sold! But he'll never do it, because he doesn't understand."

"Doesn't understand what?" Lori shouted, jumping to her feet. "Will you just tell me what you're talking about already?!"

"If Noah Blackwell changed an animal from one thing into another, it means that he manipulated it genetically in some way," Pete said, carefully, emphasizing each word equally so that he sounded as if he were lecturing a science class. "That artificial evolution may partially account for the bizarre nature of this super-poison the Flies seem to have. But, even if it doesn't, it still leaves the fact that genetic manipulation is today's new science. If a man was experimenting with it a hundred years ago, he couldn't possibly have known what he was doing—not even the theory of it. He was blindly playing with a fire that eventually consumed him."

Lori was studying Pete with keen interest.

"Do you have any idea of what Kyrik's fucking around with out there?" he asked.

She shook her head and whispered, "No."

"Neither does he!" Pete shouted, slamming his hand down on the desk with a bang. "Nobody can know what Noah Blackwell made because he didn't live to describe it. If he made one new life form, then how did he do it? How many more did he make along the way? How many failures? What have his successes been doing between then and now? And how will his new animal's poison impact the environment if it's sold and used?

"Whatever's out there today was made by an ignorant, but ambitious, nineteenth century man, and it's had a hundred years to breed, mutate, and grow! It could be anything by now! Literally *anything!!*"

He turned and tore the curtain open behind him, clearing the way for a flood of dust-heavy sunlight to bathe the room, slicing around him in golden purity as he said, "And that's what happened to my great-grandfather! I've got to see it!"

"See what?" Lori asked quickly and Pete spun, leaning on the desk with both hands and hunching into a staring, rigidly intense definition of determination.

"It!" he said, as an oath. "Because, in all this world, there isn't another one like it! It's a genetically altered species that's had time not only to acclimate itself to its surroundings, but to improve! It's unique. There isn't another one like it in the world . . . at least not yet there isn't!"

He was silent for a moment, as if to allow his words time to penetrate, and then he was moving toward the door.

"Where would Kyrik keep his boat?" he asked, racing down the stairs with Lori behind. "With that drop there's got to be a dock at the base of the cliff somewhere."

"Will you slow down!" Lori said, shuffling at the bottom of the stairs and grabbing his arm to spin him around. "Just wait a minute."

Pete, breathing hard so that his shoulders rose and fell, paused, one hand on the bannister, eyes glancing nervously around the room as Lori, standing two steps over him said, "What are you going to do when you get out there? What's your plan?"

Pete's lips moved silently, as if he were speaking under

water as his mind raced with images centered on a need to move quickly, and with purpose.

"You don't have a plan!" Lori shouted, shaking him. "You're just going to go charging out there and get yourself killed. Look!"

She led him to the patio doors, handing him a pair of binoculars that were hanging on the wall and pointing to the bay.

Pete lifted the glasses to his eyes and said, "Damn!"

There were five black-and-white police boats resting on the smooth water between the shore and the Island.

"What did you expect?" Lori asked.

Pete considered, and then said, "I still want to see if there's another boat down there. If not, we're going to have to find one."

When he moved, Lori didn't.

He stopped at the yellow door to the basement, turned, and said, "What's wrong?"

Lori's eyes were silently eloquent.

"Oh," Pete said, remembering what awaited him at the bottom of the stairs. "You wait here, and I'll go check."

"No," she said, moving toward him with sweat on her forehead. "I'll come. Just take it slow."

He nodded, opened the door, and took her hand.

It was worse than she'd described it, and Pete was stunned back to caution by the depth of violence the dissection room betrayed.

Leaving Lori with the caged women temporarily, he moved through the laboratory, covering the horrors displayed there with whatever sheets and blankets he could find until only stained white lumps of fabric outlined Cornichuk's handiwork. He then checked a stairwell that led down from the lab, and was soon running back to the room with the cages, calling Lori's name.

Reaching the door, he stopped dead in his tracks, speechless.

Lori stood amid a group of naked women, who were now encircling her protectively and looking at Pete with narrow, suspicious eyes.

Lori stepped forward, saying, "I let them go."

"I see," Pete said, licking his lips nervously.

"I couldn't leave them locked up. I remembered what you said about them not being able to think for themselves, so I decided that I'd think for them."

"Do you think that was wise?" Pete asked softly, seeing the way the dark women seemed to be sizing him up with a collectively appraising stare.

"Yes, I do," Lori said.

"Well," Pete mumbled uneasily. "Now what?"

Lori turned and the women immediately gave her their complete attention. Raising her arms, she said, "Remember, from now on, you listen to me. Only to me. Don't listen to anybody else anymore. Just to me. Now, go upstairs and wait. I'll be back soon. Just wait. But don't let anybody hurt you anymore. If anyone comes, if anyone tries to do anything to hurt you, don't let them. Fight back. Fight for yourselves. Don't let anyone hurt you anymore. Now, go upstairs and wait."

Pete watched as the women nodded, turned, and began filing through the door and up the stairs to the main floor of Kyrik's house. He had to smile thinking of their dirty feet on the old man's perfect carpet, their soiled flesh on his fine furniture. Kyrik would die if he knew.

Kyrik would die. . . .

The women were gone and Lori turned, looking into the dissection lab for a moment and setting her features.

"Okay," she said. "What'd you find?"

Pete blinked, awash in that one disturbing thought of Kyrik's impending death.

The man was doomed, he suddenly realized. Kyrik would never admit it, would argue his way around the inevitable, but he was a dead man from any way you looked at it. The things he'd done would land him in jail, or the electric chair, if they ever came to light. The families of the women who had just climbed that lonely staircase would string him up from the church steeple and leave his body to the crows, given half a chance, and then there were the Flies. . . .

"Hey," Lori said, "let's see your big discovery."

Pete came out of his fog and looked at her, saying, "You should leave now. This isn't your problem. I did it."

"No you didn't. . . ."

"Yes, I did. You said so yourself."

"I was upset."

"You were right."

"Are you going to show me what you found, or am I going to have to go looking for it myself?"

Pete paused for one more stubborn moment, and then gave up, leading her through the dissection room and down the stairway, to the docks.

The room was large, with a ceiling at least thirty feet high, cut right into the rock and shaped like a dome. It was dingy and damp, with water sounds liquid in the air and long, slimy lengths of moss hanging from the walls, right down to the planking that started at the door and ended where the lake came into the cavern. There were two docking posts supporting the platform, one empty, and one holding a black-and-white police boat identical to the ones Pete had seen guarding the Tower.

"The discovery," he said, holding out his hands.

"We still don't have a plan," Lori said.

"That's true," Pete agreed. "But we do have a boat."

Two

THE BOAT RAN smoothly over calm water, but Kyrik was still having a terrible time getting the top off the cyanide bottle.

Cornichuk, who was piloting as straight a course as he could to the Tower, watched apprehensively as Kyrik fumbled, nearly losing the bottle, only to regain his grip and try again. He got nervous every time the old man went for the cyanide.

Kyrik had been careful in his handling of the Blood Fly venom, which he called BF-V for short. The active, mind-altering agents in the poison were very easily absorbed through the membranes of the body, and Kyrik had always worn protective clothing, goggles, rubber gloves, and even a surgical mask whenever he collected samples. But the mask had not filtered out the airborne particles of toxin, resulting in an amazingly slow process of poisoning that had finally manifested itself just a month before, in a display of rage and hallucinatory ramblings that would have resulted in the old man's suicide had Cornichuk not intervened.

Kyrik should have seen it coming, Cornichuk thought, glancing to his right and seeing that the old man had gotten the first vial open and was now working on the second. He knew how the venom reacted in the test subjects, and he knew how dangerous the poison was. But it wasn't until that night when he screamed, ''Corky! Oh, Christ! Corky!'' from his upstairs office in a blood-curdling voice, that the truth had become known.

Cornichuk had been in the living room, watching a video tape of one of the newer test subjects, a woman who had just allowed her hand to be scalded in boiling water without offering even token resistance, when he responded to Kyrik's call by jumping from the couch and hurling himself up the stairs.

He found Kyrik behind his desk, blood smeared over his face and pouring from two, jagged wounds he'd punched into his temples with a letter opener, screaming, "Corky! Get me out! Get them off!"

Cornichuk moved quickly, taking the letter opener from Kyrik's hand and nearly breaking one of his fingers in the process. For the next hour, he sat atop the old man, amazed at his hysterical strength, and chilled to the bone by his screams.

"Tunnels! Oh, lost in blue! Lost forever and ever!" he snarled, desperately trying to break Cornichuk's hold to claw at his own face. "God, the Blood! Oh, the Blood!"

Later that night, after Kyrik had calmed, they made the decision to implement the cyanide treatments.

"We've got to do it," Kyrik had said weakly from his chair by the fireplace. "It's dangerous, but I've inadvertently ingested enough toxin to build up a critical residual mass in my fatty tissues. If we don't begin using the cyanide, I'll die."

The reason for cyanide was that it entered the nervous system and instantly blocked the receptor sites on critical nerve endings in the brain and muscles. With these nerve endings blocked, the venom was left with no way to affect the functioning of the brain or body and was then re-absorbed into the fatty tissues from which it had been drawn by adrenaline, thus rendering it harmless, for the time being.

The problem with cyanide was that it's nasty, and it blocks nerve endings so well that, normally, a person exposed to it dies within just a few minutes.

And Cornichuk sincerely didn't want Kyrik to die.

He loved the old man, looking at him as a father who had taken him in and given him a job after the State of Ohio had condemned him to rot in an asylum for the "crime" of conducting research into the very nature of life itself, research that required dissection and study.

And what was the use in dissecting something dead if you were studying life? Cornichuk had reasoned.

Kyrik had understood that reasoning. After hearing about his case, he went to the hospital with false documents identifying himself as Cornichuk's uncle. The state released Cornichuk into Kyrik's custody—after Kyrik turned over a substantial donation to the mental health organization—and Cornichuk became a vital part of Kyrik's wonderful work, work that utilized his unique and specific talents.

To some, vivisection is an abominable thing. And even Cornichuk had to admit that it was messy: all that screaming and writhing around as he carried on with the task of laying open layer after bloody layer of flesh to expose the trembling, steaming organs within. But Kyrik understood the beauty of it as well as Cornichuk did, and was soon providing him with *human* subjects—human subjects who, because of the Blood Fly venom, seemed almost *willing!*

For that one act, Cornichuk owned Kyrik his life. So, every time the old man raised that vial to his nose to inhale the lethal fumes of cyanide, Cornichuk cringed, and was afraid.

He was afraid now.

"Be careful," he said as Kyrik popped the top off the second vial, the vial that contained the antidote to cyanide.

Kyrik turned and nodded, revealing his face. The skin was stretched so tightly that it pulled his eyes into slits and his mouth into an unwilling smile. The closer to delirium he came, the more his skin seemed to shrink. Now, he was very close, and, instead of an answer, he simply nodded and lifted the cyanide bottle to his nose, breathing deeply, as if savoring the sweetest perfume on earth.

Cornichuk tensed, preparing to lunge should the old man fall and flinching as Kyrik's muscles went immediately rigid when the poison blew through his body, petrifying his lungs and temporarily neutralizing the effect of the BF-V in his system. He was at the brink of death now, Cornichuk knew, and would die in moments without the antidote. But it was the risk he had to take to cleanse himself of the poison he had so carefully collected.

Completely pale, not breathing, his mouth open and a thread of saliva hanging from his lip, Kyrik lifted the second vial and drank.

A slow second passed.

And, then, another.

And, then, just when Cornichuk thought that this would be that one time when it wouldn't work, that this would be the time when the old man's eyes would roll back in his head and he'd collapse, Kyrik's chest quivered and exploded with a huge gulp as the chemical defrosted his lungs and heart. He slumped into the leather captain's chair to his right, laying his head on the instrument console and breathing fast as Cornichuk sighed, relieved, but no less tense.

"Okay?" Cornichuk asked, after a moment.

Kyrik nodded without lifting his head from his folded arms.

At least for now, he was still in control.

It was almost two in the afternoon when they docked at the foot of the Black Tower. Kyrik had regained most of his color, his eyes were round again, and there were even a couple of wrinkles around the corners of his mouth. But, as was usual after a cyanide treatment, he was physically sluggish and weak. He spoke in a soft voice, instructing Cornichuk to remove the heavy equipment they'd stored on the forward deck and telling him how to arrange it in front of the door at the Tower's southern base.

There were no gulls here, which was strange. There were always gulls on anything stationary in the lake, but here, on Black Island, there wasn't even a dropping. There weren't any rodents or insects to speak of either. Anything living had long ago been consumed by the ever-growing population of amphibious predators nestled in the caves below.

Cornichuk swung big, aluminum boxes from the boat and then heaved them up the steps cut into the Island's rock. After five trips, he'd moved everything into place and, wiping sweat from his face, sat down on one of the crates next to where

Kyrik was resting in the shade and testing the battery light on a khaki colored, army-style walkie-talkie.

"Why do you need a walkie-talkie?" Cornichuk asked, pointing absently.

"We still have a lot to do," Kyrik said without taking his attention from the radio.

Cornichuk nodded, noticing how the police boats arranged in a perimeter on the Island's southern side formed a blockade between shore and the Tower.

"Do we have enough time?" he asked, wiping his face again.

"Plenty," Kyrik said, placing the radio down and pointing to two wire-mesh boxes at his feet. "Bring those," he said, and turned abruptly away.

He's in one of his I'm-the-boss moods, Cornichuk thought, lifting the boxes and following the old man as he unlocked the door and stepped into the Tower. But that was all right—anything he had to do to keep himself together was fine. Normally, when Kyrik's tempers started to swing, they'd dope him up with tranquilizers for a few days and get him back down to an even level. But, today, he had to stay alert, and couldn't afford morphine, or any of the other chemicals he regularly used. Today, it was a wing and a prayer and a vial of cyanide.

From shore, the Black Tower looked large, heavy, and solid, but the simple physical distance between an observer and the stone masked the structure's true magnitude. To fully appreciate the size and oppressive volume of the Tower, it was necessary to stand where Cornichuk was now, at its base, looking straight up the rough, patched-stone surface that perspective seemed to suck miles into the sky. You had to see its dark stones and crumbling mortar that way, close enough to touch, close enough to feel the Tower's bitterly cold breath wash over your skin when the door creaked open, welcoming you into dark halls and damp tunnels where thousands of living things, unlike any other animal anywhere, slid, and watched, and waited. . . .

"Come on!" Kyrik said, and Cornichuk quivered, settled

himself and nodded, falling into step as the old man led the way to the breeding room.

They entered directly into a winding stone stairway that spiraled up to the beacon room at the Tower's tip, and down to the basement below. The Tower was actually just a stone tube, with a room at the top, a room at the bottom, and a connecting, concrete shaft running up the center, around which the stairs were wrapped. There were no windows on the structure's surface, except for those in the beacon room, which had been boarded up tight. Kyrik lifted an electric lantern from its hook by the door and held it high over his head, illuminating the stairs and heading down, one hand on the inside wall, and Cornichuk at his heels.

They'd only gone a few steps when they paused, listening.

"Hear it?" Kyrik said.

Cornichuk nodded, sweat beading on his upper lip, the sound of distant drumming, like thousands of feet slapping pavement, filling his head.

"Right on schedule," Kyrik smiled and continued on his way.

Cornichuk followed, cages in hand.

Soon they arrived at a huge door with a small window cut into it at eye level and covered with a sliding panel. Kyrik opened the panel and looked inside, holding the lantern away from his body so that his face was illuminated only by the light bleeding through the spy-hole. His eyes sparkled, and his teeth flashed.

"Fantastic!" he whispered, stepping aside so that Cornichuk could take a look, and adding, "Amazing, isn't it?"

Cornichuk's eyes adjusted to the chamber's dim light slowly, and he was confused for a moment as a single, formless curtain of shadow became a million individual bodies, intermingled dark on the sandy floor, and hanging from the walls in squirming disarray. The room was filled with huge, glistening toads, lying atop one another and crawling as more poured from the tunnels above in a steady stream. Those already inside were slamming their wings into the toads around them, producing the drumming sound that was so completely vibrating the air.

"What are they doing?" he asked, pulling his face from the opening and finding that Kyrik had continued on, to the collection cage, the one place on earth that Cornichuk hated more than his cell at the asylum.

Descending the last few steps, he found the old man already dressed in his orange rubber suit and surgical mask, holding out his hands to take one of the wire-mesh cages and turning to step through the last door on the stairs, into the breeding chamber itself. Normally, when he did this, the phone-booth-sized cage that was built over the inside of the door's opening was immediately covered with biting, furious Flies trying to protect their sanctuary. But, this time, the Flies all but ignored him, intent only on beating each other and being beaten, forcing the old man to bang his knuckles on the bars to get their attention.

But, once he did get their attention, the very thing that Cornichuk hated more than anything else, happened:

The Flies came.

In just seconds the cage was covered with furious animals that moved so fast that Cornichuk was never really sure if they flew, or just appeared, materializing from thin air. They hissed and snapped in screaming attack, biting and pressing their wet, dark flesh against the wire mesh, willing, it seemed, to slice themselves into little octagons to win the opportunity of touching the man in the cage.

And poison fell like rain.

As the Flies stung out in frustration, their tails struck the steel with blunt thuds and sharp clangs, shaking from their stingers deadly drops of venom that glazed Kyrik's clothing and beaded on his goggles.

Cornichuk's stomach turned, as it did every time he watched this display. He couldn't stand the sight of the Flies—their slimy skin, their soft, giving flesh. They disgusted and terrified him, and he felt no relief when Kyrik successfully caught his first specimen, because it meant only that he would have to take the cage and feel the quivering fury of a Blood Fly trembling in his hand.

Set into the center of the collection cage was a door into which one end of the wire-mesh, carrier cage that Kyrik held fit exactly. Securing the cage into place, Kyrik lifted the handle and opened the door, pulling the front of the carrier cage up and allowing one of the Flies to squirm into the container. Then he let the handle go, the door snapped shut, and he was kicking the cage across the floor to where Cornichuk crouched in the hall, prepared to slide the second, empty cage, to him.

In just a few minutes both cages were full, and the two men were back up in the sunlight near where they had docked the boat, with Cornichuk mechanically dumping buckets of water that he scooped from the lake over Kyrik's head, and rinsing the venom from his rubber suit before they attempted to take it off.

"What's wrong with them?" he asked, lifting another bucket and keeping his attention on the cages, which they'd placed in the shadow of the Tower to protect the Flies' sensitive skin from the sun. "They never did that before."

Inside their cages, the two captured Flies were banging back and forth, hard, and incessantly, as if they meant to do themselves some terrible, internal injury.

"It's what we've been waiting for," Kyrik said, slipping his hood off and unzipping the front of his suit. "The urge to move is consuming them, and soon they won't be able to resist it anymore. I took these two so that you can breed the Flies again, after we kill the rest of the group."

"Me?" Cornichuk asked, confused.

"I'm an old man, Corky," Kyrik said, stepping from his suit and wiping his face. "I couldn't leave you without a way to keep your corner on the poison market after I'm gone. These two Flies will ensure you unlimited wealth for the rest of your life."

"Thank you, Mr. Kyrik," Cornichuk said, looking down at the cages and thinking, The last thing I need is to be growing these things forever.

"But now," Kyrik said, breaking Cornichuk's train of thought, "we set the trap."

"Christ!" Cornichuk said, dropping the last crate on the dusty floor.

The beacon room was huge, and dim, with new plywood

planks nailed into place over what used to be windows and exposed beams running up the walls to crisscross the high ceiling like a web. In the center of the floor sat the rusted pedestal upon which the lighthouse's immense lamp had rested until about 1951, when the two-ton, pineapple-shaped system of intricate mirrors and machinery was purchased by the Lake Erie Historical Society for some museum somewhere, leaving a precise series of jagged holes around the pedestal's rim and a grimy trap door, which had been pad-locked shut.

Kyrik climbed the four steps up to the top of the pedestal, stood on the trap door, and surveyed the room. His white clothes were almost comically contrasted with the gloom of his surroundings, and it seemed to take him a very long time finally to say, "We'll set the nozzles around this altar and point them at the ceiling."

Cornichuk nodded, scratching his head and saying, "What's to stop them from just flying right back down the hole after we turn on the gas?"

"It should only take twenty seconds to saturate the im-mediate area," the old man said to himself, placing his hands on his hips and ignoring Cornichuk's question. "But, with the high ceiling, it'll be almost a full minute before the entire chamber loses atmosphere."

"Why should they just stay and die?" Cornichuk asked, raising his voice to get Kyrik's attention.

"Of course, we can't even turn on the gas before the whole group enters the chamber."

"Hey?"

"They can't smell it," Kyrik said, turning and levelling a cold, impatient stare across the room. "And by the time they realize something's wrong and do try to escape, they'll have received a lethal dose. Now, let's get started."

And Cornichuk did.

First, he strung incandescent lights along the perimeter of the room and connected them to a series of car batteries for power. Once the room was sufficiently illuminated, he took the six four-foot-long, stainless steel, high-pressure tanks from their crates and laid them out on the floor. The tubes looked like polished scuba gear and were filled with an incredibly harsh pesticide most commonly used on rats. As Kyrik watched from above, the big man arranged them every three feet or so around the pedestal and then constructed a complicated network of hoses and aerosol nozzles that were designed to move the entire gaseous contents of the tanks into the atmosphere at a swift rate. A sturdy network of aluminum rods held the structure together, ensuring that nothing would shake loose once the Flies started panicking. And a small, black, computerized triggering device was activated last, blinking a green light amid a nest of wires and connected by radio to a remote control switch that blinked green in Kyrik's hand.

"The system's hot," Cornichuk said, wiping dirt from his face and checking his watch. It was nearly eight P.M., and they'd been on the Island for almost six hours, which seemed like a long time. Stepping back, he added, "Looks good."

"Now, open the door," Kyrik said, stepping down and handing Cornichuk a key.

The big man fit the key into the padlock, grabbed the huge, iron rig, and heaved. The trap door squealed shamelessly as he lifted it on its hinges, revealing a perfectly round, perfectly black hole which, he knew, led straight down over a hundred feet, to the ceiling of the breeding room below. Holding his breath, he heard just the hint of a steady, wet, drumming, drifting up from darkness.

"And now we leave," Kyrik said, heading for the door.

After one last quick inspection of his work, Cornichuk turned off the lights and headed down the stairs, with Kyrik at his back, and the trigger light blinking green behind.

Kyrik snapped off the electric lantern and hung it back on its hook by the door as Cornichuk emerged outside, surprised to find that the sky was still light and the air still warm. Silently, he was grateful for the early evening heat. He'd never really appreciated just how cold the Tower was inside until now. . . .

"Shit," Kyrik said, just as he was about to lock the door.

"What's wrong?" Cornichuk asked, wanting very much to sound casual because Kyrik's eyes looked funny. The old man had already had two cyanide treatments today—one in his office and one on the way out to the Island—and Cornichuk didn't want him getting upset over anything.

"We left the specimens in the beacon room," Kyrik said, snapping his fingers.

The specimens? Cornichuk thought, looking back at the black hole in the Tower. How the hell did we forget the specimens? I don't even remember taking them up there.

"I must have carried them up by mistake," Kyrik said, as if reading the big man's mind. "I'm sorry. I was just trying to help."

"Okay, I'll get 'em," Cornichuk said, trying to mask his irritation and stepping back into the chill of the Tower. Lifting the electric lantern from its hook, he climbed the stairs, shaking his head, and thinking about how glad he'd be when this night was over.

At the top of the stairs he stopped, narrowing his eyes, digesting what he saw, and, in a rush, realizing that trusting Kyrik had been a tragic mistake.

On the floor near the blinking green trigger sat the cages for which he'd come, and, on top, the walkie-talkie Kyrik had been playing with earlier. A light on the radio glowed red and the Flies in the cages sat, watching him as sweat ran down his face.

They were perfectly still.

He swallowed.

They didn't move.

The walkie-talkie buzzed and Kyrik's voice said, "Corky? Are you up there yet?"

He stepped forward, lifted the radio, and pressed the signal switch.

"I'm sorry, Corky," Kyrik said through the speaker, his voice miniaturized into a thin, plastic buzz. "But the treasure's mine. And we do need bait in our trap."

He'd trusted him! He'd trusted the son of a bitch! For going on ten years he'd treated the old man like a king, done his bidding, done his dirty work and, now, this! To die this way! To die!

Black flesh and moist green eyes, pressing deeply against

wire mesh and dripping silver, sweaty drops of poison from wormy tails: the image filled his mind, unbidden, unwelcomed, and uncontrollable.

"Bastard!" he screamed, squeezing the radio and trembling.

The Flies in the cages hissed when he shouted and he kicked out, sending one of the boxes skimming into the wall with a bang.

"I'll tear you apart!" he screamed, crushing the radio in his hand and hurling the pieces into the wall.

The Flies would be coming, soon, maybe right now, stretching their wings—their thin, wet, cold wings—and lifting themselves into the air, into the tunnel and into the room where Cornichuk stood, paralyzed with rage and a new, nauseating wash of abject panic.

"They're coming!" he shouted, to himself, to the walls, to the darkness and to the captive Flies. "Dear God, they're coming!"

Lunging and sliding in the dust, he moved to the pedestal and leaned his weight back, pulling the trap door and slamming it violently down to cover the tunnel's entrance before the Flies could emerge. But, as it came toward him, the door stopped, snapping hard at the end of a thick iron chain padlocked to its ring. Moving around, he found the chain taught, bolted to the floor, and only long enough to allow the door to swing three quarters of the way toward its place, leaving the tunnel open, and his situation desperate.

"Damn it, damn it, damn it!" he hissed, pulling the door up and smashing it back down again, quivering the chain but unable to break it. "I never saw him lock the fucking thing! I never even saw him do it!"

He stopped.

His heart shuddered.

Deep shadows moved, thrown by the confined Flies as they climbed wire mesh and displayed their stingers. The electric light was sitting on the floor by the door as dust swirled in tiny layers, thinning its glow, muffling his breath, settling as . . .

It was soft, so soft, the hiss, at first—like air escaping from a punctured tire, like a snake on ice, like a blade slicing fat.

Cornichuk jerked two steps away from the hole.

Hissing, steady, close, and wet.

Fluttering, irregular, thrumming, and loud.

Birds.

Birds in flight.

Birds in flight in the dark!

"Christ!" he screamed, scrambling around the pedestal and hooking the lantern's handle as he dashed through the door, hitting the stairs and nearly pitching forward with uncontrolled momentum as behind something leathery and soft flapped and slapped stagnant, then exploding air.

He was running in circles, down a dizzying spiral leading around and around. He struck the stone-block wall with his shoulder, hard, huffing thick breaths and stumbling only to regain his feet, but never his wits as, from somewhere out of his sight, the sound of a breaking wave washed heavy, and sudden.

The intensity of the blast seemed to charge the air, pushing a great, rolling bubble of wind before it and catching Cornichuk in its momentum so that he stumbled one last time, and fell. The lantern clattered down the stairs with him, squeezing his movements into twisted, double-jointed shadows that bounced and struggled in concert with his bone-jarring impact.

His arm struck something that was not stone and the lantern wedged itself against a broken block, ten steps down so that the passage was almost entirely dark.

Almost dark, but not quite.

He lifted his head, his neck stiff, his back screaming, and saw, in the gloom, that he was in front of the door on the one landing between the beacon room and hell.

"Mr. Kyrik?" he cried, his voice high and thin. "Please! Mr. Kyrik!"

He tried to lift his hand to the doorknob, but it was just too far away.

"Mr. Kyrik?!"

Nothing.

He knew that Kyrik was there, listening behind the door, listening as he begged.

"Mr. Kyrik! Please! Oh, God, please!"

Cornichuk was on his feet now. He'd lifted himself, hand over hand, despite his battered limbs, and had set his shoulders. Taking a deep breath, he pushed his hands into the ancient wood, hard, with all his weight and concentration, producing an awful *boom!* and shaking the door on its frame.

"Kyrik?" he screamed.

Boom!

"Kyrik?"

Boom!

With each blow the door shuddered, and his bruises and fractured joints howled painfully with impact. But two of the door's beams had parted slightly, allowing a thin shaft of light to bleed onto his face, sparkling his eyes and focusing his intent beyond the pain as he pushed again, harder than before, shaking the door more than ever and howling, "I'll kill you, Kyrik! You're a dead man, Kyrik!"

One more push and the door would fall.

Just one more push . . .

His breath freezing in his throat, Cornichuk turned in time to see the stairwell above him fill with a descending, writhing mass of something that looked like dark foam. A roar washed through him and his mouth opened silently under his wide, terrified eyes as he stumbled back one step, lost his balance, pumped his arms, and was caught in the stomach by the first flying animal of the group, that hit him like a train and forced an *"oooff!"* from his gut as it lifted him from the floor. With a terrible crash he collapsed through the observation room door, landing on his back with shattered planks sharp beneath him and his head ringing with impact.

But the ringing was not the only sound he heard.

Scrambling to his feet, the big man stumbled back, away from where the Flies had come to rest outside the doorway. Looking himself over, he wondered why they hadn't stung or bitten him, why they were waiting outside. There were thousands of them, and, through the dark passage to the stairs, he could see their eyes sparkling, thick on the stone, perfectly still, and a deep, emerald green.

Something moved overhead—he saw it in his peripheral vision—and his eyes snapped up.

Thousands of yellow eyes were watching him from the tunnels above, and long, dark streaks of something wet were dripping out of the holes and down the damp concrete walls.

There were the Flies on the stairs. . . .

And things in the walls.

"Kyrik!" he screamed, and the Flies buzzed out a roar in reply. *"Kyrik!"*

The wall shook behind him and he spun, his fists hard and at the ready.

The Flies buzzed and he spun back.

Something barked overhead.

The wall behind him shook, and a tiny crack formed in the stone.

"Kyrik!"

The ground was trembling—he could see the tremors made visible as ripples in the pool. . . .

The pool!

Without another thought, he lunged for the dark water, remembering that the pool exited into the lake and giggling a little as he ran.

But then he stopped, knee-deep in water, his jaw dropping and his face going pale.

To his right, the smooth, concrete wall just disintegrated, starting with a tiny point about ten feet from the floor and spreading out into a spider's web of cracks that crumbled the stone in seconds and sent huge chunks of rock clattering to the floor. Mud swelled through the cracks, pushing outward as if something huge were behind the wall, surging up from below and spilling into the breeding room in response to Cornichuk's presence.

He couldn't move. His legs had gone stiff and his arms were trembling. Around his knees, something living splashed in the dark water, but he didn't even care. All he could see was the wall. . . .

And it was falling into a heap on the floor.

Overhead, the tunnels exploded with the sound of barking and burping snarls. The first misshapen silhouette of the something with burning, yellow eyes was just emerging into the light and starting the long climb down the wall, to the pool.

But he didn't care.

As he watched, the bulging mud broke, and a great quantity of watery earth was belched into the breeding room, sliding in a mound that spread out from the hole and releasing the first slashes of light from below. The whole room was blue now, and a misty haze drifted out of the new tunnel, carrying with it a smell of deep decay, and wet, slimy flesh. Long, greasy drops of mud formed along the tunnel's upper lip, silhouetted against the shimmering light and hanging suspended as a wash of something invisible found the air and rushed out, blowing around Cornichuk where he stood in the pool, rustling his hair, bringing tears to his eyes, lifting his trousers over a sudden, and desperate, erection and communicating one simple concept directly to his brain—without words, without sound, and without even the hint of a doubt.

"Welcome," the sensation seemed to say.

That was all.

Just *"Welcome."*

And, in the face of something so big, and so glad that he had come, Cornichuk did the only thing that he could do: he screamed.

Outside the Tower, standing with his ear pressed to the door, Kyrik waited for the screaming to stop before he pressed the trigger that released the gas.

Three

THE SHOWER HAD been running for so long that Pete had gotten used to its sound; it wasn't until the water stopped that he looked up from his reading.

Rubbing his eyes, he pushed himself back from the desk and noticed that the slash between the curtains had grown dark. Walking to the window, feeling stiffness in his legs and a dull ache in the pit of his back, he parted the draperies and saw the Tower, black against the early evening sky, surrounded by a nest of glowing water upon which triangular sections of light vibrated out from the tiny flotilla of police boats arranged side by side across the bay.

Search lights searching for what? he thought with a sigh, allowing his eyes to relax after five hours of reading. "No good," he said, shaking his head. "I just can't accept it. It's impossible."

Behind him the door opened and Lori padded across the carpet, stopping close by and saying softly, "Well?"

He turned, and caught his breath.

Lori had been occupied with bathing the women they'd found in Kyrik's dungeon. She'd taken them, one at a time, into the shower and gently scrubbed their wounds, distributing clothes from Kyrik's closet and cleaning out his pantry afterwards to find things for them to eat. Pete had half-listened to her activities—the splashing, the thuds of dropped soap and slaps of bare skin on linoleum—and he'd been amazed

by her lack of speech, and silent resolve. She hadn't chided
or babied the suffering girls, but had gone about her nursing
duties solemnly, and with an economy of talk that hinted at
the respect she must have felt for the pain her broken sisters
had endured.

Now, this woman stood before him, radiant and fresh from
her own bath, her eyes alive and her scent strong with perfume, transformed by her exposure to suffering from the
tough-looking, street girl he'd first encountered at Rages to a
powerful, healing angel. Her blond hair hung wet and tangled
on her head, she was wrapped in a Burgundy towel, and she
offered him a steaming, china cup.

Taking the cup and smelling coffee, he smiled, glanced
down briefly, and said, "You're beautiful."

She watched his eyes without comment.

To break the ensuing silence, Pete sat down and opened
the brittle volume of his great-grandfather's notes, saying, "I
don't know where even to start trying to explain all this, and,
even if I could, you'd never believe it."

"Whether you can explain it or not, and whether I believe
it or not, isn't going to stop us from going out there, is it?"
Lori said, leaning on the desk and crossing her perfect legs.

"No," Pete responded, trying, unsuccessfully, to keep his
eyes off her. "But *we're* not going. *I* am."

"You're different," she said, combing her fingers through
her hair. "Something's changed you."

He nodded, pursing his lips and feeling a sudden intimacy
with the woman perched, half-naked, on the desk beside him.
He felt as if he'd known her for years, as if his entire life had
been somehow paralleled by hers, and as if they'd always
been together. It was a common phenomena for strangers
who had shared some trauma to bond to one another, but,
somehow, his emotions felt deeper than that, more genuine,
and stronger.

"There's no other way to put it, other than to lay it flat
out," he sighed, setting his cup down and leaning back. "I
understand what's happening now, or at least I think I do.
But I won't believe it . . . I can't believe it . . . without proof.

And there's no reason for you to expose yourself to the dangers of my finding that proof.''

"Because you love me?'' she said, her hands folded on her knee.

"Because I love you,'' he agreed. ''And for another reason that you'll probably find even harder to believe.''

Pete paused, and then continued, ''Lay it flat out—it's gonna sound crazy.''

"I'm listening,'' she said, taking a seat by the fireplace.

Pete leaned forward and rested his elbows on the blotter, hanging his head over Noah Blackwell's ancient book and reading aloud, '' 'The Beast residing within this ill-tempered lake is unlike any other on the face of our globe, for, by means wholly mysterious to this witness, It can utilize the features of other living creatures unto Itself, thus transforming It, in body, and modifying It, in character.' ''

He glanced up.

"Go on,'' Lori said.

And he did, carefully.

'' 'As in accordance with certain understandings set forth by practitioners of medieval physiology, the Beast holds within the very fluids of Its being certain humors, or talents, which allow It to mate the essence of Itself, with the spark of another creature's life, thus creating new species where once there were none.

'' 'It is therefore in truth that I, William Noah Blackwell, say that it is within this Beast's Blood that Creation's hidden secret lies. And it is through the very heart of darkest night that that Blood Flies!' ''

"Blood Flies?'' Lori said softly. ''So that's where the name came from.''

Pete nodded, closing the book and lifting his coffee cup.

"Now, tell me what it means,'' she added.

"I can't, really,'' he said with a frown. ''But I'll tell you what I *think* it means. But remember, for this shit to sound reasonable at all, you've got to keep what's happened to us so far in mind the whole time. If you just take it on face value, it's going to sound like I've been taking a nap in here all afternoon and now I'm telling you about my dream.''

"Or about your movie?" Lori asked, with a grim smile.

Pete frowned, and sighed, saying with a resigned tone, "What Noah meant when he talked about humors and all that is that he believed that the blood of the Blood Flies contains a secret so powerful that God hid it in a mysterious, unappealing animal to protect it from ever being uncovered. He thought that the animal's body was just a vessel for its magic blood, and that its blood was responsible for all the weird things the animal could do.

"Apparently, what he discovered is an animal that breeds in a way different from what he would call normal. Now, he didn't put it that way—he rambled on and on, making up cute little rhymes and things and attributing everything he didn't understand to God's will. But what it boils down to is this: as near as I can figure, the Flies reproduce by placing a fluid containing tiny 'eggs' in a host womb, or incubator. What I think Noah found is an animal that uses a virus to replicate itself. Its 'eggs' are really incomplete DNA helixes that attack the genetic material of their host and use it as a pattern upon which to grow."

Pete sat forward, and his eyes sparkled a little.

"Now I know that sounds pretty wild, but I say it because of what Noah wrote about the way these things work. He says that he found them out there on the lake somewhere, living as a sort of colony. He's pretty vague about the particulars, but he did say that when he found them they stayed pretty much together, and that bringing them all to the Tower wasn't too hard.

"Well, he studied this colony for a long time, and among the things that struck him as strange about the animal was that it never mated. As a matter of fact, it didn't seem to have any way to mate: no males, no females, no way to make more bugs.

"But one night, something happened, and Noah describes it very carefully. . . ."

Pete paged through the journal and said, "Yeah, here we go, now listen:

" 'Upon the ground laid down one of the Beast, and the others did, into Its mouth, place their eggs. For many hours did nothing of this union emerge, until, upon the sixth hour, did crawl forth from the mother's mouth hundreds of healthy young, all identical to the rest.' ''

Lori blinked, and said, ''Joshua mentioned something about laying eggs in your mouth, didn't he?''

Pete nodded.

''Apparently, the viral fluid attacks its host after decomposition of the host's tissue begins, which must mean that one of the gases produced by the actions of degenerative bacteria triggers the 'eggs' to life. That's why they lay their eggs in the host's mouth: because the brain is the first organ to rot, allowing them to hatch faster.

''So, what Noah seems to be describing is an animal that clones itself by laying its eggs in the mouth of one of Its own. By breeding that way, this thing would keep its gene pool absolutely clean, and never change.''

''Its?'' Lori asked, her eyes narrow. ''That's what Joshua called this thing. You sound like you believe that there really is just one animal out there.''

''With a million pairs of eyes, and a hundred million teeth.'' Pete nodded. ''Theoretically, Joshua's description is right, because in normal reproduction, the male and female share their chromosomes, producing offspring with dominant and recessive genes from both parents. But the Flies are asexual, so there's no sharing of DNA. If you cut one open and put Its cells under an electron microscope, It would be genetically identical to every other Fly you studied that way. They're all absolutely the same. There's one Blood Fly, a million times.''

''Like a disease,'' Lori said.

''Like a virus,'' Pete responded. ''Or at least that was the case before my great-grandfather stuck his nose into it.

''One day, as an experiment, he removed the eggs from the host incubator, and they never hatched, which proves what I was saying about the DNA helix: this animal needs a pattern upon which to base the completion of its genetic structure, or It can't grow.''

Pete stood up and pointed down at the journal.

''The next thing Noah did,'' he said smoothly, ''was to

place the eggs in the mouth of a frog—typical laboratory animal, right? And, guess what? When they hatched, they ate the frog and grew into a kind of half-frog, half-Blood Fly thing, similar to what Joshua's got in his jar.

"That's how Noah created new animals! And that's how he created a potentially disastrous environmental freak, completely unprepared to survive without impacting its surroundings over and over again.

"By artificially altering the Fly's reproductive technique, he destroyed what the Fly had been, and twisted It into God knows what. He introduced foreign chromosomes into a static gene pool, and with each alien piece of material came some new physical feature for this animal to assimilate. I think that, whatever the Blood Fly was, It isn't stable any more. It's changing . . . struggling to settle into something that can utilize this jigsaw of genetic codes It's been bombarded with.

"But now, since Noah started the genetic ball rolling, every time the creature finds some inadequacy in Its present design, It'll naturally seek out new codes to compensate. And, with every new code, comes some new problem. To fix those new problems, It'll look for new codes . . . and on and on. Which, I'm afraid, is where I come in."

Pete stood up, turned to the window, and laced his fingers behind his back.

"In a way, we're all immortal," he said, carefully. "We carry our parents' genetic codes and pass them on to our children, who do the same, so that as long as we reproduce, our DNA continues, intermingling with the chromosomes of others of our species until you could say that all of mankind is essentially an intricate series of brothers and sisters. Not individually, of course, but on a molecular level."

He turned, his eyes firm and his posture rigid as he thought, Here we go, the big one.

"That thing out there digests DNA the way we digest protein. We break protein down to amino acids, which literally become part of our bodies. In a sense, we are what we eat. The Fly incorporates the exact DNA structure of what It consumes, thereby assuming the characteristics of Its initial food source, which, I think, included my great-grandfather in July of 1907. If that's true, his DNA is a part of the animal's makeup, which means that, genetically speaking, I'm related to that Thing out there, whatever It is.''

Lori placed one finger on her lip.

Pete stepped forward, lifting his hands to punctuate his words.

"Have you ever known, just known, somehow, what your mother was going to say before she said it?''

Lori nodded.

"And have you ever felt that, because you're her daughter, your mother can almost see into your head and read what you're thinking—and sometimes does?''

She nodded again.

"Well, that's how I feel!'' Pete said, placing his hands over his heart. "That's how I've felt since I first saw that sign on the freeway, the one about Sharthington being 'Your Summer Town.' I feel an intimacy with something here, just the way Joshua described it: I can feel the Call! It's as if something very close to me—so close as to be a part of me—is reaching out and begging me to come closer, begging for my help.

"Randolph Kyrik stumbled onto this Thing and intends to slaughter It so that he can sell Its poison and make a fortune. Somehow, and I really can't conceive of the particulars, that Thing is crying out for help. It's going to die, and It's afraid. So, It called me, Its 'brother,' to save Its life.''

"Do you have any idea at all of how crazy that sounds?'' Lori asked, and her eyes were icy, and cold.

"Okay!'' Pete nearly shouted. "Then you explain it! You tell me why Kyrik panicked like he did and had Danko try to scare me out of here, had Kennedy almost kill me! Kyrik might be screwy, and he might be your childhood memory of the Boogey Man, or whatever, but he isn't careless. He's a damn good businessman—and businessmen who're worth their paychecks don't panic!''

"Okay, if there's something out there, what's It look like?'' Lori asked.

Pete's eyes flashed as he said, "Don't make fun of me! I'm serious about this.''

"So am I,'' she said, rising from her chair and taking a

step toward him. "What does this Thing that's calling you look like?"

"I don't know."

"Is It a monster?"

"God doesn't make monsters."

"God didn't make this! Your great-grandfather did."

"What difference does it make what It looks like?"

"You saw what was under Joshua's coat."

Pete was shaking his head.

"You saw it and you know you did!" Lori said, loudly. "Don't act stupid."

"So what?" Pete asked, bristling at her obvious anger. "So what if there is something under the old man's coat? If there is, it only proves what I've been talking about: the Flies can physically alter DNA."

"You've been analyzing and theorizing for hours, making everything so clean and interesting that you've forgotten the bottom line!" Lori shouted, really shouted, now. "People are *dying* because of this Thing!"

Pete's mouth fell open and he stared at her as if she had suddenly begun speaking Chinese.

"Whatever this Thing is, It didn't hurt anyone. Kyrik did!" he shouted in return. "If there's a monster here, It's got a human face!"

"Those women downstairs, and God knows how many more!" Lori said with tears in her eyes. "Their children, their husbands, and for all we know, Clay Mallard too! This isn't a laboratory, it's real life, and people are dying! Can't you see that?"

Pete licked his lips, mentally trying to explain to himself why he suddenly felt the need to defend the creature in the Island.

"If what you said is true, and this Thing really does exist, and It really is calling you, well, what's It going to do when you go out to the Island?!" Lori said sharply, stunning Pete's expression blank.

"Open your eyes," she continued. "Joshua's alone and afraid, and what do the Flies offer him? Just a chance to be king! Kyrik lives for money, and nothing else, and the Flies offer him a poison that'll make him richer than even he can imagine. And you, a scientist who can't say no to a puzzle, what do you get? Just a chance to see something that seems to hold the key to the puzzle of life itself! Each of you has found something that'll make it impossible for you to leave the Tower alone! Is all that a coincidence, or did something plan it? *Could* something plan it all and make it work?''

She stopped, her eyes wide, her lips trembling.

''I said earlier that nothing bad ever happens in the movies,'' she whispered. ''Well, this movie's leading up to a big ending, and, in it, bad things are going to happen.''

Pete suddenly found himself approaching her, wordlessly, feeling a liquid sensation running through him that prickled his cheeks with heat. Placing his hands on her shoulders he drew her close—and she let him—her satin skin warm on his face, her full, gentle breast pressed to him, sending wires of electricity through to his spine. He closed his eyes, and felt his own tears, running into her hair.

''Don't worry,'' he said, his lips brushing her ear, her sweet, clean smell finding his every nerve. ''It won't hurt me.''

Her arms holding him tightly, she was silent.

''I can't explain how I know,'' he said gently. ''But I'm certain that It won't hurt me—because It needs me.''

She drew her face back.

''But It will hurt *you*,'' he added grimly.

She frowned.

''And I'll die before I let that happen,'' he whispered as her lips came so close that he couldn't help but kiss her.

The sense of contact he found was overwhelming, filling his senses and washing through him to obliterate everything but her—her, encompassing the whole world, for that one moment; her, soft and vital; her, so strong that he imagined himself folded up, eyes closed and confident that she'd shield him, because, from her, came all that was good in this world, all that was genuine, and all that was worth protecting.

And something else.

In that instant of communion, Pete suddenly saw the error of his thoughts. He suddenly saw the ''Thing'' he had so recently defended for what his heart knew it to be: ugly, dangerous, and evil.

But when his eyes fluttered open to find her again, he didn't breathe, holding onto that one breath that had intermingled with hers, his vision of the Beast as beast already beginning to fade.

Lori opened her mouth, and a horrible, piercing scream filled the room, shattering the air and driving an invisible wedge between them, sending Pete running, and leaving her momentarily flat-footed before she too headed for the stairs.

Pete stumbled in the doorway, sliding to his left and making the tight turn as he slipped on a throw rug on the hard-wood floor. As he hit the steps, he noticed one of the north rooms shimmering red, then blue, then red. . . .

Someone screamed in the living room again. Someone different. Not a woman this time, but a man. A frightened man.

Pete heard Lori's bare feet pounding behind him as he raced down the stairs and came to a dead stop, nearly dislocating his shoulders when he hooked the bannister like an anchor.

Lori's hands were on his shoulders almost immediately, and her breath was hot on his neck as she shouted, ''No! Don't!''

The frightened man screamed again.

He was young, wearing a powder-blue policeman's uniform and standing with his back to the open patio door. He didn't seem to notice Pete and Lori, but continued scanning the group of women dressed in trousers and Oxford-cloth shirts, hunched and advancing, step-by-step, over upended furniture and the body of another woman, dressed like a man and curled on the floor. His face was pale, his eyes wide, his body covered with lacerations and ribbons of blood as if he had been rolling in broken glass, which, Pete realized quickly, he had.

The front door was open and the puddle of glass slivers surrounding the wrought iron lawn chair had been scattered and stretched into a long, twinkling nebula across the ivory colored, blood-speckled carpet.

Like the rooms upstairs, this one was flashing red, then blue, then red. . . .

There was blood on the ceiling.

Pete didn't know why he noticed that, but there were blossoms of red—that turned purple when the room changed colors—splashed and hanging in rubbery threads on the white plaster over where the woman's body had fallen by the overturned couch.

"Leave him alone!" Lori screamed just as the first woman of the group let out a frightening snarl and pounced, her hands held like claws and her sisters hot on her heels.

She and the policeman tangled into a sudden vine of arms and legs as they stumbled back, onto the patio, the man's screams drowned in the frenzied cries of the women who pressed themselves into the doorway as two more joined the twisting fight and a crack snapped through the din like a gunshot.

From where he stood, Pete caught a last, fractured glimpse of the three, or was it four? people as the railing gave way and they hung, suspended in air for an instant before the fall. Disappearing under a horizon of bobbing heads, catching the failing living room light, one bloody female hand protruded stiffly up from the writhing cocoon, and the night exploded into silence.

Lori muscled her way around Pete, knocking him into the wall and rushing forward, as if she believed that, with proper haste, she might still prevent what had already happened.

Except for a worm of nausea right under his heart, Pete felt nothing.

Numbly, his feet swollen to clubs, he stepped into the room while Lori moved through the cluster of women by the patio door as if she were parting stalks of corn in a field. And that was exactly how much emotion the women displayed now that the young policeman was dead, now that at least two of their own group had died, maybe three—and the one on the floor: the one Pete was approaching, that made four—now that four of their group had died. Lori disappeared among them and Pete stepped forward.

A sharp crackle of radio static frizzled through the broken picture window from the police car parked by the front porch.

The room went from red to blue to red. . . .

Just moments before, Pete had been in love, inside love,

luxuriating in a touch and lost, wandering through the joyous, unexplored pathways of a glance.

And now . . .

She wore a pair of dark blue trousers, with cuffs—Kyrik always liked cuffs, Pete didn't think, he just *knew*, somehow, without thinking, he wasn't thinking, he just . . . *was*— and her shirt was pink.

The other women were more scattered so that, from where he stood, he saw just a few bloody, glass-cut feet under Kyrik's beloved cuffs, staining ivory carpet and leaving red prints, like a map of some demented dance step, around the dead woman's head, which was turned away. Her left knee was pulled up, and her right leg was straight, the crease on her pants running sharp from seat to heel. Her left arm was twisted around her back, and her right was bent into an L, as if she were about to take an oath. She looked like any murder victim in any cop show ever; all she needed was a chalk line running around her on the floor.

The spit in Pete's mouth was cold.

The dead woman's head had been bashed in with the nightstick that now lay bloody where it had bounced, leaving two red lines on the floor just a foot from what was left of her face.

Pete stopped, stared down at the purple and red swelling, the shattered rendings of flesh over the woman's eye, the jagged, gaping chasm that was her fractured skull and flecked grey brain, turned, and vomited—right there on the floor—in choking, retching knots of violent release until he had emptied himself completely and his eyes were red, and painful.

Then he stood up, wiped his mouth, and went outside to turn the flashers off on the police car and kill the engine.

And kill the engine.

They worked in silent haste, Pete clumping around the dock, undoing the lines securing the police boat to the dead eye and Lori priming the engine, which rumbled and coughed, belching oily black smoke that hung heavy in the cavern and greased the inside of Pete's nostrils. Jumping onto the boat's front deck, he carefully worked his way to the little pilot house, which was open aft, and slid in beside Lori, who gunned the motor and cranked the wheel, sliding the boat away from the dock. Sitting down, he noticed a hatchway on the forward bulkhead between the seats, assuming that it led to the compartment under the front deck, and seeing Lori's cold eyes reflected on the instrument's eerie, green dials.

Silently, he remembered the exact instant when those eyes had lost their warmth:

Stepping back into the house after turning off the flashers on the police car, he had found her standing over the dead woman's body, her face slack, her eyes like ice. But it wasn't just her eyes that had lost their heat; from that moment on, her voice and manner were chilled as well, as if her emotions, having been stretched to their limit, had snapped, leaving her flat and without passion. Now, her movements were calculated, efficient, and mechanical.

In moments they had cleared the cavern's opening and were gliding northwest, hugging the shore without running lights and using the twinkling fog lamps of the police flotilla as their reference point.

The sky was very dark—it was nearly nine at night.

"If one cop came, there'll be more," Pete had said, standing on bloody glass by the beached lawn chair. "Kyrik didn't have burglar alarms because he didn't think anyone would ever dare bother his house. But if a cop doesn't come back from patrol, he may as well have had an air-raid siren on the roof."

"You're not leaving me here alone," had been Lori's stern reply.

And Pete hadn't argued; he didn't know if she'd be safer on shore, or with him, but selfishly he'd decided that he needed her close.

Lori dressed quickly in one of Kyrik's shirts and her cut-off jeans and then sent the remaining women off, into the night, telling them to hide in the trees across from the house until she came back for them. They were to hide, without approaching anyone at all while she was gone. They were only to hide.

And before she left, Lori threw the nightstick over the

patio's broken railing, heaving it high and far into the night with a vengeance that made Pete believe that he had missed the object's significance somehow—a fact for which he felt silently grateful.

"There aren't many lights west of town," Lori said, checking the port side and laying her pistol on the ledge by the window. "If we stay in close we'll ride the shore and then run up north. They're watching the bay, and I don't think they'll be expecting anyone to come in off the lake."

Just get me out there, Pete thought, half-listening and sliding open the hatchway under the console to investigate the forward compartment. He hoped to find some weapon—like one of those big, riot guns that the cops propped up in their cruisers—but he switched the light off again an instant after he'd switched it on, and slid the hatch shut with a bang.

"Problem?" Lori asked without looking his way, her attention firmly on the shoreline.

"No," he answered without elaborating.

There wasn't any problem in the forward compartment. There was just a dead police lieutenant named Danko wedged tight in the narrow crawl-space amid life jackets and Styrofoam coolers, his face blue, and his head turned all the way around.

"No problem at all," he added, holding onto the arms of his chair.

Just as Lori had predicted, the police were blockading the southern side of the Island, and the north side was dark and clear. They followed the shoreline for nearly three miles, until they were well out of sight of the bay, and then turned north, racing the engine wide open and bouncing in a rough circle back around, until they were positioned in a direct line with the Island, using it to hide their approach from the bay and gliding in quietly to dock next to Kyrik's big yacht.

Perched on the bow, Pete worked the police boat alongside the yacht with his feet until Lori jumped to shore and secured their line. From where he sat, the Island was a dark horizon and the search lights of the police boats on its other side formed an arch of glowing haze that resembled a tiny sunset.

Lori's silhouette emerged on that horizon as Pete jumped from the police boat to the yacht's deck.

Except for the occasional gurgles of the lake, and the hollow thuds of the two boats bumping together, the air was quiet.

Pete was sweating and his breath was ragged. In the dark, his movements seemed unnaturally loud, as if he weighed a thousand pounds and was walking across a huge drum, wearing a pair of wooden shoes. The deck shimmered silver under the three-quarters moon, and he moved in a bent-kneed crouch, like he'd seen people do in the movies.

The smell hit him the instant he opened the aft door on the pilot house. It was strong, fishy, and fresh.

He recognized that smell, thinking, Joshua?, and peering into the unyielding blackness of the cabin.

In his mind he saw the old man's intense eyes and crazy expression; in his mind he saw the old man's coat—or, more specifically, he saw what he'd glimpsed beneath it: the shimmering blue light, the funny, swelling . . . something. It wouldn't take on a real shape in his head: it just hung, quivering, shining blue, and wet.

"Joshua?" he whispered, still without entering the cabin. "Where are you?"

The boat creaked.

"Joshua?"

A light snapped on inches from his face and Pete jumped to his right, banging his head on the cabin wall and lifting his arm with a shout as a bright, white ball bounced and a voice said, "What's the matter with you?"

"For Christ's sake," Pete said, snatching the flashlight from Lori's hand. "You trying to kill me or what?"

"I'm sorry," she said in the dark. "Did I scare you?"

Pete ignored her, sweeping the flashlight's beam over the cabin's interior and finding a room cut into two levels.

Two captain's chairs were set before an instrument console on a floor even with where he stood, to the left of which ran a parallel lower deck, dropping five steps down and cluttered with huge, glass jugs, filled with some thick, black liquid. Beyond the jugs was a closed door, marked with glistening, hand-shaped stains, similar to the mess smeared over the floor.

"Stay here," he whispered, easing himself down the steps while Lori aimed her gun at the door.

Carefully, so as not to slip on the slimy floor, Pete crept up to the jugs and read "BF-V: July 2, 1987" scrawled across little white labels stuck to the sealed containers' sides. Putting the flashlight up close to the glass, he examined the liquid inside one of the ten-gallon drums and saw tiny white specks and ragged bits of something dark suspended in what looked like spoiled stew.

Straightening up, he counted the jugs.

Ten.

A hundred gallons!

A hundred and five, he thought, turning his flashlight on the door and finding another jug, half-full, under a stainless steel machine with a spout and funnel. The funnel was marked with running black streaks leading down into the machine's blades, and the spout was thick with lumps of ground, glistening meat.

So that's how they're doing it, he thought. They're just grinding them up.

Ten more empty jugs lined the wall by the machine, and, draped over one, was a white shirt, and surgical mask.

"Find anything?" Lori whispered from above.

"Oh yeah," Pete answered softly, picking up the shirt and wrapping it around the greasy doorknob. "Just stay up there; this shit's nasty."

Beyond the door, he found the boat's sleeping quarters, and, running the flashlight over the bunks and dressers, he frowned and let the shirt drop to the floor. He was about to leave, when something struck him as strange: a trail of black spots was splattered under the door to a compartment at his left—but there weren't any marks on the knob.

Carefully, he crept to the door and pulled it open, finding a toilet, sink, and, as he had expected, a thick puddle of vile, black juice smeared out into the trail that led through the sleeping compartment.

"Joshua's on the Island," he said, climbing back up to the

control platform and squeezing past Lori to the main deck. "He must have walked down the beach from his place to Kyrik's cavern. He hid out in the head and they brought him along. Cornichuk's probably killed him by now."

Lori followed as Pete jumped from the yacht and made his way up the stone stairs toward the Tower. When they were close to the crest of the Island, he snapped off the flashlight and placed it in his pocket, relying on the moon for light and asking, "Can you use that gun you've been waving around?"

"Absolutely," she answered flatly.

"Good," he said. "Because Kyrik's not going to like us busting up his party. If Cornichuk makes a move, you may have to shoot."

Lori didn't comment, but grimly followed him until he halted at the Tower's battered door.

There, he paused abruptly, staring into the beckoning darkness, the skin on the back of his neck crawling in response to the feeling of something—strange, strong, and waiting, just for him—raising its attention in dangerous, predatory recognition.

Something was pleased that he'd come.

Lori ran into him from behind when he stopped.

"What's the matter now?" she asked after catching her breath.

He didn't answer, but stared, unblinking, into the Tower's mouth as the sickly wave of welcome bleeding from the very stone slid up and down his spine like oil.

"They've touched your mind," Joshua had said, and Pete now knew that it was true.

He closed his eyes, and the sensation became stronger, crawling through his flesh and curling obscenely in his skull. It was a wet feeling of age and silence, like a draft from a butcher's cooler, or damp visions dreamt in a morgue.

So why did he savor its caress?

Why did he feel as if he'd come home?

"They've touched your mind."

He squeezed his eyes closed more tightly and tried to just let go, to just let it happen. . . .

Unfocused puffs of faceless thoughts, dim memories and

suppressed desires, hovered seductively at the brink of his subconscious, like visions in a glass. They were real, but unreadable, threatening and sensual, teasing at intimacy, but untouchable in some foreign, alien way that hinted at knowledge he'd never realized he possessed, experiences he had yet to remember, and potential he was still to realize.

"Hey?" Lori said, nudging his shoulder. "Are you all right?"

He was *huge*, absolutely *immense*, stretching out with powerful, irresistible branches of himself, branches that thought and touched and breathed in concert with the pulsating vortex of sheer will that was *him!*

All that was, all that would ever be, was his to explore, absorb, and judge because he was . . .

Life!

New life!

Life unlike any other!

Life that would bring together the pitiful bits of flesh that aimlessly swarmed the earth into one perfect, living entity of beautiful, harmonious unity.

"Hey?"

Soon, everything would be him!

He was buried in the safe, warm ground, where he was happy—but someone was trying to dig him up. . . .

"Pete?" Lori said, loudly, shaking him hard.

He blinked twice and focused on her face, silhouetted against the sweeping sheets of light on water where police boats lay protectively as he cleared his throat and said, "I'm okay."

"You froze."

"I'm just scared, I guess."

"Don't do it again," she said sternly. "It was spooky."

He nodded, thinking that she didn't even realize the wisdom of her own advice. He knew that, somehow, he had to keep the Call from his mind, or he might be overwhelmed, washed, kicking and screaming, into the whirlpool of the Beast's hunger.

"Okay," he said, taking her hand, pulling out the flashlight, and concentrating on the feeling of her flesh.

His flashlight's beam illuminated the cracked and gloomy stairway before them, but not the dangerous, black passages to their right and left.

"Now, this is important," he said carefully. "That shit in the jugs back on the boat was the poison we were talking about. Chances are that its going to be splashed all over this place, so don't touch anything. Understand? No matter what happens, try to keep that crap off your skin. Okay?"

Lori, her face harsh in the indirect glow of the flashlight, nodded.

"I'm going to go first," Pete continued, still holding her hand and trying to ignore the sensation that seemed to be drawing him down the stairs, into the dark passage beyond where his flashlight could reach. "From what I could figure from his journals, Kyrik's a very sick man—sick in the body, that is. But Cornichuk, he's sick in the head. I'll try to talk Kyrik into stopping this thing before it's too late, and you keep your eye on Cornichuk. Hold that gun up high and don't let them see that you're afraid. Make them believe that you'll shoot if they don't do what we say."

"I'm not afraid," Lori said, her eyes firmly fixed on Pete's face. "And I will shoot."

Pete believed her.

"Ready?" he asked.

"What does 'Before it's too late' mean?" she said sharply, squeezing when he tried to let go of her hand.

"I'm not sure," he answered, hesitantly.

"Then why'd you say it?"

"I don't know."

"What exactly are you hoping to make Kyrik do?"

Pete paused.

The question startled him a little because he hadn't taken the time actually to spell out to himself what he was hoping to accomplish by coming out to the Tower in the first place.

He'd been thinking about seeing the creature Noah Blackwell had created, allowing his imagination to run wild with silent pictures and possibilities that had overcome him with an urgent sense of transitory opportunity. He also suspected that the Fly's poison—the product of artificial, genetic mutation—would adversely impact the environment if it should work its way into the system. But he didn't know exactly how he was going to go about preventing that from happening.

"I want to keep Kyrik from moving the poison off the Island," he said, for lack of a better answer. "And from destroying what I'm sure is going to prove to be a very important species of animal."

"And what about those women in his basement?" Lori asked, her voice bleeding through the darkness like his conscience, reminding him of other, more significant responsibilities.

He lifted his eyes to hers, as if to imply that she'd vocalized something that went without saying.

"Okay," she said, releasing his hand. "Then let's close down this fucking freak show once and for all."

Pete nodded, and together they stepped into the Tower's mouth.

Under the flashlight, the stone stairs were a greyish, dead-flesh color, swirl-patterned with shadow and thickly stained with heavy spots of black ooze leading up and down, but the stains seemed more heavy on the right, going up, so Pete set his jaw and began the climb, with Lori moving carefully at his side. There was a breeze coming down the spiralling passage, bringing with it the smell of rot and dead fish Pete associated with Joshua in a warm wash that hinted not at the cloistered confines of stone but of the open sky.

Weren't the upper windows boarded up? he thought, running his hand along the wall on his right and trying to visualize the Tower in his mind. Sure, the beacon room was sealed. He remembered that clearly. Where the hell would a breeze come from?

Lori caught her breath and touched his shoulder.

Pete stopped.

They'd found the first dead Fly, lying bloated over the edge of a step and leaking darkly from its eyes.

He looked at it, imagining long, pink fingers, lying in bloody mud.

"There's gonna be a bunch more," he said, nervously. "Can you take it?"

She nudged him silently, urging him to continue.

He stepped on.

The stairs twisted higher and the fishy smell intensified until Pete felt as if he were swimming through it, his flesh parting waves of stench like an icebreaker on the lake.

More Blood Flies appeared, dead on the stone, mouths open, legs frozen in panicked postures, tails rigid and stingers exposed, ready for the fight, ready to kill. Some were crushed, as if Kyrik and Cornichuk had grown complacent about their value with so many from which to choose, and had stepped on them like garbage in the street, and others had fallen upright on the steps, now sitting with their green eyes open: watching, and waiting.

Pete touched Lori's arm when the first sound slid down the tunnel from above.

Voices.

He snapped off his flashlight and noticed the glow on the steps.

Not voices, one voice.

In the gloom he motioned with his hands for her to stay behind him, and then, arms out, feet carefully placed between dead animals, he moved up the last few steps, and into the beacon room.

He'd thought that he was ready.

He wasn't.

He couldn't ever be.

Touching a wall for support, he exhaled, long, and slow, feeling his stomach lurch and his brain protest.

There were so many Flies littering the floor that it was impossible to form even an idea of their number. They were thinner where he and Lori stood, and thicker close to the pedestal, or platform, next to which a figure dressed in orange rubber and a hood mumbled and spoke to itself. They squirmed with the man's repeated shadows, which radiated out from him like a flower's petals beneath the encircling line of bright lights attached to the walls—the dark, beaten walls, splashed with running tentacles of black that dripped slowly in uneven lines.

The man, knee-deep in the vile mound of death, and the shimmering waves of stench that rose visibly from the animals like heat off pavement, bent, picking up Flies, holding them close to his face, and either dropping them back on the floor, or into a large, white, plastic bucket.

"No, this one's much bigger," he said in a voice rough and unsure, lifting a heavy, black toad and holding it up so that the tail swung back and forth. "Nice fat one here. . . ."

Something was wrong with the man, Pete knew, taking a step into the beacon room. His voice was twisted, uttering ill-defined thoughts, without purpose, like a child.

"Sloppy, sloppy . . . oh, now, you're a beauty, aren't you?"

Pete glanced around; where the hell is Cornichuk, he thought, seeing the dark blur of Lori's gun in his peripheral vision. She was just behind him, holding her gun up stiffly with both hands.

The breeze Pete had noticed earlier was coming up from the opening in the pedestal. Up, from the pedestal.

And some of the Flies were not like the others. Some seemed . . . *different!*

Which they were!

"Something's wrong!" Pete said aloud, suddenly, unwillingly, his jumbled thoughts splitting the pall hanging in the room so abruptly that the man in the orange rubber suit snapped upright, dropping the Fly he'd been holding and turning to confront Pete with a hot, furious expression of shock and loathing.

"It's all wrong!" Pete shouted, moving two steps closer to the pedestal and holding his arms out, palms up. "Everything . . . all of it. It's not the way it should be!"

If Pete had not been so completely entwined in the horrific contradictions he was witnessing, he would have been amazed by the face Randolph Kyrik displayed across the hazy, lamp-lit room. And, even amid the tumultuous roar of his own reeling thoughts, a tiny voice, deep inside his skull, seemed to whisper, "Look at him. Look at his face!"

And Pete did.

The flesh was white, almost translucent, stretched over fibrous ridges of muscle and tattooed by prominent blue arteries that seemed to pulsate and move. The old man's skull was so intimately displayed that his eyes appeared twice their normal size, bulging as if they might pop from their sockets as tiny layers of pink muscle teased out from beneath their lids. His lips were pulled thin and grey, revealing protruding teeth that parted and snapped together several times before producing words spoken in a high, straining register.

"Good!" he said, cocking his head to one side as a tiny line of blood emerged from his left nostril and crawled lazily along the rim of his mouth. "You can help me! Take this bucket to the boat."

Pete couldn't move. His feet were rooted to the floor and his eyes were frozen on Kyrik's deformed features as reasons and explanations flitted uselessly through his head and the implications of his doubt took shadowy, tenuous form.

"It's a trap!" he screamed, a blistering sweat breaking out over his forehead so quickly that it was painful. "All this time . . . all those women . . . all the pain . . . just to get us here, just to make it impossible to leave the Tower alone!"

"Come on, boy!" Kyrik shouted, straightening up and waving his arms stiffly. "There'll be plenty of money, more money than you ever imagined. No sense arguing when there's work to do!"

"It's wrong!" Pete nearly exploded, his face flushing red and his eyes wild. "Some are bigger than others! They're different!"

"Of course they're different," Kyrik responded with his ridiculously wide, completely unnatural grin. "The males are bigger than the females."

"But there aren't any males and females! There shouldn't be. . . ."

"The males are more poisonous."

"Impossible! They're all the same, all alike, all one animal!"

"Take this to the boat before they rot away."

"They should be the same! My God, it's all over!"

"Does this look like its over?" Kyrik shouted, picking up a Fly in his gloved hand and hurling it at Pete with a grunt.

Pete slid to his left as the Fly struck the wall with a bursting-wet plop. Lori gasped, following him as he moved along the curving wall, away from the open stairs, with Kyrik's riveted, bloodshot eyes almost leading them as he bent to lift another Fly.

"It's not over. It's only just begun!" he screamed, squeezing the dripping animal in his fist and shaking it so violently that one of its moldering legs dropped off. "I'll sell so much that it won't be worth anything to anyone. The ultimate sale: what they don't need, for more than they can afford to pay!

"They'll use it on each other and erase the minds of millions! They'll sneak it into the air, and the water. They'll soak a generation in it until they ban it like they did nerve gas! And after I've taken their money for my poison, I'll sell them the empty tunnels under the Tower to bury it in!

"And if you help me, I'll give you a share! How would you like a piece of the future?"

"The tunnels aren't empty. They're alive," Pete said, his back touching the plywood behind him as he continued stepping to his left and Lori moved in close at his side. "There's no room to sell."

"Take this to the boat!" Kyrik shouted, plopping the dead Fly down. "And then we can discuss the terms of our partnership. I should have included a Blackwell in this from the beginning. And now that I have, I'm glad it's you, Peter. I've always liked you, ever since you were a boy. I've always thought of you as my own son."

Cornichuk's dead, Pete thought while the old man trembled and jerked his head around expectantly. Cornichuk's dead so Kyrik's going to bargain for time while whatever's going to happen overtakes us.

"Didn't you read Noah Blackwell's journal?" he said, trying to mask the growing alarm in his voice. Pete had led Lori so far down the wall that Kyrik was now standing between them and the door. "Didn't you even try?"

The question seemed to stun the old man for a moment, and he stood perfectly still, his eyes glazed, the tightness of his skin accentuated by the brightness of the light he faced as he said, "How do you know about the journal?"

"The tunnels aren't empty!" Pete said desperately. "Don't you understand? The animals you killed are just the tip, the crust of the . . . *Thing!* Didn't you read any of the journal except the parts about your precious poison?"

Between Kyrik's incredibly white teeth, a pink tongue probed aimlessly—and the old man's eyes narrowed.

"We're being used!" Pete screamed, his voice cracking with emotion. "We've been drawn here *by* something, *for* something! And the poison was the bait that maneuvered you into killing a generation of Flies that should have been identical to one another, but that weren't. You wiped out a bad batch. . . . You erased a mistake! You served your function and now it's time for . . ."

Pete's voice was chopped off by a short gasp that stuck in his throat, and stiffened his lips.

"For what?" Lori whispered at his side. "If you know, tell me. Please."

"And the women . . ." Kyrik said, as if an idea were forming in his mind and spreading to his mouth slowly. "How do you know about the women?"

"It's time for what?" Lori repeated.

"That," Pete said in a thin, defeated voice, nodding once and indicating the gloomy, arched doorway behind Kyrik where a dark form was lifting itself into the light.

"Joshua?" Lori whispered, placing her hand over her mouth.

"The last one," Pete said to himself, watching Joshua, blinking and holding his hand over his face, shamble to a halt just three feet behind Kyrik, who, impervious to the new arrival, was digging in a zippered pocket and jerking his head around violently.

"We're all here," Pete said, turning to Lori as disjointed pieces of his dream teased at his mind again, playing slowly, like a silent movie, with long, white cracks and dizzying sections of bursting snow.

Through shovel blades and bloody ground, twisting tunnels

and streaming blue light, the beacon room seemed unfocused around him, as if *it* were the dream, in which he saw . . .

. . . the tangled series of tubes and glistening silver tanks becoming a spider's web, surrounding the dark hole to the killer's lair.

. . . Joshua's coat, like a curtain hiding the final, shocking surprise in a drama of which he suddenly found himself a part.

. . . and Lori, pressed close to his side and holding her gun.

She was *his* bait—like Kyrik's poison and promise of wealth, like Joshua's dream of revenge and power—she was his gold, his desire, and the means by which he would be manipulated.

"You've been inside my house!" Kyrik suddenly roared, dismounting the pedestal and producing from his pocket two amber colored vials. "That's trespassing! You broke the law! You can't do that! You were in my house, where I keep my money . . . my money . . . *money! We can be rich. Help me, and we'll both be rich. We'll all be rich!*"

Kyrik's fingers danced over the little tubes as he worked his way through the nest of aluminum rods and the deep, splashing layer of dead Flies that rolled and split around his knees.

He's finished, Pete thought, watching his eyes bulge and his flesh strain incredibly, impossibly tight over the vibrating tendons and sinews in his neck. His part's done and he's going to die.

"I've got a hundred gallons!" Kyrik screamed so hard that something seemed to tear in his throat, buzzing in time to his words. *"And I've got room for a hundred more! Help me!"*

He was clear of the tubes and his hands were shaking so badly that Pete didn't think he was in control of them any more. His left, holding the amber vials, remained over his stomach while his right flickered up to his face, and then his neck, brushing desperately, as if something annoying were crawling over his skin.

"God damn things!" he hissed, pausing to unscrew the

caps on the vials as Joshua reached out, and slapped him hard on the back.

Spinning and twisting into prancing convulsions, Kyrik threw out his arms with a cry and launched the two glass tubes into a graceful arch that ended at some invisible point in the pile of rotting Flies he'd been planning so many years to create. From his eyes burst two lines of streaming, bloody tears, and his voice was hysterical when he shrieked, *"Look what you've done!"*

In an instant, he'd hurled himself into the pile, where he crawled through the bodies, sobbing and digging furiously for the vials where Joshua shook his head sadly, and said, "Poor man. Reduced to this. It's a fucking shame."

He turned his attention away from Kyrik as if he'd simply ceased to exist, and, Pete saw it: the change, or at least a part of it.

Crawling up from under Joshua's collar, from the left side of his neck, over his jaw and across his face, through his blind eye and ending in a point near the middle of his forehead, was an inch-wide welt that looked like an earthworm. It was thick, and tinted blue, like a bruise under his flesh, segmented with evenly spaced ridges and branching off in tiny tributaries that began under his eye and slithered into the corner of his mouth. When he moved, the welt seemed to swell and shudder, as if a great quantity of blood were passing through it, and, when he opened his mouth to speak, it spread—before Pete's eyes—its ends branching out further, its ridges twisting and its color deepening as its fingers burrowed new paths across the old man's features.

"We need air," he said, blue light flickering between his lips and his good eye gleaming.

He tramped toward a plywood-covered window as if the Flies were cobble stones beneath his feet, and Kyrik were not babbling his torments just a few feet away.

Pete couldn't take his eyes off the man. Everything, simply everything about him, was different. His skin shimmered eerily—the unnatural glow of heatless light. His walk was strong, confident and even—the walk of a man in control of great power. And his face . . . oh, that hideous, ancient face. . . .

Joshua buried his fingers into a sheet of plywood, producing first a series of cracking shrieks, and then a long, yowling groan of vibrating nails and splitting wood. The sheet came free, leaving a perfectly black space in the wall for a moment before the lamp secured to the wood erupted into a million bright, falling stars as its wires snapped, flickering the rest of the series and plunging the room into abrupt, screaming darkness.

It was Lori screaming.

Joshua flipped the plywood through the opening like a playing card and turned triumphantly, his flesh absolutely ablaze in the gloom, radiating harsh blue light from beneath his jacket in sharp knife blades that made everything appear suddenly two-dimensional and black and white. He focused his shining, white eye on Pete, and, when he spoke, his mouth became a dark blue hole, squirming beneath the welt over his eye, which was crawling like an ebony snake and entwining his head.

"I told you to run. I warned you. Now, it's too late," he said with a lizard's voice as he lifted the jar—that awful, glowing jar.

Kyrik's head came up suddenly from where he had disappeared amid the Flies, his hood gone, his bloody skull revealed beneath tiny, thread-like licks of torn muscle where the back of his scalp had split under the strain. He trembled, head and shoulders above the pedestal, his chest and body submerged, his protective suit running with smeared black moisture and bright streaks where the rubber itself seemed to be melting.

Joshua held out his hand, and, as if in slow motion, the jar he held shattered, spraying a silver blast of alcohol and glass shards in a flowering burst and dropping the Fly inside onto his upturned palm.

"*Shawnita shea negarik,*" he said with a grin. "To partake of Shawnita is to take part in Shawnita."

No! Pete thought, shaking his head and feeling his jaw drop. It was impossible. After everything else, the prospect of this old man with the scarred face actually eating the plump, black thing that lay limply dripping in his hand was simply beyond his ability to believe. Taking Lori's arm, he fixed his attention on the image of the deed in his mind and forced it to disintegrate, hoping that, through the sheer strength of his will, he might change what was real, just as Kyrik stood up.

Joshua froze, his eyes narrowing and a hint of something— Surprise? Fear? Anger?—washing his expression into unreadable stone as the room vibrated from bright blue to a sickly shade of green.

The floor trembled.

Did Joshua do that too? Pete wondered, his stomach lurching under his ribs. How powerful is he? How far has he changed from man to . . . what?

The floor trembled again, and plywood panels twisted under a light sprinkle of dust, snowing from the ceiling as big, aluminum light pots went crashing on the left and right.

What had Joshua changed to?

What had Kyrik changed to?

Change!

Everything was changed! Nothing was the way Pete had expected it to be! Nothing was what his mind had led him to believe was true!

Nothing!

Dark, liquid streaks of rubber dripped from Kyrik's clawed hands as he stepped through the Flies, approaching Joshua with intent focused solid in the air.

At the exact instant when Kyrik screamed and lunged forward, Joshua dropped the Fly he was holding and snapped out his hand in a smooth sweep that caught Kyrik's throat and lifted him high into the air. Silhouetted by undulating shadow, Kyrik twitched silently as chunks of something that might have been either his rubber suit, or his flesh, scattered like birds, and a blast of air exploded up from the pedestal and blew a hole in the ceiling and also, it seemed, the sky.

Sailing, twisting planks and broken, falling shingles littered the air, as an amazing sound, like a *thrummm!*, sucked the breath from Pete's lungs and pasted him flat against the wall, where Lori pressed atop him.

As quickly as it had come, the rushing air was gone, leaving the room nearly dark, and the evening sky star-spangled overhead.

Pete's ears were ringing and, when he spoke, his voice sounded tiny and muted inside his pounding skull. He pushed Lori aside and blinked and, then, blinked again.

A sudden, rending crunch cracked the air and a new, thicker wash sprayed from Kyrik's neck when Joshua's fingers ground through his flesh, locking around his spinal cord and twisting until that bone broke. Pete cried out and turned away as Joshua shook Kyrik's limp form like a rag doll until the sound of splintering bone suddenly stopped and Kyrik's body dropped to the floor, leaving his head perched atop a handle of shattered spine in Joshua's hand.

Screaming, Lori was stumbling toward the stairs.

Joshua examined Kyrik's head for a moment, pitched it aside, and bent, fishing from the pile of Flies the one he'd kept in his jar. Straightening up, he looked directly into Pete's eyes from across the room, and bared his teeth.

Pete was moving toward the stairway as Joshua lifted the limp, black form closer to his face.

Something . . .

What was it?

Something flashed up from the pedestal, something small, and fast, and white, like a tiny meteorite falling into a hole in the sky.

Thrripp!

And another.

Thrripp!

And again.

Thrripp!

Joshua's eyes sparkled with delight.

Lori stopped in the stairway door and Pete bumped into her. She was heaving huge, trembling gulps of air, and, when she turned to speak, her voice teetered precariously on the brink of irrationality.

"We can't go down there!" she cried. "*It's* down there!"

And It was.

Up through the darkness swelled a deep, gurgling sound, like a lion's roar, building, falling, and building again. Something big—something that had to be absolutely *huge*—had awakened below, and was drawing its first breaths of consciousness after a long night's sleep. To Pete, the howling message was spine-chillingly clear: fresh sensation had brushed away the cobwebs of a century's slumber, and the Thing, whatever It was, had come awake hungry!

"Dear Jesus," he whispered, taking Lori's arm.

They turned together and found more of those white balls, streaking up from the dark pedestal and disappearing into the night sky like Roman candles as the Tower trembled, hard this time, and the last three plywood panels twisted so badly that they popped from their places and sailed out into the night like kites.

Whatever the white missiles were, there were more of them now, and they appeared steadily . . .

Thrripp!

Thrripp!

Thrripp!

. . . as Joshua danced, screaming, "Come my children! Come meet your king!"

And Lori lifted her gun, and fired.

Four

THE DARK WELT on Joshua's face was multibranched and thick, and Lori's bullet tore a large chunk of it from beneath the old man's good eye. He flinched when the shot struck, pausing with the dead Fly just inches from his lips and trembling as a stream of dark blood poured down his cheek and over his clothes. The bleeding was aggressive, and unnaturally firm, as if the old man's arteries were under some kind of internal pressure, and his blood had been waiting for this opportunity to escape.

But soon something stopped the bleeding—something weird.

From beneath his hair slithered an extension of the black welt. Full, pulsating and segmented, the wormy length of flesh squirmed down Joshua's cheek, ending in a moist, pink mass that swelled inside the bloody wound, filling the hole at the welt's tip and forming its own, tentative roots.

The old man smiled, ran his tongue over his bloody lips, and bit into the Fly.

Pete pulled Lori—who stood silently amazed, the gun dropping from her hand—toward the opening left where the plywood sheets had been blown from the windows. Outside, on the narrow walkway that ran around the Tower's top, they bumped a creaking railing, turned briefly, found no hope of escape, and spun to find Joshua standing splayed before them, his head back, the mangled Fly falling from his hand into the heap at his feet.

Time stood paralyzed.

The air hung heavy, still, and charged.

Joshua swayed, his arm climbing up over his head and freezing there, his chin pointed at the broken ceiling.

Lori trembled.

Pete held his breath.

Joshua swallowed, and then pulled his head forward, bringing his face into view and tearing Pete's sense of reality into irreparable shreds in one chilling instant of undeniable revelation.

The lower portion of the old man's face melted before Pete's eyes, running like wax near a flame and leaving his upper teeth in a jagged ridge, glistening amid the mass of squirming, rotting flesh that gouged out his lower jaw and scorched his throat into a hollow, black maw that disappeared beneath his coat. His eyes were wide and panicked as he clawed out his hand, sending a dark spray up from the hole in his neck and shaking his head. The pink swelling that had repaired his wounded cheek appeared from behind his teeth to slide down, into his jacket, like a new, animated artery.

As if in answer to Joshua's deed, the floor trembled, really trembled, and the Tower groaned, leaning to one side and then back while the pedestal spit up a new wave of blurred streaks that disappeared through the ceiling.

Pete clutched at Lori when the Tower moved and the walkway upon which they stood collapsed, dropping two feet before stopping abruptly and sending them sliding into the railing in a tangled heap that would have gone easily over the side had not Pete's leg struck an upright post, giving him a chance to anchor one arm. Old wood splintered and nails squealed as Pete lifted himself carefully, snaring the window ledge with his fingers while gripping Lori's shirt with his left hand.

His muscles stretched to their agonizing limit, his teeth clenched tight, and his eyes flicking from the shimmering blue beacon room to the steady stream of white flashes climbing into the night from the Tower's roof, Pete bore down and heaved, sliding Lori up six inches before the Tower lurched again, and her shirt tore loose.

"No!" he screamed, looking down and bending so that his grip was ruined and the scrap of her shirt he had held went sailing free. "Lori! Oh, God! Lori!"

Rolling down the rough planks, Lori scrambled desperately with her hands as her legs slid under the railing and over the walkway's edge. For a hopeless moment, she snagged an upright, but her momentum was irresistible, and she entered free space completely with one final scream for help as her hair billowed around her white face and her arms twisted uselessly at her sides. Almost a hundred feet below, the water burst into life with thousands of wormy lights before the black, predatory shape of a police boat slid close to the Island's edge, skimming its search light to outline her body as it shrank with sickening speed.

"Lori!" Pete screamed again, reaching for her as she disappeared. *"Lori!"*

He covered his face with his hands and felt the tears come, hot and thick.

He pulled his hands away.

He was lying on an incline.

The walkway had torn from the Tower's side and was just barely hanging on, its outside edge a good four feet lower than that part attached to the wall.

He looked at his hands.

Both his hands.

Why hadn't he fallen?

Turning his head slowly, he found the answer.

Joshua stood over him, holding him by the shirt and staring down, his good eye transfixed on the spot where Lori had died and his expression terrible. Devoid of a lower jaw, his neck looked far too long, the black flesh having coagulated to form a bumpy layer of leathery skin that ended in a flap at the back of his upper teeth. That flap was opening and closing rhythmically as he puffed, distressed, it seemed, by Lori's fall, while a steady stream of saliva dripped from the toothy ridge of his lower skull.

Effortlessly, he leaned back, and heaved Pete onto the floor of the beacon room.

Pete landed hard, sliding on the Flies and climbing to his feet. Black ooze tingled his skin, sending prickling spirals of unhealthy sensation up his arms and numbing his hands. Verifying his balance for an instant, he clenched his fists, and spotted Lori's gun lying near where Joshua stood with his tangled hair and trembling, creeping layers of dark, swollen flesh.

"What are you?" Pete screamed, his thoughts uncontrollable and his entire body trembling.

The volume of Pete's question seemed to startle Joshua, and the old man froze for an instant. But, then, glancing around the room one last time, he turned with a flourish and leapt over the railing, his seaman's jacket ballooned and his arm outstretched in the night.

Pete was left suddenly, and shockingly, alone.

He stood, staring at the place where Joshua had been, feeling the floor vibrate beneath his feet and making a conscious effort to talk to himself. But his mind had forgotten every word it had ever known, and he knew it would be impossible to compel his mouth to move.

He'd become mute, and paralyzed—so much so that, when the Call came up from the pedestal, he couldn't have responded, even if he had wanted to.

Unlike the uneasy, unspecified nature of his dream, this time the Call was as overwhelming as surf on a beach, or wind through the trees. Its power blew through him, deepening his paralysis and filling him with disjointed images and emotions. He was at once terrified—being in the presence of something so powerful that he felt dwarfed and insignificant—while at the same time he was elated at the sense of need he felt from below.

Whatever the Call's source was, It needed him, loved him, and wanted him, very, very badly.

"Peter?" a voice said slowly, and Pete's forehead blistered with sweaty goose flesh that seemed to suck all the moisture from his mouth, leaving it painfully dry.

"Come, Peter. I've been waiting so long."

In an act of sheer will, Pete lifted his hand to his lips.

"Peter? Can you hear?"

They moved!

His lips moved!

Just like Joshua had described, something was speaking through him, using his mouth to form its words.

"Look at me, Peter," the voice commanded, and Pete could not refuse.

He turned from the window and the pedestal burst into his view with brilliant, stunning clarity.

There was light below. . . .

Blue light. . . .

Pulsating up from the pedestal's opening and calling out to him with promises of open skies, and deep, fresh freedoms that would be exclusively his own, the light drowned his mind and illuminated his soul with a blue like every sky on every summer's day he'd ever known, condensed into a perfectly symmetrical portal that led down to a place of unparalleled implication.

It was the color of potential, boiled to its bone.

It was the exact hue of ambition unbridled.

And it was that impending instant when everything, all of it, would surrender to . . .

Him!

The light was the color of . . .

Life.

New life.

Life unlike any other!

And, there at his feet, that amazing color, swirling with ancient dust, yielded a steady stream of tiny white spots that inflated with incredible speed and disappeared through the Black Tower's ruined ceiling like the immense seeds of an endless, evil orgasm.

It was dazzling, and it filled him with a sense of wonder so complete that it washed everything from behind his eyes except a burning, undeniable desire—a swollen, bursting *need*—to see all there was to see, to be all there was to be, to answer the Call!

"Come to me, Peter," a seductive voice said sweetly from

so very close that he wasn't sure if he was in fact being used or was initiating the words himself.

"Come, Peter. Come to me."

It was insane.

It was irresistible.

It was what he had wanted all along.

And, as the Tower shuddered with drumming concussion, sending sharp-edged chunks of stone and long, bony stalks of rotting wood crashing down around him, Pete stepped onto the crumbling pedestal.

Walls collapsed, mortar chipped to powder, and Kyrik's decapitated body joined the thousands of dead Flies he'd murdered in a tumbling river that ran like mud into yawning chasms in the floor.

But Pete saw the light.

Only the light.

Turning around carefully, he eased himself into a crouch and groped with his right foot before settling it on the first step of a series of metal loops, set into the concrete and spaced two feet apart down the inside wall of the pedestal. His back was rigid and soaked with sweat, and his hands left moist prints on the stone before sliding on the cold steel of the ladder's rungs. Closing his eyes, he took a deep, deep breath, let it out, and began his long climb, feeling concrete shudder inches from his nose and hearing the echoing yowls of cracking rock. Air rushed over his neck when more of those strange white balls whistled up behind him, and his knees trembled.

But he didn't hesitate.

At least not until Lori's face, framed by dark, sparkling water and frozen in her final, desperate scream, flashed through his mind.

His eyes snapped open and Lori's face disappeared.

Hanging there on steel rungs, he felt something big, and close, swoosh past him on its way down.

He looked up and another chunk of rock, this one the size of a manhole cover, tumbled inches from his left arm, causing him to close his eyes reflexively and . . .

. . . Lori was screaming and clutching out with imploring hands, her flesh pale and her beautiful body spinning in air.

He opened his eyes and . . .

. . . he was *huge* and in control, fulfilling his destiny and answering the Call.

Eyes closed: he was alone with his fractured memories of Lori's death.

Eyes opened: he was anything and everything; he was powerful and perfect. . . .

The Tower screamed and an immense gash opened in the wall directly over him, sending lightning cracks through the stone that split off into a complicated network of fatal damage. Concrete crumbled, and the white balls no longer climbed the shaft to the sky, but yielded open space to hurtling bits of dismembered rock that streaked down, into the Tower's marrow.

Pete released a primordial shriek when the steel to which he clung pulled free and gravity claimed his body. Pumping his legs and waving his arms, he emptied his lungs with a howl and saw Lori's face one last, fleeting time, before he fell, into the Beast.

PART THREE

Sharthington, Your Summer Town

One

"LORI! OH, GOD! LORI!"

Lori heard Pete cry as her tenuous hold on the walkway's railing was ruined and her fingers tore free, leaving streaks of blood and broken nail on the wood, and one last, hopeless scream hanging in the air like mist.

Sinking tremors of acceleration shuddered through her entrails as she entered free fall. Her breathing, instantly halted by the rushing air, died in her chest, and the world became a spinning, dizzying memory, offering no support or comfort.

Reaching out with grasping hands, she twisted and turned, her muscles useless, her bladder and brain both swelling to the point of rupture as, unable to so much as form a thought, she watched slivers of external detail flash past her riveted, terrified eyes in a senseless, incomprehensible collage of darkness and color. . . .

Lights below: sparkling lights.
Lights above: blue, blue lights.
Lights behind: shining white stars.
Lights in her mind: impact scars.

"Jesus Christ, lady!" someone said.

She'd never felt cold like that encasing her body now, and she'd never felt heat like the fire that burned in her lungs when she tried to breathe. Her throat closed up tight and her chest clenched into a knot as every muscle from her neck to her knees locked and hands plunged down to squeeze her arms.

"Lenny! Christ. Gimme a hand, will ya?" a shrill, hurried voice called, and the hands pulled her up a little, twisting her flesh painfully and then slipping so that she dipped back into the cold.

"What the fuck?" a faraway voice was shouting, thin with terror and moving closer with each word. "They're up there. See 'em? Fuck this shit!"

"Goddamn, man! Come here!"

Water ran from Lori's nose.

She felt it.

She felt water.

"Lenny!"

A hellish sound rose and fell in time to the bobbing of the police boat's black and white side as the worried face of a young man in a powder-blue uniform came into focus for an instant before bleeding into a perfectly white blaze, criss-crossed with delicate, black veins as Lori's eyes closed when a searchlight passed over her face.

"It's that barmaid with the tits," the second voice said, closer now, as another hand found Lori's other arm. "She musta fell a hundred feet."

The hell-sound was a siren: up and down, louder and softer, bobbing like water . . . bobbing.

Lori's stomach flexed and she heaved painfully, chocking out a steaming stream of dirty lake water the instant the two policemen dropped her on the boat's deck.

"There's gotta be a million of 'em!" a voice said.

On her hands and knees, she felt a sinking feeling ooze up her chest, and she vomited again.

"I don't care what Danko said, I'm getting my ass outta here!" the shrill voice called, suddenly far away.

"Christ, here comes somebody else!"

Lori had lifted herself off the deck and was hanging on a rail, her legs half-folded and her head lolling on her neck as she looked up in response to the young policeman's call. Her muscles ached, her chest burned, and her skull felt so cracked and ruined that she didn't even try to identify who or what the dark figure was that plummeted from overhead and crashed into the lake on the boat's port side. She simply saw it, along with a blurred shape that dropped with a thud onto the deck before her.

She looked down.

The thing was as big as a grapefruit—maybe a little bigger—and was white, round, and moist, lying there on the wet planks after having dropped from the sky. Before her eyes, it unfolded a pair of spindly, spidery legs and turned itself over, lifting its ''face'' to hers and aiming a small, sharp beak at her throat.

The fall had fractured her skull, she decided, hanging there on the rail and breathing quickly, her chest gurgling with residual water and her blood pounding in her ears. She had a concussion, and it was making her hallucinate.

She touched the side of her head, and her hand came away bloody.

The thing on the deck paused, and then turned, cocked itself like a spring, and was gone.

Someone screamed.

Thud.

Thud.

There were two more white lumps on the deck, walking with weird, jerking, insect movements.

The policeman who had first grabbed Lori's arm stumbled into her line of sight and spun, his hands at his throat where he clutched at the first white ball, which had attached itself just below his chin, wrapping both its skinny legs around his neck, and turning his face blue.

Lori turned and leaned on the railing, looking out over the sparkling water, her eyes drawn to the point on the lake where the spotlight rested. There was no one moving the beam anymore, and it lay like a silver coin, rolling with the tiny waves and holding the incomplete form of a man floating face-down.

''Lenny! Open the goddamn door!'' someone screamed behind her before the voice disintegrated into a gurgling cry.

Lori blinked, and frowned.

All her teeth felt loose.

Something brushed her foot.

Glancing down, she found another white ball, hobbling along blindly. The thing bumped her again and she examined it, finding its hallucinatory precision fascinating, and impressed with her own imagination's creativity in conjuring such a disgusting picture with which to torment her.

The thing looked boneless, its albino flesh that greyish white shade of pale so unique to undersea animals that never see the sun. Its legs were crab-like, with tiny spines running along one edge, and little pairs of claws at each tip. And the area she had first thought of as a face was actually just a blemish near the front of the sphere, a milky patch of bristling hair surrounding a needle-like beak that was lightly veined and made of an almost clear, hard-looking cartilage. It had no eyes, and no other feature that might sense the outside world for it, but only legs with which to move, and the beak, which reminded her of a bee's stinger.

It bumped her again, and paused, one of its legs sliding in a pool of dark water on the slippery wood, its tiny claws opening and closing.

She swallowed.

Her head pounded.

She swallowed again.

It touched her!

The thing actually *touched* her!

It was *real*!

The realization washed through her with almost fatal force and she slid back along the railing, still facing the thing on the deck and seeing her surroundings with new eyes.

Brand new eyes.

The boat was bobbing only thirty yards or so from the Island, its siren blaring and its engine idling so roughly that it sputtered a cloud of greasy smoke to hang over the water and obscure a second boat that had stopped a little farther back. The second boat's searchlight was poking a hard, blue ray through the exhaust, but no one seemed to be aboard her, or, at least, no one was moving.

Overhead, the Tower's broken roof was spewing more of those hideous bugs, shooting them up into the night so that they appeared white against the deep-grey sky, black against the silver moon, and then white again as they increased their altitude before turning in a descent that took them toward the shore, and town.

Toward town!

"No!" she whispered hoarsely, staggering away from the railing and turning her face up to the beacon room.

When she moved, the thing on the deck scuttled out of her way and over the chest of the young policeman, who was lying on his back near a bulkhead, his features still, his throat swollen from ear to ear. The creature under his chin had shriveled into little more than a wrinkled sack after having deposited the contents of its pulpy body into the man's neck through its needle-like stinger, and what was left of the thing was dead.

"Pete?" Lori said, louder, trying to call to mind her last sight of him. "Oh, Jesus! Pete!"

The Tower released a grinding series of sharp cracks that were plainly audible, even over the infernal shriek of the boat's siren, and Lori's eyes fixed on a sudden black wound that formed just below the point where the walkway from which she had fallen was attached. In seconds, the wound shattered, splintering out through the masonry and yawning wide as chunks of dark stone slid free and fell, landing like bombs near the boat and sending up huge plumes of spray and deep, hollow thuds that shook the deck.

Lori didn't move, but stared, transfixed, at the crumbling stone monolith.

Pete, she thought, seeing him step in front of her, shielding her with his body in Joshua's cabin when the old man turned dangerous.

Pete, she thought, seeing his face gently illuminated by a shaded desk lamp in Kyrik's office, his expression so sincere, his eyes so worried as he explained a madness for which he assumed personal responsibility.

Pete, she thought, seeing his sweat-stained face, flushed red and straining as he hovered over her, gripping her shirt and holding her when the walkway broke free beneath them.

He'd risked his life for her, she hardly even knew him, and, now, he was going to die.

"Oh, Pete," she whispered, tears streaming down her battered cheeks as the entire Island seemed to lurch and the top of the Tower collapsed in on itself. In moments, the beacon room was gone, and the Tower was left stricken, half its height invisible rubble, shafts of splintered support beams and twisted lengths of lumber bristling up from a billowing fog of settling dust, and a heavy mound of broken rock and dirt belched into a pile through the door at its darkened base.

He was gone.

The siren wailed on and on.

He was gone.

The thing at her feet bobbed over to the hatchway that led to the compartment under the front deck and tried to flatten itself enough to slide under the door. Its bulbous body was amazingly flexible, and the creature would have made the narrow squeeze had its stiff legs been just a fraction of an inch thinner.

She watched it, a wave of nausea eating at her heart and a new, heated rush of sensation prickling the flesh on her face.

Pete was gone, but the night had just begun.

She glanced at the crippled remains of the Black Tower, and then to the twinkling lights of Sharthington, seeing, in her mind, all the people she knew there, sleeping, oblivious to what hung overhead in an obscene cloud that, even as she lifted her eyes skyward, was peeling into thousands of tiny, white, falling stars.

She looked at the young policeman who had pulled her from the cold lake: dead; another officer was draped over the bow railing: dead; the second police boat was lying straight aft: dead in the water; and Joshua, his body still floating within the searchlight's beam: also dead.

Oh, yes, she thought, her eyes hardening with the same chill that had begun in Kyrik's dungeon, and that had frozen to ice in the Tower's tip. Oh, yes, the night's still young.

The thing at the compartment's hatchway turned, aimed its stinger back at her, seemed to think better of it, and leapt overboard, landing with a splash somewhere out of her view.

Glancing back to the sky, she watched the trajectory of the speckled, white cloud as it descended on Sharthington.

She thought of all those sleeping people again . . . and the dead officers . . . and Pete . . . and those poor, ignorant, defenseless people. . . .

She had to warn them!

She had to warn them now!

When she took a step, her legs protested, nearly folding beneath her so that she had to follow the railing to the pilot's seat.

Limping and grimacing, bleeding tears of pain and rage, she fell into the cold vinyl chair and took a second to compose herself, feeling deep aches in her chest and stomach that frightened her and made her visualize inaccurate images of damaged organs: split liver, bleeding lumps of spleen, ruptured bowels, all the things she imagined could happen inside a person at the end of a fall like hers. The pains in her chest were sharp, and ended between her shoulder blades; the pains in her stomach were dull, and gave her uncomfortable, weak feelings between her legs. When she coughed, she was sure everything inside her tore just a little bit more, and when she blinked, she saw stars. . . .

. . . impact scars.

Cranking the wheel to starboard, she killed the siren and pulled the throttle lever. The engine sputtered, and then roared, taking a bite out of the lake and clawing the aft portion of the boat down in a steaming, boiling wake and lifting the bow high, so that the policeman's body that had been draped over the railing slid across the deck and bumped the windshield just a foot from her face.

With a jolt, she jammed the throttle back to low, nearly stalling the engine. Then she stood up, one hand on the wheel, the other on the searchlight control, her eyes peeling through the drifting layers of diesel exhaust that obscured her view of the thing in the water, the thing that her light had touched for but an instant, the thing that had been Joshua.

She blinked.

It was gone.

She sat down, feeling new nausea and an anxious sensation of vertigo.

It had looked as if the old man was standing in just three

feet of water, his upper body protruding rigidly from the waves, his long hair writhing around his face like Medusa's snakes, and his arm outstretched, as if he were beckoning to her from across sixty feet of dark, swelling lake.

She glanced into the searchlight's silver puddle again.

Nothing.

Hallucination?

Like those white balls from the sky?

She held her breath.

A long, silent time passed.

Something wet landed on the deck behind her.

"Dear God," she whispered through clenched teeth.

Something wet slapped again.

"It can't be."

But it was.

Turning, she gasped, scrambling for the throttle lever behind her back, without even considering the steering wheel, as Joshua, one arm over the port side of the boat and one . . . thing, one thing that wasn't an arm, but that acted like one, with long, milky lengths of torn flesh hanging in wet ribbons, pulled himself up from the lake.

His face wasn't human at all, and his eyes were gone, swollen shut by the thick, rope-like welts of slithering tissue that wound around his head and ended in the yawning, gulping sack his throat had become.

And there were other things helping him up—pale, squirming things that fumbled for purchase from beneath the shreds that were his coat.

With the heel of her hand, Lori slammed the throttle down, opening the engine wide. But when the engine bit the lake again, the rudder, still aimed to starboard, etched a groove in the water and leaned the boat into a hard circle, directly toward the second police boat, lying ahead.

As Joshua pulled his chest up even with the railing, the cruiser's bow missed the second police boat's stern by a yard, but its aft portion didn't, and with a terrible report of smashing wood, accompanied by an unearthly, inhuman scream, the boat slammed the portion of itself where Joshua hung into the ghost ship.

The force of the collision sent Lori crashing into the window behind her, and her elbow cracked, but didn't shatter, the glass. A terrible, grinding roar gurgled from under the lower deck, and the boat leaned dangerously to port, where more wood splintered and aluminum railings twisted as Joshua's body was dragged between the vessels and Lori's ship scraped the full length of the second boat.

When the boats finally did part, Joshua tumbled over, disappearing into the bubbles churning up behind, as water rushed onto the deck, producing a hiss and cloud of steam from below and depositing something bent and dark. . . .

Lori pushed the throttle down again, pumping fuel into the drowning engine, which howled and chocked while water poured in over the broken port side and the boat sputtered in a wide circle.

Water was collecting aft, and the dead policeman's body drifted and bumped amid shifting debris and one of Joshua's legs, which somehow floated nearby, dark, severed at the thigh, and bleeding an inky stain into the swelling pool.

"Come on you fucker!" Lori hissed, spinning the wheel and working the throttle. "Come on!"

The diesel sputtered, coughed, and languished on the verge of collapse. But, remarkably, it didn't die. It kept running.

Aiming the boat's nose to shore, she pressed her teeth together hard, concentrating on the pain in her head, the tremors in her hands, and the twinkling, feeble lights of an unsuspecting town.

TWO

THE WATER WAS warm, and shallow. Pete's face was pressed against something cold, and there was a weight lying on his back.

Two sounds: the moist, repeated echoes of water dripping nearby and the raspy rattles of hurried, frightened breathing.

He lifted his head.

The breathing he heard was his own, and the dripping was water, oozing over freshly turned lumps of black earth in the mouth of a new tunnel, gouged into the wall before him.

The room was round, and had a sandy floor that ended in smooth, concrete walls. When he looked to his right, he found two kerosene lanterns on the wall ten yards away, burning feebly and illuminating the shattered remains of a heavy wooden door, lying on the ground near several rows of sagging shelves upon which the silhouetted forms of featureless bodies were arranged in quivering shadow. Farther to the right was some kind of cage, and, high overhead, there was a row of dark, round holes, each three or four feet in diameter, drilled into the continuous wall just below where the buckled ceiling hung, the shaft in its center and other, wide gashes clogged by a tremendous load of stone rubble, and timber.

Pete moved his hand, sliding it along the mud in which he was trapped, and pushing against the length of wood that rested on his back. The wood groaned and tumbled to one side, clattering against a large chunk of rock before splashing down and disappearing under water.

The pool was only six or eight inches deep where he was lying. It got deeper, farther out toward the wall to his left, but where he was it was shallow, and soft.

He rolled himself into a sitting position and propped his back against a block of concrete, running one muddy hand over his face and waiting for the pain either to kill him or to go away. It was an unidentifiable pain, decentralized, and lacking any real point of origin. If someone were to ask him right now, "Where does it hurt?" he would've pointed to his body and said, "There," meaning, All of it, the whole thing.

"My body's broken."

He narrowed his eyes.

"My body's broken," he said again.

He hadn't meant to say it the first time, but the words had come out anyway, echoing through the empty cavern and decaying into liquid drips of dying sound.

Gingerly, he felt himself over, pressing sore spots with sore fingers and wincing. He wasn't *huge* anymore. Not even a little bit. He suddenly felt human, mortal, inadequate, and very, very small. He suddenly felt as if he'd been raped.

He closed his eyes.

And then he opened his eyes.

Nothing in particular happened: Lori's face didn't burst out at him, dizzying images of expanse and power didn't bedevil him, and his equilibrium wasn't ruptured by unpredictable shifts in perspective or attitude.

He closed his eyes: it got dark.

He opened his eyes: it got a little lighter.

The Call had disappeared.

He tried to remember exactly what standing there on the stone pedestal had felt like. He tried to get that sensation back, like an addict trying to remember being stoned so clearly that he wouldn't need to score again. But the feeling was impossible to describe, even to himself, and his failure to achieve it made him doubt that it had ever existed. All he knew was that the Call was gone, and he was alone.

He caught his breath at the thought of just exactly how

alone he was. He could scream here—under a million tons of rock, two miles from shore in the lake—he could scream and no one would ever hear. He could climb up the tangled heaps of broken stone that surrounded him and bash his face to bloody pulp on some sharp corner and there wasn't a soul to hinder him because he was completely, and irrevocably, alone!

He'd delivered himself to his own grave, and he'd sent Lori to hers in the process. He'd answered the Call, and was now lying just a few feet from a new tunnel, made just for him.

He didn't understand how he knew that the tunnel was new, but he did, and he didn't doubt the accuracy of his knowledge for a moment.

It was a large hole, and it looked as if it had been dug from below because on either side of its mouth were piles of fresh mud that had been pushed up, from the inside. The tunnel stretched straight for a few yards, and then dipped down, proceeding deeper under the lake, and glowing with a dim, blue light.

Just like in his dream.

Reflexively, he glanced up, expecting to see shovel blades pocking through the ceiling, but instead finding rough stone edges packed in the center of smooth, concrete walls into which holes had been drilled like ant tunnels. The holes were dark, and perfectly round, with machined edges stained underneath by dribbling, oily streaks. There were ten of them, and they were all sparkling with the tiny, yellow glints of something moist, watching, and alive.

Alive!

"Oh, Christ!" he said, the volume of his voice startling him into thinking, Now they know I'm here!

They?

Who were They?

What the hell was he thinking?

The first form to emerge from a dark hole seemed to unfold itself, thrusting out a face that appeared embryonic, and canine, with bright, yellow eyes, and teeth—a lot of teeth: tangled and misdirected, filling its mouth and forming an insane grin that Pete immediately realized was too toothy to be useful. The thing was emaciated, its flesh adhering to its twisted skeleton as if under the pressure of suction; and it was weak, its movements coming slowly, and one at a time, because its teeth were so large that they blocked its jaws from opening wider, closing farther, or letting food pass to its throat. Its flesh was nearly as yellow as its eyes, and bristled with a sparse series of hairy tufts that gave the beast the appearance of having been plucked.

Flopping one paw-like appendage out of the hole, it spread out a pair of loose, membrane-covered bones in apparent preparation for flight, and, flapping feebly, tried to catch a breeze. But the exertion seemed to ruin its balance, and, for an instant during which it nearly fell, it struggled to right itself before folding up its "wings" and dragging the rest of its body, which looked to be about three feet long and shaped like a cone, down the wall. Gripping the smooth stone with its tiny nails, the thing began sliding, headfirst, producing scraping, skittering sounds, thin, reptilian barks of exertion, and a long, greasy stain of saliva, darkening the concrete beneath its jaws.

Pete stared up from where he lay in the pool, his mouth hanging open, his eyes transfixed on the holes from which appeared more misshapen creatures, deformed in ways that made it impossible to identify what they were, what they might have been, or what they were supposed to be.

For a full minute he watched—just watched—the connection between himself and what he saw fitting together inevitably over his most violent mental protests. And, when the pieces finally did snap, so did his composure, and he was crawling through the mud, bumping into blocks of stone and continuing automatically, his progress slow, his eyes flickering along the ceiling in hypnotized, repulsed fascination.

A long, spidery "arm" groped its way from a hole, its bird-like bones visible through scale-covered skin, its hand pressing four soft, jointless fingers against the concrete, where they flexed and folded like tongues.

A thing with what looked like a baby's head—round, less than firm, and mapped with blue and pink veins—aimed four shining, insect eyes, two up and two down, trying to judge the distance it would need to hop.

A ratty nose sniffed the air before something with seven legs, and a naked body so weakly gelatinous that its belly dragged, began chattering hungrily, giving voice to its own emptiness and inciting a cacophony of frenzied grunts and screams from the other creatures, the volume of which froze Pete like a statue and left him on his hands and knees, his peripheral vision filled with images of baggy, crawling flesh, while quivering drops of sweat bled off his chin.

Something cold and smooth brushed his left hand, which was buried in mud up to the elbow, and he reflexively jerked his arm away as something with fins and tiny spines split the murky water's surface and hurried quickly from his path.

"F-F-Flesh!" he jibbered, holding his hand before his face so that plump globs of mud swelled from between his fingers. "It's only flesh. . . ."

All around him the water flashed with the backs of swimming, spiny things and the breeding room's walls squirmed with the progress of a solid, descending wave of impossible animals.

"Flesh! It's just meat!" he cried, splashing madly to the pool's edge, pulling himself over a ridge of broken stone and slapping at his trousers where pale, fishy things with whip-like antennas and grasping, stumpy fingers had attached themselves.

"Jesus Christ!"

Spinning, he slammed his back into the moist side of the new tunnel's mouth and felt his way with his hands a few steps before turning and focusing his eyes on the center of the room he'd just left behind. Atop a grey pile of concrete chunks, two of those dog-like things were digging furiously and howling.

He should have run. He should have turned and followed the tunnel wherever it led. But he didn't. He couldn't.

Instead, he hung in the tunnel's mouth, breathing so quickly that his head swam, watching limping, scrambling animals plop themselves down on the sand and scurry over to the mound of rubble already occupied by the dog-things. There,

they joined the digging, or, in most cases, began batting uselessly at sections of broken stone, whimpering, salivating,
jostling for position and barking or hissing their excitement,
while more monsters emerged from the holes overhead and
the rubble mound disappeared beneath an undulating layer of
countless, pale mistakes.

"Mistakes," Pete whispered to himself, his eyes wide, his
body craning forward.

A fishy thing hanging on his right leg dropped to the ground
and flopped there like a beached trout.

He looked down at it.

It was maybe a foot and a half long, shaped like a catfish,
and marked by a double row of silver blisters running down
its spine. From the center of each blister protruded what
looked like a stinger, and the antennas on the thing's nose
were just longer specimens of the same bristles as were on
its back. When it slid itself over in the mud, its underside
briefly wiggled with rows of finger-like feet, all moving like
an insect's legs and ending at a gulping mouth, that was filled
with tiny teeth.

Overall, it looked dangerous enough to survive, but,
watching it squirm, Pete realized that its movements were
unorganized and pointless. It could have easily walked back
to the pool, if that's where it wanted to go, but its legs seemed
to be jerking randomly, as if the connection between its body
and brain were scrambled, and its natural state was a kind of
endless fit, or seizure. So, instead of simply returning to its
pond, the beast rolled around helplessly in the mud until it
grew tired and stopped, lying motionless on its stomach with
its blank eyes staring into space and the two gills that ran
down the center of its forehead opening and closing quickly
to reveal the pink interior of its skull.

It's a mistake, Pete thought with a frown. It's a fucking
mistake, like the Flies Kyrik killed, the thing Joshua had in
his jar, and everything else down here. It's all one immense
mistake!

A unanimous roar of triumph shook lumps of earth from
the tunnel's ceiling and caused him to look back up to the
breeding room's center, where the creatures on the mound

were fighting each other, wrestling over one another and furiously pushing themselves forward. A glimmer of something flashed briefly amid the writhing mass and then disappeared.

Pete squinted, concentrating on the spot where he'd seen something orange, and then . . . his neck jerked and he caught his breath.

Kyrik's headless body erupted from the group, rolling and tumbling over itself in the grip of one dog-thing and one beast with spider arms. As the two animals shook their heads and snarled, other dog-things were rubbing their useless mouths against Kyrik's flesh, their tongues working frantically behind the cage of teeth that prevented them from eating while other creatures struggled for a chance to bite.

Pete turned his head away and found the fishy thing at his feet whining sadly, its eyes fixed on the spectacle on the mound, its antennas trembling.

One hundred years, he thought, despite himself. For one hundred years the creature that Noah Blackwell had tampered with lived under this tower, roaming these dark passages and using the new abilities that crazy old man had given it. Here, in the dark, the Thing sought new genetic codes to incorporate into itself, experimenting, like Noah had, stabbing blindly without any idea of what it was doing and producing the freaks on the mound, the monsters, the *mistakes* that were now howling out their agony and frustration after having been hidden from the world by their own inadequacies and failures.

Pete had known that they'd be here, he realized now. Though he hadn't given it conscious consideration, he'd known, since reading Noah's journal, that these beasts absolutely had to be.

And now they were fumbling out to greet him, fumbling out to show themselves to him and to say, "Yes, Peter Blackwell, great-grandson of the man responsible for us, you were right! Here we are! Every time we'd lay our eggs in a different animal's mouth we found a new genetic code, and, with every new genetic code we found, came some new problem. We tried and tried. And when one of us didn't work out, we tried again! But it never worked out! Why? Why didn't it work out, Peter Blackwell? Why?

Because the chances of randomly combining the genetic structure of one animal with another and producing something functional are about one in a zillion, Pete thought, his eyes losing focus for a moment and his lips pressed firmly together.

It never worked out because, without the action of natural selection and the orderly combination of compatible genes, there's no restrictions on what physical features might bond together: take a wing here, a claw there, an eye, a tail, a tooth, throw them all in a bag, shake it up, spill it out, and see what you get! Forget nature. Forget logic. Forget the evolutionary cycle of life, which, whether it's convenient or not, developed on this planet for a reason. Sidestepping that cycle leaves chance as the master of species. And with chance in control there's no plan, no rules, and no God.

He blinked, and sweat prickled his neck.

The room had fallen absolutely silent, and that silence deafened his thoughts and tore his attention back from where it had hidden at the rear of his skull.

He blinked again, and his eyes readjusted, presenting him with a blurred mountain of featureless shapes that became perfectly detailed so quickly that he experienced an instant of vertigo that climbed into his stomach and blossomed into nausea.

Every beast on the mound, every creature hanging from the walls, and every stalled monster in the mouths of the holes overhead had frozen, turning every eye to the shelves near the door where kerosene lanterns flickered feebly, and the black shapes of dead human beings lay blanketed by shadow.

Pete was trembling, but he forced himself to take a step forward, and his shoe made a loud sucking sound when it lifted from the mud.

Not one animal paid the slightest bit of attention.

Something was happening on those shelves; something that could only happen here, and something that could silence the feeding frenzy of countless hungry predators.

He was still trembling, as he took another step.

He was still trembling, but he wasn't afraid.

And why should he be?

He was trapped under the lake with no escape, Lori was dead—and he'd killed her—he was surrounded by thousands of nightmarish creatures that, though misshapen, could tear him to pieces, and probably would eventually, and, at the bottom of the tunnel that was the only place left for him to go, waited something so powerful that it had drawn him here from halfway across the country.

He was already dead, so why not see all there was to see? Why not open that last wooden doll—as he had as a child—and see what lay inside?

Why not see?

Why not?

His steps sounded like huge, moist kisses in the new stillness of the room. His back was like a ramrod, and sweat ran freely down his face in creeping, muddy tattoos that outlined his mouth and eyes. He could feel the gaze of the beasts on the mound, propelling him toward the shelves, where something was moving, not a lot, but enough. There was a charge hanging in the air, a current of expectation and excitement that caught his heart and made it beat faster.

It was like reverence.

It was like church.

And, as he took that final step that placed him directly before what lay on the shelves, he felt as if he were a priest at some altar, an attentive, worshipping congregation assembled at his back, anxious for him to celebrate some dark ceremony that he didn't understand, and that didn't really require his help, or comprehension.

Lying on the top shelf was the body of a man, his face contorted in a death mask of terror and a blue swelling under his chin the size of two softballs. Pete knew immediately that his name had been Clay Mallard, and, with a grim smile, he thought, Hello, Mr. Mallard. You don't know it, but you've been an awful lot of trouble for me.

Moving his attention down to the shelf at eye level, he found the body of a middle aged man he didn't recognize. He had grey hair, a tan, and looked as if he'd been dead only a short time. His throat was also blue, but it wasn't nearly as swollen as Mallard's.

The next shelf was empty.

But on the one below that, the lowest of the four, Pete found something quite different—he found the remains of a naked woman, almost a girl, but twisted and no longer beautiful. Mottled with greenish patches of diluted bruise and peppered with black gashes and split wounds that were fuzzy with two days' growth of mold, the girl lay nearly obscured by shadow, her throat purple and distended into a sack the size of a basketball that hung down on either side of her neck in stretched, lumpy acquiescence to gravity.

And, inside the sack, something heavy was moving.

With a jolt, Pete became of two minds.

One part of him was ready to run, pumping his muscles full of adrenaline and squeezing his stomach into a painful knot that made his shoulders sag and his knees feel watery.

And the other part of him, the part that was probably responsible for him being here in the first place, was drinking in what he saw and storing it, analyzing it, trying to identify it in relation to the things he'd learned about the Beast so far.

Swollen throat: egg sack, he thought.

Discoloration: decay.

Decay: the product of the degenerative bacteria that the Fly's eggs need to grow.

Movement in the egg sack: birth!

His heart lurched, and that part of himself that wanted to *run* temporarily assumed control. He retreated two or three reflexive steps before that part of him that wanted to *see* slammed on the brake and left him standing there with his heart kicking in his chest.

He was seeing it! Right there: the actual process of reproduction unlike any other on earth! One of the creatures behind him, or some other beast he hadn't yet seen, had placed the incomplete DNA helixes of itself inside this poor woman, and, judging by the way her throat was squirming, the product of that union was about to make itself known. The product of that union of Beast and man would soon emerge, and Pete was going to *see* it!

He couldn't move, could hardly breath.

Whatever was inside the sack was struggling violently now, pushing out tiny, flesh-covered bumps that made him think of bees behind cheesecloth, made him think of blisters.

He held his breath.

The beasts behind him were perfectly still.

The only sound left in the room was the moist splat of tearing skin as the girl's neck succumbed to a split that started just under her chin and ran to her right shoulder.

Without thinking, he stepped forward, his breath still locked in his chest and his neck craning as he looked, really *looked*, calling on every ounce of his courage to keep his legs from dropping the rest of him onto the sand, and opening every passage in his mind wide.

In that posture, he suddenly became a vessel to be filled, a roll of blank film begging for exposure, a computer chip ripe to remember; he became the eternal scientist, the immortal impulse of fearless curiosity personified, offering himself as witness and saying, "Yes, it happened. It happened, because *I saw it*!"

Simply by his presence, Pete was fulfilling the most ancient of all demands mankind has ever placed on his environment: he was exercising his right to *see*. Verifying existence and confirming it, bestowing legitimacy on a thankless world and making it *real* because nothing can happen unless *seen* by man. If man doesn't *see* it, it can't be true.

So Pete looked.

And he *saw*.

And what he saw nearly stopped his heart.

He'd thought that the syrupy mass pouring over the girl's deflated breasts was simply a jell. But as he approached, he realized that the substance dripping down her arm and onto the floor was actually a closely pressed colony of tiny, wiggling creatures the color of raw fat. It was thousands of wet, fleshy worms, about an inch long each, oozing into the world helplessly and glistening in a trembling, spreading lump that masked all but their most general features.

Glancing up, he fixed his eyes on one of the kerosene lanterns, and, taking a second to retrieve it from its bracket on

the wall, lowered it over the girl's head, allowing its yellow
flame to produce a circular spotlight and seeing the truth
about this newest addition to the Blood Fly's store of experimental animals.

During the second or two that it took his mind to understand, the lamp remained steady. But then it slipped from his
limp fingers and tumbled to the ground, splashing out oily
licks of flame from its shattering globe that engulfed the girl's
upper body with a *whooosh*! and sent Pete dancing back, his
spine stiff and his lungs emptying themselves in a gurgling
expulsion of shock that prodded an answering roar from the
beasts on the mound.

He fell, pumping his legs and pushing himself backwards
a few feet before he bumped into something and started
crawling on his hands and knees.

All around him, creatures jabbered and barked, hissing and
moaning, climbing over one another in a frenzied display of
enthusiasm that seemed to erupt as a result of his understanding—as if his horror had been their reward.

But he didn't hear their cries.

He didn't really hear anything because his mind was full
of what he'd *seen* in the bright spot beneath his trembling
hand.

Within the lantern's yellow glow had squirmed the spawn
of man and the reptilian version of the Beast that Joshua and
Kyrik had held in such high regard. Small and smooth, the
creatures had ignored the light because their swollen eyes
were blind, milked over by membrane and useless. They
looked something like tadpoles, with tapering bodies and
smooth skin. But, sprouting from a frog-like thorax, four,
misshapen human arms groped with minute fingers beneath
a huge, dangling brain that looked far too heavy, and that was
exposed like the meat in a prepared lobster's tail, bulging in
a row from a split in the creature's skull and laced with deep
folds and fissures.

Stumbling into a half-run, Pete collapsed in the tunnel's
mouth, rolling in a heap in the mud and coming to rest against
a moist wall. Burying his face in his hands he clenched his
teeth and trembled, trying, through a sheer act of self-control,

to banish the image of tiny fingers, with impossibly small nails, grasping and squeezing clear fluid under yellow light in his mind.

But the image would not be dispelled. Instead, it evolved, first to the creatures full-grown, six feet tall and monstrous, lumbering in lopsided hops from dark holes in the ground and carrying people back to feed the beasts under the Tower that couldn't hunt for themselves, and then to the creatures full-grown another way: two feet long and hiding behind branches in trees, creeping through gardens, watching children undress behind pink curtains in pretty little houses and waiting for them to fall asleep so they could use their big brains and little hands to unlock windows.

He looked up.

The fire had spread along the base of the shelves and was now burning brightly up the wall, obscuring all three bodies there, and consuming the newborn monsters.

"Now you see why you were called here, Peter," Pete said aloud, tiny reflected images of fire burning in his eyes.

Black smoke was filling the chamber fast, hazing over both the flames and the lantern by the door, dimming the room and washing everything grey. Sound seemed to die, falling mutely into an oppressive pall, under which the beasts on the mound contentedly dismembered Kyrik's headless body and consumed it: those that could eat, doing so, those that couldn't, watching jealously, rubbing themselves against one another for consolation and occasionally charging the feeding areas in blustering, hopeless displays of bravado.

And over the whole scene hung a nearly transparent, superimposed image of little white worms, with tiny fingers, squirming in the air.

"Peter?" he said, his voice strong, and soothing. *"It's time, son."*

He wasn't going to fight It any more.

He wasn't going to squirm.

He wasn't going to deny that the Beast was inside him, and had been all along.

He understood why he'd been called here now. The breeding room and its twisted occupants had explained everything to him more eloquently than any journal could ever hope to, and with his understanding of the Beast's desires came the knowledge that there had never really been any hope of escape for him, never anywhere to run, and no conclusion other than that planned.

Climbing to his feet, he turned and faced the new tunnel, his tunnel, the tunnel that had been dug from below especially for him. His long hair hung heavy with mud, his eyes were red-rimmed and flat, his skin was drawn, and his fate, which he had once thought of as his own to determine, was assured.

The tunnel was wide, and shaped like a cylinder, stretching out a few yards before him and dropping into a slope that could have descended a hundred feet, or a million, to a place where a pool of light vibrated around a silhouetted, human figure, its tangled hair blowing round its head and its clothing hanging in flowing, tattered rags. Pete watched it lift one arm in welcome and beckon for him to approach with a slow, easy motion.

He hesitated only for a moment, expecting his traitorous mouth to speak again, and surprised when it didn't.

Glancing back at the burning shelves one last time, he frowned, swallowed, set his shoulders and took that first step forward.

Placing his shoe down, he screamed, really screamed, when his body pitched forward and the secure, level ground before him was transformed into a steep, muddy slope. He landed with a splash and a skid, fast, hurtling through flying mud and struggling as acceleration buffeted him from side to side and his body spun in full spirals along the inside of the tunnel . . . around, and down . . . and down, and around. . . .

While a voice in his mind that wasn't his own, and no longer needed his mouth to form Its words, said, *"Welcome, Peter Blackwell. Welcome home."*

Three

LORI KILLED THE struggling diesel and allowed the crippled boat to glide into a row of old truck tires hanging along the police station's dock. Soft, liquid gurgles licked the sinking craft's hull, and a hissing cloud of steam lifted abruptly from the engine compartment's vents, dissipating quickly in the cool night air over a patch of oil, spreading through the water flooding the aft deck.

The boat bumped the tires again before she climbed from the pilot's seat. Her skin, slick with a glaze of nervous sweat, and smeared with dark patches of lake grime, glistened in the moonlight as she clambered up to the forward deck and examined the yard behind the police station.

A small rowboat with the name *Leviathan* painted across its back was overturned to her left, half-hidden by a green tarp that was washed pale in the yellow glow of a single floodlamp. The lamp cut a bright, triangular tunnel of amber through drifting diesel exhaust, harshly outlining the sparse grass in the yard and cheap aluminum siding on the wall. Garbage cans stood next to a basement window that had bars over it, and a black police car with a large gold shield painted on the driver's door was parked on dusty gravel, both its front windows rolled down and its headlights reflecting yellow like big, uninterested eyes.

She held her breath and listened.

No sound.

Nothing moved.

There weren't any shadows behind the police station's frosted windows. No cats sniffing around the garbage cans or dogs barking down the street. There wasn't a single mosquito hanging over the water, or one moth fluttering near the glowing haze of a streetlight shining by the liquor store. There wasn't any traffic on the street beyond the parking lot, and no late-night-duty officers rushing out to see who had just limped in one of their bay cruisers after five had left earlier in the day with most of the Sharthington police force aboard. No amazed crowd was pressed along the shore, staring at what was left of the Tower, which stood like a broken tooth against the moon, and none of those baggy, white creatures that had killed two policemen before Lori's disbelieving eyes were anywhere in sight.

Nothing moved.

Nothing.

It's dead, she thought, as a series of loud, bursting bubbles burped from the submerged engine compartment and the boat dipped deeper into the water. I'm too late. Sharthington's dead.

She'd never thought of a town as something that could die before. Maybe it was just the pain in her head, or all the blood she'd lost in warm trickles from her right ear, but now, alone and frightened, she felt as if she were standing at the foot of an immense grave that started at the lake's edge and stretched out before her in a tangled, mysterious maze of silent passages and unoccupied homes. The image was precise, almost hallucinatory, and in it everyone she knew was dead, and a steel freeway sign that read, SHARTHINGTON, YOUR SUMMER TOWN, R.I.P., leaned like a tombstone on a bent post somewhere in the dark.

Pete had called the Blood Fly a virus, she remembered, realizing that, from where she had stood in the pilot house of this sinking boat, she had seen that virus climb up from the broken Tower and kill her town. It had been an unfair race, with her pressing the throttle lever so hard that it had cut a T-shaped groove into her palm as she willed the sputtering engine to keep running despite the water rushing in over the ruined deck; and those soft, bulbous monsters, hanging in a cloud overhead, falling like snow before she could reach the shore. After that cloud had disappeared, she'd been left to finish the final portion of her short journey across the bay in the company of dreadful, gnawing frustration and a bitter, creeping sense of hopeless foreboding.

She was to have been Sharthington's savior, and, now, Sharthington's savior was mourning at its grave.

"Bullshit!" she hissed, jumping down to the dock, which made a deep, hollow thud under her tennis shoes, and produced a lightheaded feeling of impact in the pit of her brain. "Towns don't die!"

Another series of groans boiled up from the boat, and, glancing back, she watched its aft portion slip even deeper into oily water, leaving life preserver rings, a wooden paddle, and lumps of shapeless junk that she couldn't identify floating aimlessly into the darkness beyond where the police station's floorlamp reached. But the body of the dead policeman who had pulled her from the icy water after she had so nearly died, which had been curled against the aft bulkhead just moments before, was gone, and so was Joshua's leg.

Joshua. . . .

Suddenly, the old man's image burst through her mind, overwhelming her with a new, intimate tingle that prickled her skin and tensed her already tender nerves. Through the gentle sounds of water lapping the posts beneath the dock, an invisible weight, like animal eyes studying her every move, pressed in on her, creating an undefined tension that hung in the air and convinced her that some deadly, personal threat was lurking just beyond her awareness.

Inexplicably, the sensation drew her eyes down to the dock, where, under the combined glow of feeble moonlight and bug-lamp yellow, the bleached-wood planks took on a sickly, naked shine that was regularly interrupted by bands of black. She could have sworn that she heard something moving under there, creeping through the darkness and clumsily trying to use the licking waves to camouflage the sound of its approach.

She bent and lifted a five-foot wooden pole, tipped with a

spear point and hook, that had been lying at her feet. Bouncing the docking pike in her hands a couple of times and feeling slightly less exposed because of its firmness, she glanced at the police station again, and said aloud, "You're being paranoid."

The sound of her own voice seemed to help settle her nerves a little, so she added, "Cool out. Just let it go," as she turned her back on the sinking boat and tried not to think about anything slimy and green reaching for her ankle from the dampness under the dock.

But she couldn't let it go, and she knew she never would, because Joshua's face, his black flesh segmented like the underside of a huge snake, his throat gulping like a fish, and his hair squirming as if it were alive itself, was seared into her memory.

He wasn't dead yet, she knew, somewhere so deep inside that she wasn't sure if it was a conviction or simply an eternal truth understood by the flesh. She'd slammed him between two police boats and chopped him in half, but he wasn't dead yet, and the moist slits that hid his hideous reptilian eyes were somewhere close by, watching her with deliberate, predatory satisfaction.

But she wasn't going to let him win, she decided, her teeth pressed together so firmly that her jaw ached. She wasn't going to let that son of a bitch beat her. At least not yet, not as long as she could make her bruised muscles move.

So, squeezing the pike hard, she bent herself into a hunter's crouch, and, with a bead of sweat crawling down the left side of her nose, she aimed the spear out before her, and started for the police station.

Each step of the thirty yards she covered reverberated up her spine and ended in a sickening blast of concussion between her eyes. Her wet tennis shoes made a soft, swishing sound on the grass, and her breathing rose and fell quickly, like the soundtrack to a film about surgery. Her eyes jerked nervously from place to place, and the door through which she had seen Cornichuk heave Pete into the rain so many centuries before came within reach.

She pulled the screen open with the pike's hook and paused.

Inside, the station's lights were on, and a high-pitched whistle whined steadily, like a cry.

"Hey?" she said, rattling the door with the pike and moving up the stairs. "Anybody here?"

The building didn't answer, and Lori, her fists hard and her eyes icy cold, stepped through the foyer.

At that same instant, crouched in warm darkness thick with the smell of his own sweat, Lenny Kennedy was pressing his ear to the hatchway between the police boat's pilot seats, listening to something awful flopping around somewhere close by and feeling the boat leaning aft as gulping eruptions shuddered the planks upon which he was kneeling.

He'd been aboard when the Tower had started spitting those weird, white things into the night and Lori had come sailing down from the sky. He'd watched an officer named Tom Stanley lift the girl from the water as another person, a man this time, also fell from the balcony a hundred feet overhead, landing yards away and lying as still as death. He'd even been the one to aim the searchlight at the man's body, floating face-down off to starboard in a classic dead man's posture. But when that first lump of pale flesh had landed on the deck and unfolded itself like a bug, he'd locked himself in the crawl-space, holding the hatch firm while men screamed for their lives.

It wasn't pleasant, hearing men die like that, but he'd held on tight and, when the boat started moving, he'd almost smiled. When it rammed something, throwing him against the bulkhead and bruising his face, he'd prayed. And when it bumped the dock so that whoever was piloting it could get off and leave it to sink, he'd crouched at the door, buckling up his courage and thinking that now it might be safe for him to make his break.

But just as he was about to slide the latch free, a new, and terrible, sound froze him like a cat, riveting his attention and stimulating his sensitive pulse. Whatever it was that was making the slow, dripping slurps that reminded him so much of mud squeezing between his toes, it was big.

Really big.

And it had apparently been hanging on the side of the boat, because, as soon as the person who had been on the forward deck was gone, it dropped from the port side with a splash that sounded as if a hundred pound bag of cement had fallen overboard. Now, it was dragging itself up on the dock, slapping soft, wet skin on empty wood, and sliding slowly away.

Lenny waited.

The sound faded.

Still he waited.

Nothing.

He gave it another couple minutes, and then opened the hatch, stepping carefully between the pilot seats, and listening hard.

Whatever he'd heard crawling out of the lake was gone, which he found difficult to understand. The closest thing to the dock was *Leviathan*, and it was probably fifty feet away. Whatever he had heard, it must have moved fast once it hit dry land, because the wet, glistening smears that led from the far end of the dock ended at the grass.

But Lenny didn't care about that. His eyes had settled on the police car parked in the yard, and his mind had become fixed on the idea of escape.

So, with his right hand squeezing his service revolver's handle, and his trembling lips forming the silent words, "Thank God! Thank God!" over and over again, he glanced furtively from the car to the shadows, and gently set his foot down on the dock.

But, in his excitement, he didn't notice that something on the station's roof—something small, round, and pale—was moving.

The thin whistle of the teapot died the instant Lori lifted it from the hot plate, and the station became silent again.

She was standing at the reception desk, behind a pane of bullet proof glass that had a rising sun cut into its lower half so that people could slip things to the secretary from the lobby—which was well lit, painted white, and looked as if it had been hit by a bomb.

Every window in the place had been broken, and glittering glass chips littered white tile beneath overturned orange vinyl furniture and scattered copies of *People* magazine. The window on Lieutenant Danko's office door had also been smashed, and a great quantity of blood was splashed in a flowering pattern down the door, vividly contrasted, red on white, and ending in a puddle that smeared outward, as if someone had dragged himself away—or had been dragged, more likely—after having been badly cut.

All that blood made Lori's already uneasy stomach feel a little queasy. It was so fresh that some of it was still running down the door, and it was so thick that some still hung from the shiny gold knob in long, stringy lines, and, frowning, she placed the hot kettle on the secretary's desk, thinking, It couldn't have taken me more than twenty minutes to get here. Where the hell is everyone?

Stepping around the bulletproof partition, she forced her eyes to follow the sticky red trail from Danko's door, across the hall, and around a corner, to where it disappeared down the basement stairs.

The basement stairs . . .

She wasn't ready for the basement yet, so she took a closer look around the station's main floor.

In an office across the hall, she found a telephone hanging at the end of its curled wire, beeping urgently and turning first one way, then the other. Lifting the receiver and pressing the handle, she got a dial tone and was about to punch out her mother's number, when she thought, What am I going to say?

"Hi, mom. Just thought I'd call and see if you were still alive. Lock your windows and hide in the basement 'til I get home, okay? Yeah, love you too.''?

No way.

She laid the receiver down and tried to think of someone else to call. But she was already in a police station; if she called the police in some other town they would probably think that she was just a crank. And she couldn't bear arguing about her sincerity, or sanity, with some self-satisfied public servant who didn't like his hours. So, for at least the time being, she decided to forget the phone.

The next room she entered was apparently used for meetings; it had a big, rectangular table in its center and chalk boards on all the walls.

The gun rack on the wall in the next room was empty.

And someone had apparently tried to climb right through the window in the little bathroom just beyond the gun room, because, when she opened the door, she found more blood running down the wall and a knotted-up uniform shirt lying next to the toilet, looking as if someone had unsuccessfully tried to use it as a tourniquet.

Her search led her inevitably back to the basement stairs.

"Hello?" she called, placing her foot down carefully on the first step and holding her spear out stiffly.

As hard as she tried, she couldn't keep the memory of the stairs in Kyrik's house from her mind, and suddenly her head was filled with unwelcomed images of pathetic female faces behind ugly sheets of rusty chicken wire. . . .

"Anybody down there?" she nearly shouted, forcing herself to be strong, forcing herself not to stop moving. "Hey? I'm coming down!"

On both her sides, the walls were smooth, and free of any disturbing marks. But the stairs, burnt-orange linoleum with white swirls and metal runners on their edges, were blood stained and slick. Her tennis shoes squeaked desperately, her knees trembled as she moved, and her mind filled with questions—the answers to which she already suspected but refused to entertain.

"Hello?" she called again.

The stairway ended with a wall to her right, one straight ahead, and a doorway to her left that was dark, and open. As she reached the final step, she noticed that the wall opposite the door was black and bumpy, scorched and peppered with what looked like a thousand tiny holes.

The air smelled of sulphur and smoke.

She froze, her foot inches from the landing and her heart racing as she called, "Hey! Don't shoot! Okay? Don't shoot me!"

In her mind she saw a dozen cops, huddled in the dark to her left, aiming the shotguns they had taken from the rack upstairs at the landing, scared out of their wits and trigger-happy.

"Hey! I'm on your side! Okay?"

She waved the pike out before herself.

"Okay?"

There wasn't a sound.

Breathing fast, she clenched her teeth and stepped down, facing the dark rectangle on the wall and exposing herself to the void.

Nothing happened.

Carefully, she entered a short, dim hall, her eyes adjusting slowly to the gloom, and what little light there was fading as she moved farther from the stairs. By the time she reached the second doorway, the area before her was completely black and she had to grope on the wall for a light switch while she said, "Is anyone in here?"

Snap came the lights. . . .

"Jesus!" she gasped, dropping her spear on the concrete floor where it clattered and rolled noisily.

She'd found the night shift.

Here they were.

Hiding.

It was the cell room, a long, narrow place with four cages, arranged two to the left and two to the right, with a small, bar-covered window high up on the wall straight ahead. It was the deepest room in the building, and it was probably the one that everyone thought of as the most secure, being cement, steel, loud, and dark. It was where the cops had headed when the creatures from the Tower had attacked. And, it was where they had died.

"You poor bastards!" Lori whispered, stepping back slowly. "Oh, you poor, stupid bastards!"

They were in the cells. All of them. Why? Who knew? People do crazy things when they're scared. When windows break in the middle of the night and screams fill the air, when open, bloody wounds gape in bright halls and disembodied voices call—

"Holy shit!"

"They're coming in off the lake!"

"Hide in the basement!"

—people do crazy, automatic things.

And, "Hide in the basement!" was about as automatic as you could get in Sharthington.

You learned to hide in the basement early, growing up by the water, like these cops had. You learned to do it the first time spring blew a big, black storm in off the lake. Maybe you were just six years old the first time your mother screamed, "Hide in the basement until it goes away," over the rattling of shutters and the howling of wind. Maybe you were six; maybe you were less.

"Hide in the basement until it goes away."

It stays in your head, even after you're not six any more.

And, judging by their postures, these cops had remembered. But, this time, the storm hadn't gone away; this time, it had followed them down the stairs.

Apparently, they had dragged the two men who had tried to climb through the glass, into the cells first. There was one bloody corpse on the cot in the cell closest to Lori's left, and in the one farthest from her right. Both men's arms were twisted in the air, as if to block blows aimed at their faces, and the walls over their heads were blood-splashed and covered with running red hand prints. The rest of the group, six men and two women, were piled on the floor, five in one cell, three in another, their arms and legs tangled and their shotguns scattered like huge black needles in two small, powder-blue haystacks.

Lori's heart was racing.

So this is what it's going to look like, she thought with a jerk. This is what she could expect to find all over town: broken windows and overturned furniture, violated homes with bloody walls and people in heaps on the floor . . . children and women, men and girls, lying in the street, lying in the dark like these dead officers with their faces terror-stretched and their throats bloated blue beneath the lethal embrace of something soft, and shriveled, and empty.

They'd come from the Tower, thousands, or more.

They'd drifted across the bay, faster than she could follow.

They'd fallen on sleeping Sharthington, like poison from the air.

They were everywhere.

They were here. . . .

Lori dove for her spear as the first creeping shadow coagulated and pulled itself into the shape of a crab-like leg, clattering claws on concrete and bending beneath the arm of a dead man. More insect legs moved, and from the pile emerged living specimens of the deadly creatures, silent, seemingly blind, snapping pinchers and scuttling into the light as if they were responding to it, as if they were following it to more prey. . . .

As if they were following it to her!

Spear in hand she stumbled back into the short hall as shapes at eye level crawled up walls and into view from shadowy corners. She smashed into the blackened plaster at the bottom of the stairs as three pale sacks fell to the floor from the ceiling over where she had been standing. And, spinning to the steps, she leapt up the first three, every muscle in her body flexed and her adrenaline level high as she lifted her eyes, and . . .

Screamed!

No words, no expression of any thought, just a *scream* that shattered the atmosphere and reverberated through the stairwell like a useless personification of pure despair.

What was waiting for her at the top of the stairs had paralyzed her in mid-air, one leg straight out behind her, one bent three steps up, and her arms crooked and jutting the spear out as if she were about to lance an enemy.

It stopped her dead.

It stopped her cold.

It was Joshua—or, at least, it was what was left of him— hanging between the two walls between one human arm, and one plump, stumpy thing that was thick, segmented like a scorpion's tail, and sporting at its end two lengths of sharp, curved bone, the size of butcher's knives. He was staring down with one, open eye that shone like a black mirror at the center of what his face had become, dripping and wheezing phlegm from gaping holes that sucked like tiny mouths all over his body, which was exposed completely now, and chopped neatly in half from just over his right hip to just below the left side of his groin.

Quivering, the pouchy sack of his throat opened, shuddering and filling with hissing air as lengths of curling intestine dropped from the gaping wound where his legs had been, hanging nearly low enough to drag on the stairs.

"Sssshawwwta . . .'ooree!" he said in a rumbling, bass voice, heavy with liquid and deeply resonant. *"Sssshawwwta!"*

Lori's legs gave out—they just let go—dropping her on the stairs where, for a terrifying moment she was unable to move. All she could do was lie there and let her eyes register details about the thing overhead that her brain refused to accept and that therefore only compounded her state of collapse.

He was totally black . . . her eyes said.

He was glistening like rubber and, from the spot on his chest where he had claimed the Blood Fly had left its mark, there climbed creeping lumps of serpentine flesh, like roots branching over the rest of his body, entwining his head and shoulders and forming hundreds of squirming lengths of skin, some almost three feet long, hanging in a bunch over his stomach and ending around his penis, which squirmed like the rest. He trembled one more time, and dark, wet things fell from inside him, rolling on the stairs and steaming. The hanging loops of intestine fell, something else fell, and from inside him poked the shattered end of his spine, groping like a tail.

"Sssshawwwta!" he said.

"Noooo!" Lori screamed, scrambling to her feet and stumbling back into the wall behind her with a thud.

The floor was alive with those baggy white things, bouncing out of her way and struggling up the stairs. Out of the corner of her eye she could see that the short hall to her right was simply lousy with them, and, on the ceiling, there were some crawling out from under the Styrofoam acoustic tile. Tiny pinchers explored the landing through the holes punched in the wall by shotgun pellets, and, behind Joshua, there were more, crawling along the white tile floor like crabs in search of the sea.

There was nowhere to go!

She didn't have a chance!

And, as Joshua prepared himself, leaning back and coiling like a cat judging the distance of its leap to the kill, Lori shook her head, dropped her spear and cried, ''No! No! Oh, sweet Jesus, no!''

Diving to her right at the same instant that Joshua sprang, she slipped on something soft, slid, fell, and saw a huge black shape slam into the wall behind where she had just been standing, clattering her abandoned spear and turning her way almost instantly.

It moves so goddamned fast!, she thought, her legs pumping furiously amid scattering, pale shapes and her eyes locked on a closet door to her left. Just so goddamned fast!

Her hands slipped off the knob once, causing her to whimper involuntarily, but then the knob turned, and she plunged inside, rattling against loud, metal objects and slamming the door shut behind herself just as Joshua's human hand touched the wood.

But it wouldn't do any good, she knew. She'd seen him pull plywood sheets from the wall in the Tower's tip and she knew the flimsy closet door wouldn't keep him out for long.

And, as if to verify her thought, the closet was suddenly filled with the sound of rending wood, and, in the undependable light of a swinging bulb, two huge claws shattered through, inches from her face, sending her scrambling back, into a rack of mops and brooms as wood splintered and Joshua howled, '' 'Oooreee!'' like a fiend.

No window!

No other door!

Nowhere to go!

''Ssshawwwta! 'Oooreee!''

''Go away!'' she screamed. ''Just go away!''

The claws slid down the wood as if they were tearing fabric; and Lori ran her trembling hands over first the janitor's sink to her left, and then the objects lining the shelves to her right—knocking jars and cans to the floor and finally settling on one stained plastic container. Ripping its lid off just as the door split in half and tore free, she spun, jerking her arm up and splashing the bottle's hissing contents directly into that black, staring eye in the middle of Joshua's face.

The container was marked, ORGANIC MATERIAL SOLVENT, and had a tiny skull and crossbones grinning over the words, *For clearing metal pipes of obstructions—Caution: Poisonous and Corrosive.*

And it was corrosive.

With a howl, Joshua fell, rolling back and groping over his face with his human hand as his lizard arm curled beneath him and propped his body upright. A long plume of whisping steam climbed from between his flexing fingers, and dark, greasy slime bubbled down his arm.

Lori plunged through the doorway and hit the stairs in three strides. She was through the station's lobby and in the yard before her brain could register what she was seeing. . . .

She stopped.

And then she screamed, "Help! Help, police!"

The man in the yard—the living man—was thin, and dark; he was wearing a powder blue policeman's uniform, complete with short pants, and he was holding a gun. He had just laid his hand on the driver's door of the police car when Lori's call caused him to turn, crane his neck for an instant, and then turn away. Pulling the car door open, he jumped inside, and didn't look at her again.

" *'Oooreee!*" came a roar from inside the station.

Lori jerked violently around and found Joshua's dark figure at the top of the stairs. He was balanced on his curled, reptilian arm, which held his truncated body off the floor at a peculiar angle, bouncing ever so slightly to create an impression of impending action, and great strength. His human arm was stiffly motionless over his head, and where the pipe acid had touched his skin, bubbling patches of scorched flesh ran with dark fluid across the glassy, black eye that had been so prominently positioned over his mouth, and that was now just an oozing mess.

But, as she watched, that mess quivered and bulged, and, from inside swelled something glossy and dark. The little mouths that split his skin opened and closed quickly, as if to catch her scent, as a wash of dark juice slithered down his face and another, smaller eye bubbled up like a blister to take the place of the one she'd ruined.

He froze for a moment, as if testing his new sight, and then, in one, fluid motion, his coiled lizard arm flexed, hurling him into the air and across the foyer, directly into the station's front door.

The police car's engine was grinding, trying to start and coughing a puff of smoke from its exhaust pipes. Lori jumped from the station's porch and slammed the door, scrambling in the gravel and hearing Joshua's heavy thud of impact behind her just as the car burst into life and something moved in the sky.

The man behind the cruiser's steering wheel lifted his eyes from the ignition and threw open the driver's door. In an instant he'd piled into the back seat and slammed the door closed, squirming around and grabbing the sheet of wire cage that separated the front and back seats and watching as the movement in the sky became white balls of flesh that flew down fast, and hard, bouncing off the glass surrounding him and skittering into the car through the open front windows.

Lori dashed across the parking lot, her legs smacking down on gravel like pistons, her eyes wide, and her lips pressed so firmly together that they were blue. Behind her, the police station's door exploded and Joshua howled like a lion in the night. But she didn't stop, didn't look back or even try to imagine what he was doing. The car was just a few feet ahead, covered with writhing lumps of milky skin, its engine running, its driver's door hanging open.

"Leave me alone! Go away!" the cop in the back of the cruiser was shouting, banging on the wire, his eyes riveted on the front seat and his perfectly tanned face almost completely pale.

Lori reached the cruiser and began brushing the creatures off with her hands, simply knocking them away, grimacing at the weird, pouchy way they felt on her skin, but unafraid. They wouldn't hurt her, she knew. She didn't understand why they wouldn't, but if they were going to do her any harm, they had plenty of opportunity before now.

"Under the seat!" the cop cried, scrambling around frantically and clutching alternately at the wire partition, and the door—which didn't have a handle, so he couldn't get out. "Under the seat!"

Lori picked up squirming things, and dropped them on the ground behind herself. The front seat was covered with them, but as many as she removed, more crawled back in through the open passenger's-side window, skittering over green vinyl and down to the floor. Brushing a place clear, she finally slid in behind the wheel, yanked the gear shift to D, and pressed the accelerator, just as a wet hand plunged through her open window and grabbed her by the throat.

Blackness crept around the edges of her vision and tiny, silver stars sparkled, glazing the windshield and her eyes, as the car lurched, throwing the cop in the back against the seat and sending the crab-like creatures in its path bounding out of the way like immense frogs. Blackness washed briefly over everything in her head, the steering wheel spun, the cop in the back screamed frantically, and Joshua's fingers squeezed even tighter. The car bounced over gravel, grass, and then a curb, smashing down on pavement so hard that two wheel covers went rolling in opposite directions and a length of tail pipe collapsed, immediately producing a *boom-boom-boom* of roaring engine and a black plume of exhaust.

A tree loomed and dove to the left. Telephone wires as tight as banjo strings segmented the sky and melted away. Lori pressed the accelerator to the floor and futilely leaned against Joshua's grip, feeling something snap under her chin and seeing two very disturbing things at the exact same instant:

Joshua's lizard-tail arm teasing like a tentacle on the car's windshield, its soft skin producing doughy patches of contact on the glass and its immense, dripping stingers bone-hard and lightly veined . . .

. . . and Rages's huge, rectangular barn doors, painted red, white, and blue, snapping into brilliant proximity right at the very end of the car's hood.

The impact was fabulous.

It shattered the windshield instantly, showering her with hysterical slivers and driving her forward, into the dashboard and then back, before pulling her into a ball, wedged below the steering wheel. The engine raced as if it meant to pull the car all the way through the tavern, but then it sputtered, shifted feebly, and died, ending its brief, maniacal run with a tremendous hiss, and the flapping of what sounded like rubber straps on tin, slowing to silence beneath the rhythmic ticking of cooling metal.

A choking cough ruptured the new quiet.

And then another.

And then Lori crawled painfully up on the driver's seat, dropping a blue glaze of powdered glass off herself as she moved, and rubbing her hands over her throat while her lungs quivered and her esophagus gulped stiffly for air.

Then her eyes went wide and she snapped her head to the left, throwing her arms up to protect her injured throat from Joshua's renewed attack.

She paused.

The window was dark, revealing only the semi-familiar shapes of bar stools and nautical mementoes somewhere deeply hidden behind a heavy haze of drifting dust and gloom. Along the window's lower rim was a black stain running down the door, and the rearview mirror had been ripped from the car's side.

Tink: a tiny something fell from the ceiling.

Tick tick: the engine cooled.

Lori turned and looked through the wire partition, finding the officer in the back curled on the floor, his arms twisted in awkward, bone-snapping disarray, his throat swollen and an empty sack attached rigidly beneath his chin. Two living creatures sat on the back seat, quietly folding their arms as if they were disappointed, and ready to settle down to wait for another chance.

Her stomach turned when she noticed that there weren't any handles on the doors back there, and that the only way the cop could have gotten away from the creatures that had crawled beneath the front seat, would have been for her to have let him out.

Tick tick: the engine cooled.

But his gun was still in his hand—and she wanted it.

Pushing her door open with a jerk, she grimaced at the squeal the hinges made and set one foot down in the rubble. Then she hissed, spraying saliva between her teeth and collapsing against the side of the car, her eyes squeezed into slits and her hands groping for support.

A pain like fire was climbing through her chest.

She'd broken a rib, she knew, probably on the steering wheel, and with each step she tried to take, and practically every breath she drew, the heat of injury burned like a furnace deep inside her broken body.

Rages was almost completely dark, and there wasn't a sound other than the cooling engine. The barn door had shattered like cardboard, and lengths of wood lay like a nest around the steaming car. Everything Lori did seemed to produce some incredibly loud noise, and just the crunching of her shoes on the floor was maddening.

But where the hell was Joshua?

That was the question that drove her on. It was the thing that made her defy the pain in her chest and pull open the back door. It made her lean inside, and, with a terrible frown and cold, emotionless movements, pry the dead man's fingers apart so that she could lift his 38 caliber policeman's special and bounce it in her hand. It was almost identical to the one she had carried in the door of her Monza, and the Monza's memory produced in her a weird, yearning sense of brief nostalgia for a time before she had ever heard of Randolph Kyrik's Blood Flies, or of Peter Blackwell, which was really nostalgia for a time only a few hours past.

But having the gun helped—not a lot, but it helped—and, squeezing it protectively, she turned back to the bar, took a deep breath that made her ribs ache, and said, "I know you're in here Joshua!"

Rages was silent, dark, and lonely.

He moves so goddamned fast, she thought, afraid to stay where she was, and at the same time afraid to move.

"Joshua?" she called, her voice cool and her arm upraised to display her gun.

Just so goddamned fast.

"Joshua . . ."

Where the hell could he be?

Four

It was Cornichuk standing at the bottom of the tunnel, beckoning to him with his hand, and Pete recognized him the instant he rolled to a halt near the big man's feet. But, through waves of spinning nausea, and confused, tear-filled eyes, he didn't immediately recognize the material flapping around his face. From the top of the tunnel, before his slide, he'd thought it was hair, but after a minute he was able to blink away the tears, and he realized that it was really *flesh*!

As if a surgeon had sliced open Cornichuk's head, starting directly between his eyes and ending all the way back at the crown of his spine, the scalp had been peeled from the bone in long, thin strips, and the skull had been chipped away, leaving a bloody, folded brain exposed, and tattered threads of hairy flesh hanging so far down that his left ear dangled below his chin.

Lacerations and bruises covered the rest of his body, and his shredded clothes were so blood-soaked that they looked almost uniformly red. His eyes were vacant, staring and blank, his mouth hung open—with a thread of saliva quivering at the end of his lower lip—and, after a moment, he dreamily stopped waving his hand and allowed it to drop at his side with a slap.

Pete struggled first to a sitting position, and then to his feet, slamming into a rubbery wall for support and throwing his arms over his head frantically as he shrieked, "You're

It?!? You're the Thing?! I died for my chance to see It, and It looks like you?!''

The rage he aimed at Cornichuk was blinding, but, still, he couldn't help noticing that the walls behind him were closing up and erasing the tunnel through which he had fallen, leaving him in a space no larger than twelve by twenty feet that was radiant with harsh blue light, and wavering, slowly, as if it were a part of something very large, that was moving.

Claustrophobia washed through him like electricity and left his mind filled with racing, panicked patterns that were combining themselves into a randomly generated collage of disjointed verisimilitude so illogical that it turned his stomach and made him dizzy:

. . . a bloody night stick sprouted green reptile eyes in his mind, jutting from between Lori's naked legs while Kyrik's head rolled loose through the nightmare of Joshua's face.

. . . gelatinous bodies with crazy-big teeth quivered from his mother's sympathetic eyes as twenty-six birthday candles burned tiny white worms into shriveled fingers lying in bloody mud.

. . . something *huge* folded flesh in an *immense* arch that reached through flying blood, touching his mind and making him say, *''Life . . .*

''New life!

''Life unlike any other!

''You can't be It,'' he forced himself to whisper, cutting off the raving he felt overtaking his jumbled thoughts and relaxing his hands and shoulders.

His legs felt weak, and his spine chalky and stiff. His tongue was dry, and it moved clumsily when he finally added, ''I know there's got to be more. I can feel it.''

Licks of crackling light, like blue wires, slithered in a hundred snapping bolts from everywhere in the room, meeting and bristling over Cornichuk's head and shuddering his body. His arms jerked up and fell as his legs flopped, jerking him upright from the waist in a staggering, watery-kneed posture that made him stumble awkwardly toward the wall to his left. Like a slow-motion film of milk being poured, the wall opened, and Pete watched in amazement as Cornichuk took control of himself and the wall closed up again.

"Well?" he cried. "Why'd you bring me here?"

Cornichuk was silent.

"Come on!" Pete shouted, feeling his bile rise. "I died to get here! Lori died to get me here! The least you could do is talk to me, for God's sake!"

"It's for God's sake that you were Called," Cornichuk said slowly, evenly, and with absolute authority. "Welcome to Genesis."

"What?" Pete bellowed, the image of Noah Blackwell rising in his mind, which was the truth about what he'd been subconsciously expecting to find here all along.

After having read the journal in Kyrik's office, it was a monster with his great-grandfather's face—like out of some old movie—curled beneath the Tower and calling him down so that it could get more Blackwell DNA to play with that he had been expecting, almost hoping, to see. It was something *huge*, something so overwhelming that it would almost be worth all he'd sacrificed just for that one moment of proximity, that one instant in which he would *see* something that no one else had ever seen, or would ever see again.

"This is it, isn't it?" he said softly, his eyes wide and his convictions fading. "You've got a Blackwell, and that's all you wanted."

Cornichuk cocked his head and almost smiled.

"You're not what I wanted," he said, his eyes a blank. "You're what Shawnita wanted."

"But, aren't *you* the Shawnita?" Pete asked, swallowing and trying to organize something in his mind that would give him a clue to what was going on.

"No," Cornichuk said earnestly. "*You* are. It wasn't just any Blackwell that was required—it was *you*! And now that you're here, there can be the Beginning."

Pete's mouth was open, and his options closed. For a full minute he stared at the hideous deformity standing before him, soaking in the extent to which this man had been damaged into his very being and coming to a slow, impossible understanding.

"You're dead," he said at last, sweat rolling off his upper lip and beading under his eyes.

Blue lightning started up again, spinning around the room and finding Cornichuk's skull. Every time he spoke or moved, the lightning came, and, every time he stopped, it stopped too.

"Almost," he said simply.

"But why is the Shawnita doing this to you?"

"Because you need to understand before the Beginning."

"But It made me talk!" Pete shouted, lifting his hands and letting them drop. "It put a dream in my mind and words in my mouth! Why should It need you to tell me what It wants me to know?"

"A dream is just an image," Cornichuk said, the wire of blue crackling into a halo around his head. "And words are just places in the mind to find and touch. But knowledge is complicated, and if Shawnita were to touch your mind too many times, It would burn all words away."

"So It's using you as Its translator?"

"In a way," Cornichuk agreed. "Consciousness is a force in and of itself. Shawnita possesses a great depth of consciousness, and therefore great power. If It were to give you Its consciousness, as It did to me, what happened to me would happen to you: all you know, and all that you are, would be overwhelmed and die. All that would be left is what Shawnita knows, and, in your case at least, that would be of no value. So, Shawnita is funnelling what It knows through me so that it can enter your mind in a way that won't do you any harm."

"And what does Shawnita know?" Pete asked, hesitantly, feeling sweat running down along his spine.

"How to make everything perfect," Cornichuk said easily.

"What's perfect?" Pete asked in return.

"Shawnita."

"So for everything to be perfect . . ." Pete began.

"Everything must be Shawnita," Cornichuk finished for him. "Patterns. Everything is patterns."

Patterns? Pete thought, searching his mind for something that would explain what the Beast was trying to tell him. It had gone through a lot of trouble to get him here just so he could serve some vital function—and he still didn't have the slightest idea of what it was. . . .

Searching his mind?

He was searching his mind . . .

For a pattern!

All thoughts are patterns, he realized. A thought is just the firing of certain nerves in a certain order. All understanding is a pattern. All thinking is a pattern of patterns. All reality, if it is to be understood by man, must be organized into a pattern . . .

Understood by man?

The Shawnita was thinking like a man! It was expressing Itself through Cornichuk because Cornichuk's brain was a pattern It could understand.

"So, if the Shawnita were just to put the pattern It wants me to see in my brain, It would damage me?" Pete asked suddenly, as if he were thinking out loud.

Cornichuk's head snapped up and his mouth moved but didn't speak.

"Does the Shawnita have the patterns that Noah Blackwell had?" Pete asked.

"No," Cornichuk said. "It has his ability to see patterns, but not the patterns he saw."

Something was taking shape in the back of Pete's mind, coming together slowly as the things Cornichuk related fit, one into the next.

"So, the Shawnita took Noah Blackwell's ability to think, but not the specific thoughts that were in his head. If It were to absorb me, like It absorbed him, It would then be able to think like me, but It wouldn't retain my actual thoughts," he said.

Cornichuk was nodding, his eyes moving in the same blank way as his head.

"The Shawnita doesn't really want *me*!" Pete suddenly snapped, his eyes wide with new terror and his hand climbing free in the air before his face. "It wants what I know. . . ."

He paused, thinking, peeling back the layers of imagery in his head and laying things out flat where they could be viewed and studied.

"It brought me to the Tower, and into the pedestal. It worked very hard for me to be there with Lori when Joshua came up the stairs. It sent the Call to drag me down into that room with the shelves. And It made sure I saw those things in the wall before I ended up down here. . . ."

He stopped, his mouth moving silently and his fingers flexing.

"Those things in the wall!" he whispered. "It needs me because of those things in the fucking wall!"

Cornichuk actually smiled as he said, "Everything is patterns, and the ones Shawnita needs are in your mind."

"And It can't take them . . ." Pete began.

"So you must give them," Cornichuk concluded.

"How?" Pete demanded.

"Shawnita shea negarik," Cornichuk replied. "To partake of Shawnita is to take part in Shawnita."

Pete was watching the blood run down the middle of Cornichuk's forehead. It was thick, and it blurped out in an awful, three-branched line that was distracting, and that held his attention for the moment it took the floor to change.

Up from between his legs shot something thin and strong, tangling his right knee and climbing his thigh in a flash to slide in under his shirt. A bolt of pain tore through his chest and Pete threw back his head and shrieked, his arms jerking up, his fingers twisting into claws. His teeth clenched into a frightful grimace, the tendons in his neck standing pronounced and tall, he twisted once, turned, and then groped up quickly, tearing his shirt from collar to waist and revealing his wounded chest.

He looked down and screamed, "No! Goddamn it, no!"

The floor changed again, three more whips formed and whistled around his legs before following the course of the first tentacle and gouging their way into burrowing tunnels beneath his skin.

He tried to move, but he was literally rooted to the floor.

The tentacles dug deeply through him, crackling his nerves and overwhelming his brain with millions of firing sensations of agony . . . sensations of agony, and strangely . . . very strangely . . .

He stopped fighting.

It was strange. There was pain. But beneath the pain, he felt . . . aroused.

Cornichuk smiled.

Pete looked down, over the welted, bumpy flesh of his chest and stomach, overrun with blue worms of hidden blood, and saw that his pants had lifted over the bulge at his groin.

He had an erection.

He looked up at Cornichuk, and found that the room was very different.

He looked up at Cornichuk, and suddenly understood.

"It *is* here!" he shouted, struggling like a man wrapped in barbed wire. "It is, isn't it? *Isn't it? Isn't it??!!!*"

"There is but one Shawnita," Cornichuk said as the walls moved in closer and smoke lifted from his scorched brain. "And It's of two pieces: Its body and Its brain. Its brain remains here. . . ."

He lifted his arms and indicated the room.

"And It's body goes out into the world. Shawnita sees through the eyes of Its body, and feels through the limbs of Its body. But Shawnita thinks with Its brain, and, soon, Shawnita will think with *your* brain too."

Cornichuk's eyes closed as the electricity burned brighter and sizzled in his head.

"Until Noah Blackwell found Shawnita, It was of a different pattern," he went on, his voice sounding more ragged, and less sure. "It was content, and It was one with the world. Its brain remained hidden and safe, and Its body sought food and produced the energy that kept the brain alive. As long as the body lives, so does the brain—and, as long as the brain lives, so does the body. It's the perfect animal, and every forty years, when Its body grows old, the brain makes a new body, sending the old one away to die and leaving the new one to live on. In this way did the Shawnita live from the beginning of time, and, in this way, It would have gone on forever. . . ."

"Until It took Noah Blackwell into its body!" Pete screamed, straining against the new cords that slithered out from the wall and beneath his skin from overhead and to his sides. "It laid its eggs in Noah's mouth and produced a body that was smart! A body that could think for itself and that wanted more than just to blindly serve a brain, right!?"

"No," Cornichuk said, a clear liquid running from beneath his quivering eyelids and more smoke climbing from his fractured cranium. "Then It took Noah Blackwell into Its *brain*."

Pete kept his eyes on Cornichuk's face, realizing that the smoke he was seeing was the tissue of the man's mind melting away under the power the Beast produced to induce him to speak. He kept his eyes on Cornichuk, and ignored the things he thought he was seeing in the unsure recesses of his peripheral vision—the strange, unbelievable things . . .

. . . like his own flesh being pulled, painlessly, from his body and stretched into a nearly transparent, membrane-like film between quivering lengths of snaking tentacles, emanating from the walls.

He didn't look at that.

He didn't believe it.

And he certainly wasn't going to fight it.

"Every time Noah Blackwell stole the essence of Shawnita and placed it in some other animal, just to see what would happen, he created more parts of a bigger and more complicated body for the brain to control." Cornichuk said, blood joining the fluid running from beneath his deflating eyelids.

"Controlling the body Noah Blackwell made became more and more difficult, and Shawnita's brain was forced to grow, bigger and bigger, tunneling even deeper underground from where Noah had buried It beneath the Tower and stretching out, becoming larger, and more intricate.

"But still he persisted in making more body parts, more limbs to control, and more senses to understand, so that finally, the brain was left with no choice but to modify itself in a way that could accommodate the strain placed on it. Noah Blackwell's brain offered a pattern that could be used for such a change, and Shawnita took his pattern as Its own.

"Like so . . ."

Cornichuk suddenly fell to the floor and something big shuddered through Pete's now flexible head. It was a quick, precise image, one of the dreams the Shawnita apparently found so easy to send.

And he saw this:

The room beneath the Tower was different from the way he had seen it. It was gloomy, yes, but it was neat and, in a strange way, appealing. The shelves that he had seen used to hold dead bodies now held books and old, outdated scientific equipment, and a man, tall, thin, with whispy grey hair as long as Pete's, and a familiar face, bent over a table awash with the gentle glow of a shaded oil lamp, impervious to the danger Pete sensed was approaching from the ground.

The man was Noah Blackwell, and, in his mind, Pete gasped.

He had seen only still photographs of his ancient relative, and to be presented with this moving, animate image of vitality and grace filled him with a sense of longing, and loving pride. Noah looked a lot like Pete, except for his stiff collar and dark, strangely cut suit. He looked even more like Pete's father, and he had about him a way of moving that was intimately familiar, and that made Pete feel as if he were seeing himself, through a stranger's eyes, in another time, and, perhaps, in another life.

"Blood Flies," Cornichuk's voice wove through the scene, intruding on the simple integrity of the image and distracting Pete's attention briefly. "Through the air, and through time, blood flies."

And what the voice said was true, Pete understood.

"In a way, we're all immortal," he himself had said to Lori in Kyrik's office. "We carry our parents' genetic codes and pass them on to our children, who do the same, so that, as long as we reproduce, our DNA continues. . . ."

So, here he was merely seeing himself in another of the forms that the vessel propelling that which was the essence of his family, the common DNA that was *Blackwell*, assumed through the ages.

It was stunning.

It was weirdly reassuring.

And it was almost more than he could bear to keep from

crying out and trying to embrace himself in the past. He'd never been exposed to such depth of emotion and closeness to the past as in this exact second. He was one with everyone in his family . . . literally *one*! They were all simply extensions of the same creature, stretching through time in a single line and sharing the same genetic codes. . . .

Sharing the exact same codes . . .

Like the many parts of the Shawnita's body; like the Blood Flies, sharing the same code and reliant on the brain to dictate behavior. The Flies were simply an entire lineage born together!

Pete wanted to call out, but he couldn't, and, in horrible silence, he was forced to watch as the danger he felt threatening his great grandfather—threatening *him* then, as it was threatening *him* now—was made known.

It burst up, first through the bubbling pool, and then through the ground itself. It was huge, grey and flexing, emanating from below in tentacles that were larger versions of the same whips the Beast was using to hold Pete's body suspended over the floor. They broke the ground and blasted into the air, jerking Noah's head up and entwining his body before he could even scream.

Like Pete, Noah struggled at first. But, then, he fell limp, and stared down at his own groin, where he too had achieved an erection—like a dead man dangling from the gallows—before his head snapped back and a particularly large tentacle shot up from the floor and clamped itself between his legs.

Noah screamed as the tentacle seemed to vibrate. Then, his head was drawn, first into his neck, and then down into his chest as his entire body was sucked into itself, through his groin, into the bulging tentacle of the Beast as it disappeared under wet sand.

The room pulsed, and shuddered.

Oil lamp glow danced on abandoned books.

The ground swelled, and dust fell from above as something happened below, something terrible.

Shawnita exploded beneath the Tower, rumbling the ground and blasting out in screaming lines of nerve endings, for miles, it seemed . . . for miles and miles.

The Beast had found a new pattern!
It had found an amazing, dangerous, new pattern!

"And so started that which begins again today," Cornichuk said from where he lay curled on the floor. "So Shawnita found the intricacy It needed to control all the limbs Noah Blackwell had created for It, and more. Using what Noah had taught It about changing Itself and exercising Its new ability by taking the pattern of Noah's brain as Its own, It emulated Its God, because, to Shawnita, Noah was amazing. Here It had been living for millions of years as one kind of creature, and then, one day, along comes this man who just changes what It was. Shawnita found that remarkable, and It watched as he experimented, and It learned from what he found. So, when the day came when It absolutely had to make Its change or lose control of Its body, why wouldn't It choose the best pattern It had ever seen? Why wouldn't It choose the pattern of a man?"

Pete knew that what Cornichuk was saying was important, but he was having trouble concentrating on it because the walls were different now. They were fuzzy, and shuddering, and he had a peculiar, disjointed feeling seeping from the area that had been his stomach, up, through the area that was still his head. He felt as if he were breaking up, splitting into more than one part and then coming back together, as if he weren't sure whether he was one being, or more.

"It's the Blood that makes you feel that way," Cornichuk said.

"You mean the venom Kyrik wanted so badly?" Pete asked.

"Yes," Cornichuk replied. "The Blood brings you into Shawnita and shows you another's life. It's the essence of Shawnita, and it's the medium through which the thoughts of Shawnita travel."

"The Blood is the medium? But I didn't have any of the Blood when I had the Call in New York."

"You had the Blood then, as you have it now."

"Because of Noah?"

"Yes. Shawnita Called you as easily as It would Call one

of Its own body. You share Its Blood, because you share Its lineage.''

"But, according to Kyrik's book, if a man gets too much of the Blood, it'll kill him," Pete protested feebly.

"The Blood doesn't kill that way," Cornichuk said. "When Shawnita's body forces the Blood through the skin of another, it kills, quickly, and without pain. But if the Blood enters the body slowly, and is taken into the brain, it doesn't kill at all. It prevents the brain from functioning alone, and freezes it so that the thoughts of Shawnita can be heard. If a man gets too much of the Blood, he will see too much of Shawnita, and he may kill himself.''

"It makes him crazy," Pete concluded.

Cornichuk nodded his head.

"So then Kyrik was listening to the Shawnita all along. He was just doing what the Shawnita wanted him to do and was never any real danger at all.''

"Kyrik was good," Cornichuk agreed. "For years he protected Shawnita by keeping people away from the Island. If it weren't for him, someone would have stumbled on the truth long before you answered the Call.''

"But why would the Shawnita let him do all the terrible things he did to those people under his house?''

"Because it was what he needed to do to continue hiding Shawnita. And because Shawnita was curious.''

"Noah was curious," Pete said.

"Now is Shawnita.''

"What else was Noah?" Pete asked, moving his bleary gaze from the wall to Cornichuk's twisted body and seeing that his brain was almost completely black.

"God," Cornichuk said simply.

"Noah was God?" Pete said with a fatal laugh. "Of course. Noah was God, and now Shawnita is Noah. God's perfect, so Shawnita's perfect. For everything to be perfect, everything must be Shawnita.''

"Exactly," Cornichuk said, and his brain flopped out of his skull and onto the floor in a steaming mess, running at the end of a tangle of wet nerves and sinews.

It made perfect sense, Pete realized.

Shawnita had taken on the form of Noah Blackwell's brain, and with it had come that peculiar sense man seemed to possess of his own, self-centered importance in the universe. Just as all but a very few cultures believe that the gods have smiled on them in particular, and that the Holy has bestowed Its blessings on man by making him master of the world, the Shawnita believed Itself to be blessed.

Quite simply, the Shawnita had an ego.

Pete trembled when the logic of it all unfolded. He closed his eyes, and the room disappeared, being replaced by a weird, twisting tunnel of blue that seemed to stretch before and behind him for miles and miles. He was momentarily lost in the expanse of the Thing, and the nausea in his stomach, and the peculiar, red tint that seemed to frost the edges of his vision didn't bother him at all.

Slowly, he flexed a part of himself that seemed to lie to the left, and he felt gratified when something shuddered through the walls and down, into his flesh.

He concentrated, and suddenly he found that he could move through the tunnel and make its walls slide past him as he followed its complicated network of branches and tributaries. Its color was a constant, electric blue that apparently was produced by the brain's tissue, and its consistency and depth staggered him.

He stopped, eased himself whole again, and allowed the nagging impulse to relax to overtake him for just an instant, and . . .

Suddenly he was seeing the inside of cages, floors covered with straw, and Cornichuk, shadowy under dim bulbs, carrying naked women over his shoulder and wearing a bloody, white surgeon's smock.

He saw that. He positively saw that. . . .

He opened his eyes and pulled himself back together enough to see that Cornichuk's face had almost completely sunken in on itself and that blood was pouring from his eyes.

"The Blood is taking you into Shawnita, and yet you aren't being damaged," the big man's rubbery mouth said. "You understand what I've told you, so the pictures you see will make sense."

"I'm seeing what It saw, but I'm not losing what I know," Pete translated, hearing his own words but realizing that he hadn't moved his mouth.

For a curious instant, he wondered if he still had a mouth. He moved his eyes—he couldn't move his head any more—but he could not see what he looked like. He did notice that his fingers seemed to be somewhere very high above him, and that his chest didn't hurt.

He closed his eyes, and saw new wonders. He saw the shoreline of the lake, rough and unspoiled by the structures man would one day call Sharthington, Ohio: ancient memories of the Beast.

He saw Indians dancing, eating the dripping lengths of dark flesh that were the Blood Flies before Noah Blackwell changed them. He saw them fall and contort themselves on the ground before raging fires as the Blood was absorbed by their systems, hurling them briefly into the vortex of the Beast.

He saw thousands of places, through thousands of eyes, separately, and simultaneously, and he realized that the Beast could be in more than one place at one time, and perform more than one task as easily as Pete had been able to move his own two hands.

He saw thousands of dark slashes, glistening through sparkling water, swimming free, all separate and, yet, all a part of him. The sun bled dreamily from above, cut by the surface of the lake into bands of color through which the silhouetted forms of what the Shawnita had been, millions of years ago—sleek, strong, and pure—slid in an amazing dance, like the notes of a tune. And he saw himself playing them from below, like the keys on a piano, all at once, individually, at the same time.

It was breathtaking to feel so free and experience such a loose sensation of expanse while maintaining such absolute control and balance.

He saw, in that instant, the beauty of Shawnita.

He saw Its majesty.

And then, he saw Lori.

His eyes snapped open and he thought-said, "Lori! What was that? Was that a memory, or was it real?"

But even with his eyes open he saw more, always more, and the precision of the images temporarily seduced him back from the picture he had seen of Lori, moving through the darkened gloom of Rages's doorway.

He saw the Tower, spewing out tiny white sacks of the essence of Shawnita as the Beast took the very heart of Itself and released it—a pure elixir of the animal's life, untainted by exposure to experiments or failures, a slice of Its very soul, sent out into the world to find material upon which to build.

He saw Sharthington below, and dropped on it from the sky in a million different places, touching what seemed to be a million different people, most of them sleeping in their beds. He felt himself enter them, saw their flesh from a perspective he had previously only imagined, and understood from an instantly intimate and practical level what had been explained to him about the cell in science classes for years.

He saw into the very heart of man's DNA, and he couldn't help but look. He became the Shawnita, Its life's blood resting in thousands of human bodies, the building blocks of Its being poised to combine with those sparkling lengths of pure *life*. He felt like God, preparing for the creation.

"Genesis," Cornichuk said, and his voice was nearly lost beneath gurgling bubbles.

But Pete hardly heard him.

He didn't need to hear him, because suddenly he understood. Suddenly, it all made sense and stood crystal clear before his wondering sight.

He was to be the Beast's mind!

He was to take the knowledge he had gathered in graduate school and put it to practical use; he was to test the theories and discover the truth by simple observation, and he was to organize the combinations of the Beast's DNA with that of man, choosing the best of both and creating an absolutely new, absolutely perfect species. He was to be the brain of the world.

He was to be *life!*

New life!

Life unlike any other.

Life that would bring together the pitiful bits of flesh that aimlessly swarmed the Earth into one perfect, living entity of beautiful, harmonious unity.

Soon, everything would be him!

He boggled at the implications of it. He marveled, staring transfixed, at the simplicity of the DNA helix, observing it like a laboratory specimen, turning it in his mind and turning it back. He was already considering his course, already determining attributes and limitations from the nearly boundless pool of raw possibilities afforded him. . . .

The hand of man was good.

The eye of the bird was better.

Man's cerebral cortex was marvelous.

An insect's ectoskeleton protected it from the world.

. . . And he would begin by breaking the material offered him in the bodies of the people in Sharthington into a number of test groups. He would endow each group with a different experimental form: number of legs, eyes, lung capacity, etc., and then put them through their paces to see how they did. The next generation would be the best of the test groups combined with whatever materials were needed to correct any failings that might present themselves.

It wouldn't be a quick way, but it would be the most logical. No more blind combinations. No more mistakes like those animals in the walls under the Tower.

The animals in the walls!

He stopped his ruminations and said, "But what about the creatures that are alive now?"

"All must be perfect," Cornichuk's voice slurred, barely audible, barely decipherable.

"What about the animals, the fish, and the birds?"

"All must be perfect."

"What about the people?"

"All will be Shawnita!"

"What about the people?!!"

"All will be Shawnita!"

Pete saw it in his mind—and he saw it despite the Beast.

The experiment would begin with this generation of creatures, and continue as those things Pete created went out and began clearing the way for the Shawnita to grow. It would be limitless, spreading like syrup over the globe, insidious at first . . . just a small, Ohio town that suddenly isn't right anymore.

"All the folks just up and disappeared," the story would go.

And then strange reports would start up. Strange talk of things in the woods, weird things in the dark.

And then the killing would start.

People would die, and men would go looking, and more people would die. And the creatures Pete created that were the best hunters would be modified next—and maybe Shawnita would even take more men as raw material.

And the number of the Beast would grow.

And grow.

And *grow*!

And Pete would watch it all from the safety of the tunnels under the lake. He would see the killings and the spread of the scourge through the Beast's own eyes, until man either found a way to fight back—maybe locating the brain and destroying it, or just wiping out the body, over and over again— or, until the Beast won and all the world became one single living unit.

And then what?

What would It eat after that?

Would It grow men like cattle?

Where would it end?

Could it end?

"No," Pete thought-said. "We're talking about murder, genocide, the fucking plague! We're contemplating the apocalypse! And I won't have any part in it!"

"Too late," Cornichuk's slurping voice gurgled. "You're more than just a part of it! You're Its *center*!"

"You can't force me to do it!" Pete howled so hard that every nerve he had left seemed to burn.

"You can't refuse!" Cornichuk replied like a threat.

"You can't force me!" Pete howled again.

"Look!" Cornichuk bellowed, and his voice nearly disintegrated with emotion beneath tearing, quivering flesh.

"Lori!" Pete shouted as Lori's face suddenly came into his view.

She looked haggard, beaten, and battered. Her white tee shirt was almost completely black from dirt and grime, torn over the right shoulder where he had gripped it on the Tower's ledge and hanging down so that nearly all of her trembling right breast was exposed beneath a twisted, dirty bra. Her face was pale, her hair tangled, her fingers were bloody, and her legs were unsteady when she walked. In her right hand she held a gun, and her left arm was lying protectively over her stomach, as if she were in pain.

"Lori!" Pete screamed in his mind. *"Oh, God! Lori!"*

"She can't hear you," Cornichuk's voice buzzed hideously—barely words, but still conveying meaning.

Lori was in Rages. The bar was dark, and brooding, and she was the only person Pete could see.

But where the hell was he seeing her from?

Was he sitting on the floor as one of those baggy lumps of the Beast's vile juice? Was he some kind of ambulatory aberration that had been able to get out from under the Tower before the structure collapsed and was now watching Lori as she intruded on its haunt? Was he a corpse of an innocent Sharthington citizen, lying on the floor with a bulging throat and staring, cadaverous eyes that were serving as his windows on the world?

What the hell was he?

"Lori!" he bellowed again, but she didn't respond.

Crouching, gun cocked at her waist, she limped hard and grimaced as she drew breath. She was moving away from a dusty grey wreck of a police car that was half-smashed and crookedly protruding through the tangled disaster of Rages's big barn doors, with a shattered windshield and broken bubble lights on top. She was stalking something, moving slowly and setting her feet down gently in the rubble, her eyes running over a dusty jungle of jutting bar stools and overturned tables, her attention cat-like and sharp.

He could see her clearly.

But, something more.

He concentrated, moving his attention from Lori's figure

to the edges of his view. He was definitely seeing her through the eyes of something living because his range of sight was limited. He understood depth, and width, he saw dim colors, and he even gathered a hint of motion, as if whatever he was that was seeing the girl in the cut-off jeans and dirty tee shirt was moving, slightly, slowly, and without sound.

And mixed with the sight, was the smell—vivid, musky, and *human*. He could smell her sweat, and her fear, he could drink of her aroma and tingle with the completeness of his contact with her. He could visualize her body and her flesh just by the amazing mix of sour and sweet, clean and wet, oily and smooth hints of scent she exuded.

He had to be an animal, he decided fearfully. Only an animal could respond to a scent so deeply. Only an animal could hold so still, and wait so patiently for its prey to blunder closer—as Lori was now doing. Only an animal could remain so quiet.

"Lori!" he screamed, trying for the first time to move his body and succeeding in moving something, he wasn't sure what.

And Lori apparently knew that he'd moved it too, because an instant after he'd flexed whatever it was he'd flexed, a deep rumble that sounded like an earthquake shook Rages, dropping a spray of dust from the ceiling and spinning Lori around with a start. Carefully, she skipped over to a broken window and leaned on the sill, craning her neck to get a better view of something out of Pete's line of sight and whispering, "What now?"

And her voice stunned him.

She didn't sound like herself at all. Where before her words had been imbued with a bright timber, a crispness that had reminded him of tiny, silver bells, they now conveyed a throaty hoarseness that amazed him and forced him to understand at once how much she must have gone through, and, at the same time, how human she really was.

She was just a person, capable of corruption like any other. She was just a transitory bundle of nerves and flesh, another stop in the flight of her blood through time, and nothing more. She was born, grew old, and then died, losing innocence along the way and losing her individuality as well. She was just another example of her species—a dangerous, but interesting species in dire need of a little fine tuning.

Like those pendulous breasts, for example. What function did they serve being so pronounced?

"No," Pete thought-said, fighting the intrusion of the logic of the Beast. "She's a human being! She's alive! She has a right to herself and I won't violate it!"

He squirmed, harder this time, and the result was an even deeper rumble that sent whiskey bottles rattling behind the bar and that made Lori hold onto the wall as she peered out a window that, Pete realized, faced north.

She was looking toward the Tower and he felt like calling her name again. But before he could try, whatever he had become deliberately made a noise and she spun from her place by the wall and looked him straight on.

And her reaction broke his heart.

She was cringing from him. . . .

From *him*!

He knew that she was terrified of whatever it was he had become, and that she didn't even know that he, Peter Blackwell, was there, but still he melted into despair at the way her eyes raged against him, seethed with disgust and loathing for him, expressing hatred and panic at him: the man who had been willing to give his life for her, the man who had professed his love for her from nearly the moment they had met, and the man who wanted nothing but to be with her and to protect her. She was afraid of him, and it cut through his soul and left him feeling desperate, alone, and alienated from the entire human race.

She was looking directly into his eyes and creeping away, her back pressed to the wall as she slid to her left, her arm trembling as she pointed the gun out before herself and her eyes glazed with pure terror as she said, "No! Stay back! You stay the hell away from me!"

Broken glass crunched beneath her feet and she lurched right into an overturned chair when Pete grunted, loud, wet, threatening, and hard.

"Lori!" he mind-screamed, sending a memory of what his

voice had once sounded like when he had been capable of producing a voice through the twisting blue tunnels he now occupied but couldn't control. *"It's me!"*

"Stay away from me you monster!" she shrieked, righting herself and moving past the chair, waving the gun as if it were some kind of magic wand and working her thumb over its hammer.

Monster! Pete thought, feeling the sting of the word as if it had been jabbed into the memory of his eyes.

He moved in closer, the dimness of the bar feeling good on his sensitive skin and his body bouncing over the ground in a weird, jerking motion that seemed to be a combination of a slide and a hop. His range of vision bobbed, invisible objects went crashing and rattling carelessly outside his line of sight, but nothing could obstruct him as he wheezed and stalked, sucking in air through what felt like openings . . .

Monster! she'd called him.

. . . openings that felt like holes, or mouths, gaping and closing, kissing the air and slapping gently, pulling in what Lori was—her aroma—and filling him with such a detailed sense of contact that he could actually taste the salt in her sweat.

It was a delicious taste.

Such a delicious taste . . .

"Oh, God," he groaned, luxuriating in the sensuality of it, the pure, unadulterated bestiality of the taste of her, oozing through him and prickling his instincts so thoroughly that it made him run his tongue over his wet, cold lips. And, snapping those lips together, he thought, If this is smell, what does taste feel like?

He smacked his lips once, and then again, like a dog over his supper, producing hard snaps of contact and a feeling of perfectly natural satisfaction that bordered on the sexual. It was so powerful, so complete, that it washed his mind a blank, ripping Lori's image from his grasp and leaving him without the will to struggle or protest at all, when whatever he was pounced.

Lori screamed and lurched to the side, bounding awkwardly over a bar stool and crashing down amid a tangle of aluminum and vinyl. But in an instant she was up, scrambling over the mess on the floor and eluding Pete's grasp.

He clattered into the bar, ending a long leap in a crash that quivered the length of the structure and hurt, deeply, in a way he had never been hurt before. It was an almost distracted kind of pain, a feeling of damage done to him, but not to *him*.

Then Lori made a noise off to one side and he spun, clattering more stools and leaping up onto the bar.

And that's when he saw it!

There, surrounded by dozens of nautical mementoes, in a huge, oval mirror with a gold anchor emblazoned on its lower portion, he saw what he was, and his thoughts were paralyzed.

He could still hear Lori moving. But it didn't matter anymore. He wasn't listening—the Beast was, but he wasn't.

He was *looking*, and thinking, Joshua?

Could this . . . thing, be Joshua?

"How?" he moaned.

It's position was absurd. It had been truncated, and mangled beyond any semblance of ever having been human except for two things: its penis—around which squirmed a hairy mass of fleshy cords—and its one, perfectly formed, perfectly functioning, human arm, that had a tattoo of a maple leaf just over the elbow.

But the rest of it . . . the swollen welts, the dripping slits that opened and closed like mouths to emit flickers of pale blue light, the quivering bag that looked like a perversion of the sack a bullfrog inflates to grunt at its throat, the long, grey hair hanging in tufts on either side of the head, and the bubbled, running mess of burnt flesh and oozing muscle that was all that was left of the old man's face, looked like a nightmare made real, a nightmare made especially for him.

In the center of the creature's head, a perfectly round eye jutted, revolving like a black billiard ball that had been forced into a bloody wound and moving slightly as another eye swelled up next to it, bursting from within the creature's skull and revolving backwards so that Pete suddenly saw the mirror before him, and Lori behind, at the same time.

She was right there, standing so close and looking right at him. She had allowed her gun to drop, and it now hung limply at her side.

She was so close, he saw, so very close that he could be on her in one good leap.

She was so close, but she wasn't running any more; she was standing as if she'd had a new thought, a new image that had changed her perception of her surroundings, and, as she stood, her lips were forming the silent word, "Monster!" over and over again.

Pete could have taken her then, but he didn't. Instead, he stood, balancing on his one human hand, and his one swollen stump of flesh that looked like a club, looking at himself, long, and hard. . . .

"How?" he asked, utterly defeated.

"Shawnita," a whistling voice piped up. "For you."

Pete wrenched his attention to the sound of Cornichuk's words, barely discernible as words at all, and said, "It can do this?"

"Planted the seed, years ago. Has grown . . . years ago," Cornichuk gurgled. "Just a body . . . no mind anymore! Just a body . . . for you!"

Pete didn't look, but he knew the impact of the Beast's power had all but finished off the man's brain. There would be few words from his scorched mouth to come, and those that came he already suspected.

"Be master of children," Cornichuk commanded with a hiss. "Be master of children or Shawnita born without hope again, and again, forever . . . for you to see. Never . . . die! Never die but watch! Watch . . . kill . . . forever! *Watch . . . her take the seed!*"

The liquid pop at the end of Cornichuk's sentence was pronounced and thick, and Pete knew the man's throat had been used up. But he didn't need to have anything more explained. He understood.

His future was now standing before him, swaying in a stupid mirror surrounded by stupid chunks of man's collective memory of Lake Erie. Whatever the Beast decided he would be, wherever the Beast decided he would be, so would he be.

So would he see what the Beast showed him, like an unwilling audience, for the rest of the Beast's time on earth, which, for all he knew, could be forever. He'd watch first Lori and then countless other human beings die; he'd watch people he knew, and people he didn't, used as raw materials in a genetic experiment the scope of which was stunning.

Thousands of seeds had been planted in Sharthington already. And they were just the start. There'd be thousands more, millions more, and he'd see every one . . . he'd *be* every one. He couldn't stop it, and he couldn't look away—the Beast wouldn't let him. His eternity would be spent staring at random acts of horror and violence, forever, until his mind snapped and he gave the Beast his knowledge in a twisted, insane way that would make the world a madhouse, and all of life nothing more than the crazy dreams of its only inmate—like the loathsome dream staring at him from the mirror over the bar now . . . the loathsome dream, that was *him*.

Why fight it?, he thought.

Why not try and do what the Shawnita wanted and make the perfect species? Wouldn't that be the best thing for everyone? Wouldn't that prevent a lot of pain in the long run? Mankind was just fucking up the planet anyway; why shouldn't something else have its chance? Maybe this was the next step in man's evolution. Maybe this was what nature had intended all along, and by resisting he was just standing in the way!

A long, twisting length of spit dripped off the creature in the mirror's front tooth and dangled in the dark. The little mouths were all closed now, and both black eyes were still.

"No," Pete whispered stubbornly in his mind. "I just can't do it. No man has the right to be God! No matter what happens, I just can't be any more than what I am."

There, he'd made his decision, he'd vocalized it the only way he could, and, like thunder, the sound of his refusal seemed to reverberate for miles in every direction, filling the blue tunnels of lightning and ambition with echoes that swelled and pounded, roaring up into a wave of sound that rumbled through the ground and ended in a blast and flash of white light.

The mirror behind the bar exploded, breaking Joshua's reflection into a thousand tiny images that dropped to the floor with a titter. Replacing the glass, a black bullet hole appeared in the center of the old wood frame.

Another shot rang out and the gold greyhound vibrated and fell from over the mirror, crashing into the whiskey bottles and dragging a sheet of fishing net down with it that overturned an entire row of brass clocks and little fisherman figurines.

Pete watched the room turn as Joshua spun in response to the shots, focusing both his revolving eyes forward so that the image of the mirror frame was lost as the bar shook with a frightful, angry roar that emanated from deep inside his reptilian chest. Coiling himself like a spring, he hung for just a moment, aligning his shoulders with the source of the sound, and settling his attention on where Lori stood behind a layer of hanging smoke, her feet planted on the floor and her back stiff.

She was holding her gun up with both hands so that Pete could see only the very top of her eyes, and, before Joshua could move, she squeezed the trigger again, producing another ball of shattering fire that jerked her arms up and sent a sharp *bang* slamming into Joshua's sensitive flesh microseconds before a bullet rammed itself home.

"Yeah!" Pete screamed through those empty blue corridors. "Yeah! That's my girl! Kill the fucker! Oh, yeah!"

The shot hit him low and to the left, near what would have been his stomach if his stomach had not gone rolling down the police station's stairs. It hurt like hell, collapsing a good portion of Joshua's rib cage and shattering a Jack Daniel's bottle on the shelf behind the bar after it exited near his squirming spine.

She fired three more times:

Bang bang bang!

And every shot found its mark.

The impact staggered Joshua and almost made him lose his balance. But he was steady and moving even before the sounds of concussion had completely faded in the dark.

His lizard arm was incredibly strong, and when it flexed it

propelled him a good fifteen feet through the air, clattering him down just a foot or so from where Lori stood, the empty pistol still smoking in her hand and her eyes wide with disbelief.

"Christ!" Pete mind-screamed, seeing Joshua's human hand grasping out for Lori's ankle as she slid to the left and stumbled. "She didn't hurt it at all! Four holes didn't hurt it at all!"

Lori was crying as she fell, her legs pumping on the floor and her arms swimming through bar stools. She was crying and whimpering, kicking away Joshua's fingers and pulling herself up on a table, which she overturned to obstruct Pete's view as soon as she was on her feet.

The table caught the left side of Joshua's head and he snapped out his lizard arm, smashing the wood and spraying a hail of splinters before him as he growled, coiled, and took to the air again.

The wall beyond Lori rushed toward him and Pete reflexively cringed as Joshua's chest smashed into it, rolling him against the plastic side of a jukebox and then supporting him as he reached out for Lori, who fumbled into him with a shriek.

"Run!" Pete screamed.

"No!" Lori snarled, her right wrist tightly held in Joshua's fist and her left hand behind her as she struggled.

" 'Oooreee!" Joshua roared, the impulse for the word flashing past where Pete hung in the Shawnita's mind from somewhere he could not see, like a bird flying through a window.

And then pain blossomed through his being, clogging his thoughts and taking his attention back to the barroom.

Lori had produced a bottle from the table behind her and had planted it directly between Joshua's new eye and his old.

Joshua's grip relaxed for an instant and Lori squirmed free, clutching the bottle with both hands and immediately driving it down atop his head with all her strength. The bottle broke, slashing painful cuts through Joshua's new eye and sending him back a foot and into the jukebox again, which tipped, burst into life, and filled the room with revolving, multicolored light as a needle went *rrrzzzzt!* across a record and Willie Nelson started singing in the middle of a phrase.

" *'Oooreee!''* he howled again, spinning and bringing his lizard arm down on the jukebox, smashing through the glass and dismembering Willie's warble into one part silence, two parts gloom.

A door banged shut somewhere, and he turned, spraying slime from every mouth on his body and focusing his injured eyes on a hall behind the bar. He leapt once, smashing through the door and peering down the stairs into the bar's basement. The dark air was thick with the tantalizing smell of young girl's sweat, so close, so sweet, filling him with an insatiable, blinding desire so black that it burned through the darkness like fire and dragged a grunt up from the deepest recesses of his bowels.

"My God!" Pete roared helplessly when he saw the thought take shape in Joshua's mind. And, *"It's impossible!"* he screamed when he felt the erection swelling what was left of Joshua's groin.

" *'Oooreee!''* the creature roared, plunging headlong into the blackness of Rages's cellar. *"Ssshawta 'oooreee!"*

And, with Pete unwillingly positioned behind the eyes of the Beast, screaming his protests and raging in vain, the chase began in earnest.

Five

Hide in the basement until it goes away!

Lori heard the words ringing through her head like an air raid siren, and, dropping the shattered whiskey bottle as Joshua fell back into the blaring jukebox, she turned, and plunged for the door.

The basement stairs were absolutely dark, but she didn't care. She'd worked at Rages for two years and had climbed these stairs countless times. She knew every inch of the basement by heart, so she didn't take the time to stop and reach around behind the bar to where the light switch was on the wall. She just plunged ahead, pounding down the rickety wooden steps and visualizing the room around her.

The basement was very deep, with unpainted, concrete-block walls and a bare brick floor. The stairs had been built next to the wall, and the room stretched out to the right for almost the full length of the bar before ending in a walk-in freezer behind stacks of empty beer kegs and cases of whiskey, soda pop, and beer. Anchored between the left side of the stairs and the wall was the beer chute, a two-foot-wide, steel ramp that had a bed of wooden rollers running down its center, up which full beer kegs were pushed, and down which empty ones were sent careening into the darkness to clatter on the floor until someone had time to stack them upright. Exposed rafters ran over the ceiling, hung with wires bulging with homemade repairs of wadded electrical tape, and sweaty plumbing pipes climbed every wall to the barroom above.

With each step she took, the pain in her ribs blossomed, blasting up her spine and into her brain like sharp coils of hot wire, knotting up the muscles in her back and making her movements stiff and unnatural. She wheezed when she inhaled, and grunted with each new stab from her side, running her left hand along the beer chute and squeezing her right fist into her breast bone as if to support her lungs so that they wouldn't fall down and crush her stomach.

She wasn't thinking, running in the dark; she wasn't thinking of words at all. But she did see pictures, clear, concise pictures that went fleeting through her mind and dazzled her with promises of escape. Since she'd stood her ground and emptied her pistol into the thing that was Joshua, her entire frame of mind had changed, and escape now blared as her only hope.

She'd just put four shells flat into Joshua—flat into him!—and he'd shaken it off! Chunks of meat and blasts of dark grease had gone flying every which way, and the son of a bitch hadn't so much as flinched. That had finally driven home to her the futility of anything she could do to resist, and had transformed her from a fighter into a runner.

Across the room, straight ahead from the bottom of the stairs, there was a platform, and she saw it clearly as a picture in her mind. It was about ten feet long by five feet wide and it had a kind of cage made of steel tubes and chicken wire built over it that formed into an arch that pushed open two steel doors when the platform was raised. They used it to bring deliveries down to the cellar, and it opened up onto the alley behind Rages that ran to the street.

If she could get to that platform, she could hit the switch and ride it out of this nightmare. She could send herself up to the alley and leave that monster blathering in the dark. By the time he got back up the stairs and through the front door, she'd be gone, bum rib or not. She'd flap her goddamned arms and fly away if she had to—but, once she got to the alley, nothing would touch her.

No shit. Honest to God!

But then her foot came down on something soft in the dark and she pitched forward, shouting involuntarily and grasping at the beer chute as she fell, hitting the wall and sliding her hands over the rollers as the door overhead burst open and Joshua's unearthly voice resounded, *"Ssshawta, 'Oooreee!"*

Scrambling for some kind of balance, she planted one foot on the stairs and looked up briefly, seeing Joshua looming overhead, black against the gloom of the barroom, his human hand outstretched and his reptile arm snaking along the wall. His hair was silhouetted sharply, squirming on his head, and, as he coiled for his first leap, all his tiny mouths were tasting the air and sending out sharp, blue rays of light that stabbed through the darkness like glittering knives and frosted everything around him a sickly green.

In the feeble light, Lori saw that the thing over which she had tripped was Ralph, Rages's owner, sprawled on the stairs, head pointed down and legs askew. There was one of those bags of flesh at his throat, and, through the stairs she saw that the floor looked like a mass of big, swelling bubbles. But, seeing Joshua bent in a crouch like he was, she automatically moved, throwing herself over the railing and down, probably ten feet, to the floor.

She landed first, but Joshua wasn't far behind.

"Ohhh!" she choked as sparkling stars danced in her head and the rushing floor bent her fractured rib.

The soft thing her left foot came down on burst beneath her with a wet *plop!* and when she rolled she smashed two more invisible creatures that sprayed a sticky fluid up and into her face. All around she could hear the frantic skittering of crab-like legs on bare brick and the air was suddenly filled with an unbelievably sweet smell that gagged her as she struggled toward the ceiling-high stacks of beer cases to her left.

Joshua hurtled down the stairway and landed with a thud, rolling for but an instant before he was up and hissing. But Lori didn't see which way he turned once he had regained his balance, because she had reached the first aisle of cases and darkness blocked her view.

And then it got quiet.

She paused on her hands and knees, cold slime oozing down her face and her heart pounding out a tattoo of pain and terror in the dark. She held her breath and the effort of inflating her lungs caused a white blaze to blast up into her head, making her so dizzy that her right elbow gave out and she momentarily dipped, smacking her chin on the floor and breaking her concentration.

She froze.

Insect legs were snapping concrete around her, moving away and thick. But, other than that, the room was quiet.

She let go of her breath and tried to steady herself enough to crawl without making too much noise, but the air rushing up her esophagus seemed to chill her chest and she started choking so hard that she had to clamp one hand over her mouth to keep from coughing aloud.

Muscle spasms burned her spine to jelly.

And, through her pain, she heard something wet behind her.

Right behind her.

Racing to her feet she plunged headlong into the darkness as blue light and Joshua appeared at the mouth of the aisle, his hands outstretched and his breath coming in huge, sucking gulps, like an old man running up and down a long flight of stairs.

Lori suddenly found herself in a blue tunnel, trapped by beer cases on either side that were overhung with baggy creatures, all turning their stingers her way and clamping tiny pinchers in the air. She took two crouching steps, looked back to where Joshua was reaching his reptilian arm up, and then struck something on the floor. Pitching forward she landed hard and rolled into a second body, lying just a few feet past the one over which she'd tripped, as a wall of beer cases came crashing down where she had been crouching and everything went black again.

Lying still, she hugged the body over which she had tripped, pushing her face deep into the cold, bare flesh of someone's back—she couldn't tell if it was a man or a woman's corpse she embraced—and waiting for the clatter of cardboard and empty bottles to stop. When it did, she raised her head, and found that Joshua was gone.

Tink: an empty bottle rolled over bricks when she slid her knee up under her.

'' 'Oooree?'' a voice whispered sinfully through the featureless wall of gloom hanging around her eyes. It was an insidious voice, seductive, liquid in the dark and directionless in its naked longing. ''I come, 'Oooreee!'' it slurred, swirling through her pounding head as if it might even be originating there.

And then, joining the voice, there was Joshua, blasting through a wall of beer cases and roaring like a wild animal, rupturing the darkness with flashes of blue and swinging his reptilian arm out for the kill.

But Lori had anticipated his approach and was moving seconds before he attacked. Running down the aisle, she overturned beer cases behind herself as she went, leaving a trail of cardboard and glass through which Joshua clattered, screaming out his rage and blazing brightly in the darkness.

Reaching the end of the aisle, the Beast found a row of tee shirts and underwear hanging from a clothes line at eye level and tore down the line with his human hand. As the laundry fell from his view, a tall stack of beer kegs emerged before him, teetering once and then descending directly his way, smashing into his shoulder before he could move and ripping from his chest a wounded, painful scream.

Lori, trembling with a mix of terror and triumph, moved the two-wheeler to the next row of kegs—they were full, and weighed about two hundred pounds each—jammed the lip of the thing beneath the stack, and heaved. The sound of kegs crashing to the floor was deeply satisfying, and she couldn't help but move around to the front so that she could try and see where Joshua had been crushed in the gloom.

Peering out from an aisle, she held onto the cold metal of an empty keg and squinted, her breathing fast and sweat stinging her eyes.

The darkness was quiet and complete, and she waited a

long time before the skittering of insect legs broke the silence and began afresh.

Hesitating a moment longer, she listened to the soft scrapes of bugs on stone, hearing nothing beneath their sharp snaps and almost grateful for the regularity with which they moved.

"Joshua?" she whispered, her eyes straining hard in the black and her ears desperate for sound. "Are you here?"

She swallowed a lump in her throat and pain spiralled up from her chest.

Finally, after waiting longer than she knew she should, she tore herself into motion—feeling a little like she had just come out of a coma—turned, and headed for the stairs.

Overhead, the doorway to the barroom was filled with a dim, grey light, and, by comparison, the gloom of the basement looked inky and featureless. The light from above outlined Ralph's body on the stairway and offered Lori enough illumination to clamber halfway to the top, which was just far enough so that she could begin bursting with relief, when . . .

Joshua's human hand shot up from between the stairs and grabbed her ankle.

"No! God damn it, no!" she screamed as she stumbled, slamming into the wood with her hands and rolling, kicking and raking her nails over Joshua's flesh as little mouths opened below and blue slashes of light snapped up between her legs.

"Motherfucking . . . son of a bitch . . ." she snarled, pounding down hard with her fists and clenching her teeth. "Enough already! That's enough!"

Joshua roared, *"Hhhharrrrg!"* and heaved, pulling her leg through the stairs up to her hip and rolling her over so that she grappled first with the wood of the stairs above, then with the slippery, metal sides of the beer chute.

Her hands hooked the lip of the chute and she kicked, feeling the cold dampness of something swollen and soft sliding up her thigh. The sensation was so sickening and close that it sent her into a panic that expressed itself in a tantrum of flexing muscles and thrashing legs.

"Please!" she screamed, spraying spit and throwing her head back. *"Not there!"*

Her right foot caught something, and Joshua froze for an instant. So she kicked out into that same spot again, and again . . . and his hand slid on her ankle and she pulled it free.

Tearing back a few feet, her shoulder smashed into the beer chute and she pulled herself up, just as Joshua's glowing body emerged over the side of the stairs and his lizard arm reached out to take her back. Rolling hard, she threw her weight down on the chute and immediately felt gravity pulling her into motion. With Joshua's arm smashing the rollers where she had just been, she hurled back down into darkness, feeling acceleration yawning out a bigger and bigger gap between her and the Beast.

But the elation was short-lived, and dropped off in the same instant when she fell from the end of the chute and landed in a jumbled pile of empty beer kegs, producing a series of dull thuds and a plethora of flashing impact scars in her head. Momentum carried her over the rolling kegs, and she scrambled, head over heels, into the wire cage on the loading platform, where she curled into a ball and settled, motionless, overrun with agonizing licks of bruised muscle and almost completely disoriented.

It was time to give up, a voice whispered, closer to her ear. It was time to just hang it up, and die.

"Bullshit!" she tried to say, her voice tiny, and so weak that the word came out as "Uulshhip!"

But the intent was there, even if its expression was less than precise.

Her right hand moved when she mentally asked it to, and that was encouraging.

There was a roar in her ears that washed over everything else and created an impression of theatricality, and expanse. Things just didn't seem all that important any more, and, as she struggled over and worked her hand up to the handle on the cage's door, she was able to give herself up to a sense of unhurried ease.

Just take your time, she thought, concentrating through the ringing bells and washing waves in her head. One thing at a time: first, the latch.

It was dark. Completely dark.

But she had opened the door on the platform a zillion times over the years she had worked there, and there was nothing to it.

The platform was surrounded by a chicken-wire cage for safety's sake. It had a door in the front that had a simple latch that locked it shut. It was that latch for which she was striving, and, in a second, she felt it, cool on her fingers, right where it was supposed to be.

Life is good, she thought sardonically.

Lifting the latch, she eased her weight to the left, out of the way of the door, and swung it open, allowing herself to fall into the cage. . . .

There was blue light flickering somewhere close, and for some reason that disturbed her. It disturbed her so much that it made her pull her legs up and curl herself into a ball.

To raise or lower the platform there was a little metal box with two buttons—one red and one black—screwed into the cage's frame near the door. But there was also a foot pedal on the floor directly under the button box, and, pulling herself around like a turtle, she reached out and searched the gloom until she found it, and pressed it.

The electric motor started whining the instant the pedal was depressed and the platform lurched beneath her.

It didn't go fast; it went agonizingly slow. But it went, and she lay there, feeling unbridled gratitude for the vibrations shuddering through her as the platform climbed and the top of the cage touched the huge, steel doors overhead.

A squealing peel accompanied the emergence of a slice of silver moonlight, bleeding bright between the parting doors. And that moonlight, cutting down, across where she lay on the platform's floor, was beautifully thrilling, yawning wider with each second, beckoning her up, into fresh, open air and revealing the cage's interior beneath a greyish-white monotone that brought tears to her eyes with its simple, mundane predictability.

And then the platform stopped moving.

She gasped, looked up briefly, and then down, finding that her hand had slipped from the pedal.

She moved her hand back, the platform lurched again, and a terrible grinding sound crashed down around her, jerking her face to the right, where the chicken-wire door—that she had forgotten to close—was collapsing from the top as the platform rammed it into the ceiling beyond the opening into which the platform fit.

And then the platform stopped again, and the air was shattered by a tremendous grinding sound, like chains revolving in an automatic dryer, just before smoke wafted up from below.

The door jammed the motor! she thought, pulling her hand up from the pedal without taking her eyes from the folded wire overhead.

And then something moved in the cage's doorway.

And then that beautiful, moonlight-silver that had outlined her vision was replaced by vivid, blazing blue.

And then a voice said, ''Ahhhh!''

And then she knew that It had won.

Deep inside, she wanted to fight . . . God she wanted to fight. She was Lori Sterling, after all. She was the girl who had out-toughed a train, and that toughness was still glowing, white hot and ready, both fists clenched and feet firmly planted on the ground, deep inside her heart. That toughness wanted to fight on, and it was itching to take another swing. . . .

But her body just couldn't accommodate.

She was hurt.

She was hurt bad.

She was hurt so bad that all she could do was lie helplessly in a pool of vibrating blue light as a terrible grinding sound belched oily smoke from below the stalled platform. All she could do was watch as first a black, stumpy thing, like a scorpion's tail weighing probably seventy-five pounds, slid through the platform's little door and flattened with pressure, interrupting the elevator's assent and overloading the engine. And all she could do was watch, and whimper in frustration, as that gnarled, hideous tangle of burnt flesh and squirming hair that was Joshua's face rose from below, dripping dark streaks of fluid from gasping slits, aiming two huge bulbs blankly over the lip of the platform, and releasing stagnant breath through the shuddering sack of its throat in a repulsive, satisfied, "Ahhhh!"

God, she wanted to fight!

And, in the face of her pain, she did all she could do, which was to crawl a few inches back from the platform's door, and clench her fists.

When she moved, her hand came off the pedal that raised the platform and the motor below stopped grinding, sucking the air silent and leaving only the wet smacking of Joshua's moist skin to insinuate itself into her head.

The doors above had parted about a foot and a half, and the sky through that opening was starless, and bible black.

Where's the moon? she thought, her attention settling on the heavens. I'd kind of like to see the moon one more time.

And then something cold touched her leg, spinning her whole body around so that her legs faced the cage's opening, and her head faced away. She was lying on her back; she lifted her head, and she started to cry.

Joshua was pulling himself up onto the platform.

She had not been this close to him before without moving immediately away, and suddenly his smell hit her like a slap. It was a fishy kind of smell, like the one he had exuded in the cabin, only thicker, deeper, and much more vital. It seemed as if the smell itself were actively seeking her out, as if his aroma were the first living part of him and it wanted to touch her first, wanted to find her body even before his flesh did, and wanted to explore her intimately, making her feel dirty, and moist.

He was wheezing terribly, and he shuddered as if with anticipation, his reptilian arm acting as an anchor against the cage, and his human arm bent oddly just below the shoulder.

Lori almost smiled when she saw the way his arm was bent. She had damaged him. Probably when she hit him with those beer kegs. He was going to win, he had worn her down and beaten her, but she'd gotten her licks in, and he wasn't going to forget what it took to . . .

Her thoughts froze, and every bit of color rushed from her face.

As Joshua pulled the last of himself into the cage, the lower portion of his body bumped and bounced into view. From the center of his sternum to the end of his ragged hips, lengths of flesh squirmed like feelers, moving randomly, like grass in a wind, and reaching out around the erection that had sprouted at the center of his groin. That erection hung on a triangular flap of flesh, behind which Lori could see that one of those white creatures from the Tower had attached itself, its insect legs folded, and its pinchers snapped tight to Joshua's slippery, reptilian skin, running with lines of black ooze and smelling so deeply of fish.

When all of him was in the cage, the serpentine fingers dangling close quivered, and touched the warm skin of her thigh, running over her coolly and sliding around in the beginnings of a deadly embrace.

And Lori's mind erupted.

The firing patterns in her head were like a waterfall, tumbling as if from above and washing her into a stream of bubbling blood that hissed with one, screaming word:

Rape!

She'd been ready for death. She'd almost accepted it, almost made her peace with it, almost welcomed it. But this . . .

Never! she raged in her mind. Move, get out of the way, fight, run, anything, but don't let him do this to you! Don't let It do this to you? Fuck the broken rib—you've got a bunch more that aren't broken. To hell with the bruises and the cuts and the bumps and the aches, just *move, damn you! Move!*

And she did.

Desperately, and amid a surf of pounding aches that emanated from just about every part of her body, she flung out her hands and hooked the wire cage, pulling with all her strength and dragging herself a few inches away from the door.

The exertion was dizzying, and its effect on her placement before the Beast minimal. But she was fighting, and she continued pulling, watching the stars in her head and hissing through her teeth, feeling the cold metal on her back as she slid another six inches or so. . . .

And then the wet snakes on her legs bit down, twisting her skin and anchoring her like iron, heaving hard and yanking her back two feet, bringing her closer to the Beast and entwining her all the way around so that she could feel tentacles on her buttocks and lower back tearing her cut-off jeans to shreds.

Slowly, Joshua leaned back, lifting her hips from the floor and leaving her shoulders to squirm as she threw her head from side to side, her face covered with sweaty lengths of bloody, blond hair and her arms outstretched, as if she'd been crucified.

" '*Oooreeee!*'" Joshua hissed, hovering over her now and leaving long lines of moisture dangling in the air. "*Ssshawta!*"

His reptilian arm had its stingers hooked through the wire mesh overhead, and his human hand was outstretched before him, hanging in the air six inches from her throat. His eyes were aimed directly at hers, and the sack of his mouth was still, and limp.

When his spine stiffened, Lori screamed and squeezed her eyes shut, feeling the tentacles holding her legs flex in preparation for the final, lethal thrust.

She threw her hands over her face and began praying, quickly, randomly, grafting pieces of different acts of contrition together into a single, juxtaposed petition for mercy and deliverance that she hardly comprehended herself, and that she simply broadcasted like a distress signal in hopes of reaching anyone who might be listening.

And, as if someone were listening, something remarkable happened.

Joshua paused.

His entire body just went stiff and he paused, coiled at his peak and ready to plant the seed. His eyes stayed firm, his human hand went still, his mouth shuddered, and his tentacles eased on Lori's legs.

Lori looked up at him, watching his bulbous eyes moving first to the sky, and then down, to meet her pale blue ones in a gaze that suddenly became . . .

Gentle?!

Over her throat, Joshua's human hand hung, trembling, his fingers moving stiffly, as if he were just awakening from a deep sleep. And, beneath her shoulders, the metal sheet upon which she was lying vibrated.

And then the steel doors vibrated.

And then a rumble shook through the building, emanating from somewhere far away and shaking the ground so hard that beer kegs and cases of bottles went crashing to the floor off in the darkness of Rages's cellar, and the platform itself groaned as its steel runners twisted.

Something was happening.

Something big.

Joshua's fingers quivered over her throat, and his hand began moving closer to her face.

She flinched automatically, sweat intermingled with blood running between her eyes and breasts, her attention cemented to the dark, glistening form of Joshua's hand, coming even closer, as fascinating as a snake, and even more dangerous.

When he lovingly touched her cheek, running his finger tips over her satin skin, as if he were savoring the simple sensation of her flesh, she whimpered, clenched her teeth, and heaved her body.

Throwing her feet up, she kicked his stomach with all her strength, which wasn't all that much, but that succeeded in moving him back. He seemed disoriented, even before her attack, and he wavered, half-hanging from the cage's ceiling by his reptile arm and tumbling through the door so that he had to grope with his human hand for support as he gurgled, *"No, 'Oree! No!"*

At the end of her kick, Lori allowed her feet to fall back to the platform's floor. Her left foot came down next to the elevator pedal and she pressed it, sending the electric motor below into instant, grinding convulsions and lurching the floor into motion.

Joshua rolled his eyes, looked up, covered his head with his human arm, and screamed, *" 'Isen 'Oree!"*

The crumbling cage door descended over him like a net, folding and whining against the approaching ceiling and collapsing into a shroud that pinned his limp figure to the pedestal's floor.

"Pete!" he howled. *" 'Oreee! Pete!"*

Lori lifted her foot from the pedal.

Joshua went completely still. He was folded beneath the chipped wire of the cage's door, his head rammed down hard between his shoulders and his arms pressed at odd angles into his sides. He wasn't glowing now because all of his mouths were closed, and his eyes had stopped their sinister revolutions, having settled calmly on Lori's face.

"Pete," he slurred, his mouth shuddering and licks of blue teasing in the moonlight.

Lori pulled herself into a sitting position and worked her way back to the far side of the cage. Behind the roaring of blood in her ears, she felt a deep, bass tone, rumbling as steadily as a passing train and vibrating up through the pedestal's floor to tingle a dull spot in her chest that seemed hard, and tender. Her eyes were fixed firmly on Joshua's dark form, almost featureless beneath the yellow wire, and her lips were silently trying to form Pete's name.

"Pete," Joshua said again, and again, "Pete," as the first snaps of insect legs skittered around Lori's head.

With her back resting on the cage wall, she allowed her eyes to move to the left and right, and she found that, from the darkness below, shimmering pale bags of flesh were climbing up the cage's sides and moving steadily into the moonlight overhead. It was like the beginning of an exodus, with neat lines being formed in which creatures followed one another peacefully, and quickly, from the gloom to the open air.

"For you!" Joshua said, and Lori looked back at him. "For everyone. But, mostly, for you!"

"What's for me?" Lori whispered, watching Joshua's reptile arm slither in a pool of spreading black ooze on the pedestal's floor, moving like a huge worm and lifting its ugly, bone stingers so that they snapped on the steel a couple of times before coming down on the elevator's control pedal.

"Watch me die!" Joshua moaned balefully, and pressed

down on the pedal, causing the platform to lurch, and the electric motor to grind again.

Lori didn't want to see, but she couldn't look away. Her face remained pointed at the scene and her eyes stayed focused as the elevator rammed Joshua's twisted figure into the ceiling.

Half of him was hanging outside of the cage, and half of him was resting on the pedestal's floor. The opening in the ceiling approached quickly, and the concrete overhead caught his skull first, pressing it even deeper into his shoulders and producing a series of deep, rending snaps that cut through the engine's whine like rifle shots and preceded the Beast's dying screams by less than a second.

The mixed effect of the engine, the sounds of tearing flesh, and the depth of the creature's agony washed over Lori, pressing her even farther back in the elevator's cell and driving her hands up as she grimaced and shrank beneath the weight of the Beast's pain. Reflexively, she curled her knees up close to her chin and closed herself off, like a flower pulling back its petals in response to a blast of cold air, which was exactly what the wave of sound emanating from Joshua's throat felt like. It was chilling, cold, and meaty, turning Lori's equilibrium upside down and stripping her humanity for an instant, leaving her shriveled and exposed, sickened, and yet so alive that every sensation she experienced seemed to be swallowed whole by the very pores in her skin and transmitted directly to her brain. After a moment of hearing Joshua's voluminous screams, she was screaming too—although she couldn't hear herself—and she continued screaming as she pressed her hands against the sides of her head and watched the creature that had been Joshua die.

At first he was dark beneath the crumpled cage door, and his body shrank in on itself as the ceiling pressed down. But then a blur of spurting lines squirmed up with a tremendous belch and, like a sigh of release, the engine below coughed twice and kicked in harder, digging its drive chain deeply into the sockets on the elevator's gears and smashing Joshua's bones against dirty concrete and rusty, dull-edged, pig-iron beams overhead.

When his skull split, a brilliant flash of blue seared the darkness, spreading in an arch and climbing the gloom like solid tubes of eerie animation. Long, dripping globs of oily juice burst through the air, hanging suspended longer than seemed possible and then splashing the cage over and blowing a stench like the Devil's breath into Lori's face that not even the swirling night air, rushing in over the parting doors above, could cut.

The half of the Beast that hung over the platform's edge was peeled neatly from the half of him that remained in the cage, folding and sliding in a smear on the ceiling and dripping in wet lengths of dark meat that hung quivering as the platform continued its climb. The half of him still inside popped and shuddered against the descending steel, ripping and spreading, darkly silhouetted against a glare of blue that sizzled from its interior and squirting through the wire's twisted patterns like dough through a press.

Bang! Bang! the doors resounded, falling to the sidewalk, as the platform emerged in the alley and the last bits of Joshua were pulled from the rest.

What remained of him lay bereft of light, and life, settling moistly into a wad of meat in the cage's mouth, while the rest of him peeled from the ceiling and dangled for a moment before falling to the bare bricks below.

The elevator's engine stopped.

And, as her head spun from exertion, Lori ended her scream and sucked in a huge gulp of sweet, night air that surged through her being like some incredible drug, spinning her head and reeling the world around her so unpleasantly that she nearly threw up.

But, when she had settled, her forehead resting on her knees and her hands wrapped around the front of her legs, she noticed the sound, and her discomfort paled in comparison to the fear that flowered in her stomach.

She lifted her head, and blinked her eyes once, twice, then three times before her vision cleared enough for her to understand—or at least recognize—what she was seeing.

She was in the alley behind Rages. The platform had lifted her into the night, and she now sat, as if displayed in a cage, curled against wire mesh and facing directly north. On either side, the alley was completely black, climbing up as brick walls, featureless. Overhead, the sky was midnight blue, and, straight out from where she sat, the moon shone down on the sparkling water in squirming, silver worms and surrounding the ashen-grey form of Black Island, squatting, as if in a huge tub, and exposing its smooth back, upon which the crumbling remains of the Black Tower grew like a tumor.

Bubbling along the ground, twisted by perspective and the unpredictable, uneasy surges of concussive shifts in the girl's ability to focus and comprehend, thousands of white lumps, with snapping, groping legs of hard bone and sharp claw moved toward the bay. They seemed to be coming from everywhere—simply every dark region and undefined param- eter of her view—swarming like lemmings, bobbling, hob- bling, bouncing in that weird, insect way they had, running down the walls, groping up from the ground, sliding out of windows and sewer drains, pulling themselves over doorsteps and moving, en masse, slowly, but with purpose, toward the lake.

And Lori saw them through bent wire, framed by a tunnel of convoluted shadow, shimmering vividly beneath the moon and stretching out at the mouth of the alley, as if the entire Earth had suddenly transformed itself into a living Thing that needed to walk away from where she, specifically, was sit- ting.

"I love you, Lori," she said, and her eyes glared blankly as her mind searched itself for the motivation behind her words. *"I love you, and I couldn't let It have you."*

A tingle climbed her legs and she glanced down fearfully to find that she was sitting in a pool of the black grease that had run from where Joshua lay. Her thighs sparkled beneath the skin, feeling as if electricity were climbing the network of her nerves, following the complex pattern that was her brain's contact with her body.

Her legs were covered with cuts, and it was through those cuts that the Blood had entered her system, easing her pain by its presence, and opening her mind. . . .

"When it's over, burn Them all!" she said. *"Find Them*

all or It will start again. Burn Them all or the Brain will start as a new Pattern! Burn the Brain!''

Lori settled a little, listening to herself talk. She allowed her muscles to ease a bit, and she didn't hurt so badly. There was a closeness descending over her, a sensation of belonging, of being watched over by a great love, and a great lover—something like the feeling she remembered as a little girl, lying in a warm bed and knowing that her big, strong father was sleeping just in the next room in case anything bad happened.

Her legs stopped tingling and her entire body sagged as a vibration like a heartbeat shuddered up through the ground.

"Blood Flies, Lori,'' she said, cryptically. *"And it flew to me. I've been a part of It all my life. If I don't die, everything else will. . . .''*

"No,'' Lori whispered, not knowing why but feeling a sudden wash of loss for something she didn't quite understand.

"I love you, Lori,'' she said, regretfully. *"I love you. Goodbye.''*

"No. . . .''

Her voice decayed, her eyes went wide, and, in stunned silence, she watched it happen.

All the creatures spreading out on the ground before her suddenly stopped moving and fell absolutely still beneath the silver moon. They turned their ''faces'' to the bay and aimed their stingers in unison to Black Island, where, although no motion had yet manifested itself, something *big* was rolling beneath the ground.

Trees shimmered, a traffic light swayed on its wire, a bicycle propped against a fire plug toppled over, and everything, except the dark line that was the horizon, seemed to tremble.

Why wasn't she scared? she wondered dreamily from her cage. Why didn't this bother her? Why did she welcome the tremors, and the earthquake roar that was so suddenly filling the air? Why did she feel like jumping up and releasing a shout of praise and dancing joyfully while the earth moved?

Why did she suspect that the relief she was experiencing came from deeper in her soul than she could ever imagine?

It was as if some ancient part of herself, some memory she'd carried in her mind for centuries without being consciously aware of its presence, some dim hint of terrors past, an undefined conviction of terrors to come, was being lifted from her. She felt as if she, and everyone else, had just taken a collective step back from the edge of the Pit, becoming, therefore, one bit safer, and one heartbeat more secure. Of all the dangers in the world, one was now in the process of being removed, and it was happening because of Peter Blackwell.

She saw his face briefly in her mind, and she almost smiled.

The ground rumbled harder, and somewhere there was glass breaking. The water around Black Island was becoming agitated, gurgling out in ripples that looked tiny and intricate but that had to be four or five feet high to be so clearly visible from where she was sitting. Loud thuds pounded out from the docks as the first of these ripples ended their journey across the bay, lifting stationary boats and slamming them into their moors. Huge plumes of spouting spray blasted up along the shore like surf on some faraway, ocean beach. And pieces of the Island dropped from its ends like falling slices of bread as peculiar eruptions of bubbles sprouted first here, and then there, as if the bottom of the lake had suddenly been punched through and the water was running out.

Pete's eyes were blue, watery, and sad. He smiled at her over the bouncing traffic light and rippling waves, seeming to see her, and yet looking past her somehow so that she couldn't catch his eye. His long hair blew freely around his face, his presence was comforting, and she wanted him to speak to her so that she could hear his voice say that everything was going to be all right.

And, as if he had heard her thought, his image smiled, and nodded reassuringly.

And the first movements that she had seen that were not threatening to her at all started up along the mouth of the alley's tunnel:

There were people—real, live human beings—emerging

from houses, stepping like zombies into the street, stumbling—one step . . . one step . . . one step—their arms hanging limp at their sides and their figures silhouetted by the moon. Their faces were turned to the bay, and their ghostly forms converged along the sidewalks, standing alongside the bubbled mass of monsters in the street as if they were no longer to be viewed as unusual, or dangerous: predator and prey observing the fantastic.

There were more people left alive than Lori had expected there might be, and she was grateful to see them.

She felt like saying, "Hello!"

But she didn't.

She just watched them watching Pete churn Sharthington Bay.

"For you," she said.

And she nodded, understanding that *you* meant everyone, and ready—or at least as ready as she felt she would ever be—for the end.

Up from the water crackled a razor-thin line of blue lightning that climbed so high that she almost lost sight of it. When it finally stopped climbing, it sparkled the underside of a cloud, and a peal of thunder rumbled louder than the steady roar that she had been taking for granted. As soon as the lightning faded, another bolt snapped out, closer to Black Island, splitting itself into three groping branches and revealing that even more clouds had appeared from somewhere farther out over Erie's yawning expanse.

Suddenly, the moon disappeared behind bubbling tufts of rolling thunder that stained the sky a boiling shade of purple, and repeating slashes of light bounced up and down around the shadow that was Black Island. With the moon covered, the sky fell so dark that, just for a moment, Lori thought that she might have closed her eyes. But then she noticed that she could still see the bay, and the silhouetted people, and the alley, all dimly outlined in blue.

She lifted her hand, and it shone blue.

She lifted her eyes, and the bay shone blue.

Blue.

As if from below, the water was glowing, not uniformly,

but brighter here, dimmer there, vivid around the Island and bleeding into sparkling foam as the waves churned themselves into a lather.

More lightning snapped, and, each time it did, the people on the street gasped in unison. A couple of them had raised their arms over their heads, and some were moaning and swaying. Others stood still and clutched their children, or each other. Some stood alone and shook their heads in the face of something that seemed to Lori as alien as anything she could imagine, and, at the same time, as familiar as the lake itself.

Soon, nearly every person she could see had lifted his or her hands, and the bottom of her view bristled with black fingers, stiff in the night, as someone, somewhere, sang out fractured pieces of a couple of old hymns—including a line or two of a Christmas carol—woven together tunelessly into a kind of chant that sounded primitive, and appropriate. Another invisible singer soon piped in, foregoing words to echo the meter expressed by the first, and some people kneeled down.

A lick of foam shot up from behind the Island in a spout that had to be five stories tall. More rock fell, and the Island crumbled.

The ground shook.

People kneeled and sang.

The sky vibrated like a strobe light as hundreds of bolts of lightning climbed both up from the water and down from above.

The traffic light bobbed one last time and then tore free of its wire, crashing down to the pavement and crushing dozens of those white creatures before rolling onto its side, its three different-colored eyes dark beneath a little box, mounted on a nearby pole, flashing, DON'T . . . DON'T . . . DON'T, in amber letters.

The Blood in which Lori sat shimmered blue like the lake, and so did her flesh.

She saw the Island through a yellow cage . . . and then she saw the shore from the bay . . . and then the Island . . . and then the shore. . . .

And she blinked.

And saw blue tunnels, twisting endlessly. . . .

And the Island through yellow wire.

Something fell from overhead and bounced off the cage as the ground lurched. The front of the bank lost a granite lion, and part of Elm Street collapsed, carrying silent people down in a cloud of dust.

Lori blinked, and rolled her head against the cage's wire, a weird, disjointed queasiness climbing through her stomach and a funny, expansive feeling teasing at the back of her mind, making her surroundings seem trivial somehow.

The Island crumbled, and then rose up . . .

She knew it would.

. . . and up.

And she saw It. . . .

A wave lifted a fishing trawler that had to be forty feet long and dropped it twenty yards back, on cracking concrete surrounded by swirling, sinking muck.

People screamed.

People sank.

Lori whispered, "Pete?"

And the Island rose up . . . and up!

The blue shaft of light that blasted through the crack in the lump of ground that had been Black Island turned the night into day and blew a hole in the bubbling sky. With a roar like a tornado, the Island split open, wide, and the light defined every bit of Sharthington's petty masonry, as, from deep inside, things emerged in a churning, hazy blue vomit that ran over rock and gurgled in the water.

There were things moving in the mist, rolling and struggling like misshapen dogs, or fish, or God knew what. They tumbled and flexed, surging up in the light and then down, hopelessly fighting for some kind of stability as their cries were drowned beneath a sucking rush of wind that poured up with them to send spinning chunks of rock hundreds of feet into the air like molten matter from an emerging volcano.

Something formless briefly appeared amid the blue haze and then sank back down.

Smoke rings swirled around the blue beam as it punched its hole in the sky.

Millions of little black licks began spinning up from the hazy hole, and Lori squinted her eyes a little, thinking, Bones.

There were millions and millions of bones in there.

The first hint of the rushing wind reached her, smelling rank, and ancient, like the air from an Egyptian tomb.

"Watch me die!" she screamed, and the street before her collapsed in a rush as something that had been under Sharthington, something upon which Sharthington had rested for years and years, pulled Itself up through the yawning hole in Black Island.

The formless Thing in the haze returned, moved, bled beneath the intense light pouring from the earth, and, then, emerged, for the first time in a hundred years, into open air.

Lori caught her breath.

"Watch me die!"

It was covered with squirming creatures—Its hidden mistakes—and falling bones—more mistakes—undulating without shape and yet substantial and *huge*. It squeezed Itself like a tongue through cracked lips, a little, which was a lot, and then more.

Blood poured from Lori's ears and she couldn't hear anything but a white-noise blare that nearly cracked her skull.

The people left at the alley's mouth all fell to the ground.

Trees fell.

And Shawnita came.

It boiled, and flexed, gurgling up, towering up into a storm Its very presence pulled from the sky. It was *immense*, expanding more with every second, pushing Black Island apart and splitting it up so that each and every stone was defined black before blue light. It stretched up to the sky, pulling Itself like clay, thinner in a sudden tentacle that looked like a tiny lick of Itself but that had to be a hundred feet around and five hundred feet high. And then It deflated and fell back on Itself, only to surge again as it *roared* out, blasting the Island again so that it literally disappeared amid a churning, grinding pool of boiling water so violent that it pushed the hulk of the *Emma*, lying a hundred yards away, over on her side so that dark, dripping lumps of mud and aquatic plants suddenly squirmed in the dark. Lightning crashed all around, and thunder blasted into one steady roar over spinning chunks of something that began falling like hail.

And then Lori saw that what came from the Island was not all there was. It was simply one part, one stretching section of the Thing!

From the churning water, two hundred yards to the west, another water spout swirled up and peeled back to reveal a wavering blue tentacle as tall as the Black Tower had been, and nearly as wide. Farther out from there, another tentacle erupted—and to the east, another, and, up through the police station's parking lot, another, as big as a redwood tree. . . .

The ground rumbled, and concrete split.

People went running.

A crack yawned from the shore to McKinnley Street, splitting the earth and weaving through Sharthington's interior. It split wider, carrying layered chunks of pavement down and then sending them back up as gravel in a blue wash.

The crack groped its way to the shore and disappeared under the lake, which boiled in, rushing through town as if the flood gates had been opened.

Rocks bounced off Lori's cage. . . .

The ground heaved and, then, heaved again.

Sharthington itself seemed to be lifted—to tremble, and then, to hold itself still and high as . . .

A million years It had been alive, Lori knew.

She didn't know how. . . .

A million years It had been beneath the ground.

She didn't know how. . . .

And now It would die.

That she understood.

The ground suddenly fell, and a crashing like a thousand thunderstorms all at once and together exploded as the bay churned and a trunk of shimmering blue flesh surged up, and up, stretching so big that Lori's view couldn't take It all in.

It blasted up, folded like a brain, moving like a snake, as big as a hundred ocean liners balanced on their noses and half hidden by swirling water, mist, and lightning. It glowed an intense blue, It lifted the entire Island with It, submerged the *Emma*, and blazed so bright that every trace of the night was gone. It stretched Itself up into the clouds and exploded with a sound that seemed to say, *"Looorreeee!"* but that was incomprehensible because of its volume and its depth as It pulled Itself into the air and split Itself open so that what was inside burned the night like white-hot syrup, steaming and running in bubbling waves to hiss on bloody water as Lori's eyes squeezed shut reflexively and her hands dug her knees into her chest and her chin pressed down and her brain shut off and her lips said, *"I love you!"* as blue light burned to white and a blast of hot wind swept back her hair and sent dust and dirt slashing through the cage and . . .

Something *big*, something that had grown to be absolutely *huge*, exposed Itself to a world that It had left behind long before Its name was ever spoken by man. Folding in on Itself, the Shawnita rolled, groped one last, desperate time, and, as Lori's world went dark, died.

EPILOGUE

THE ROOM WAS white, tight, overhung with clear plastic bags filled with clear plastic liquid. It smelled like alcohol, rubber, sickness, and smoke.

Lori hated it.

She felt as if she were floating, and her vision was hazy, uncertain, and hard to understand.

There were heavy canvas straps wrapped around her stomach and chest, holding her stiffly and making it hard for her to breathe. Her head was bandaged, and her hands were wrapped. Something soft pressed under her chin, keeping her head erect, and a white sheet lay over her body, contoured to her form, and blood stained. Four clear plastic tubes ran from the bags hanging around her and disappeared beneath her sheet.

A door opened, and a shadowy figure pulled itself into the ambulance, paused, and then crouched, moving closer until it settled itself on her left.

She rolled her head, and tubes quivered.

The man's face was covered with sweat and dark, smeared patches of grime. He had a gas mask hanging around his neck, and his hair was thick with something sooty and black. He was dressed in an orange fireman's raincoat that groaned when he moved, and his features, which were rough, and limp, were vaguely familiar.

He, too, smelled like smoke.

"Lori?" he said softly. "Can you hear me?"

"Uh," Lori said, her voice sounding hollow through the triangular oxygen mask covering her mouth.

The man gently pulled the mask down and then withdrew his hand quickly, as if afraid he might touch her.

"Okay?" he asked.

She nodded.

Voices drifted in through the open door, and she glanced over to it, seeing movement out there.

"What time is it?" she asked, and the effort of speaking made her dizzy.

"Noon," the man answered.

"Noon," she whispered, trying to add hours in her mind. They had gone out to the Island at about eight . . . and then. . . .

She frowned.

"She's the same color, for Christ's sake. We're desecrating good people while she's in there giving orders! It's not right," a voice from outside said, drawing Lori's attention.

She moved her head again—spinning—and looked out through the back of the ambulance.

The big Chevy van that was her hospital room had apparently been parked somewhere close to Rages—right in the middle of the street from what she could tell—and was facing the bay.

The sun was high, and bright, and the water out there was sparkling harshly, hurting her eyes and almost masking the presence of something floating on the water's surface, something lumpy, colorless, and dead. The street was cracked, the concrete ruined; telephone poles were bent and broken, with their wires lying like huge serpents on the ground. People were moving purposefully across the bottom of her view, and a garbage truck rolled by in a ball of dust, a man wearing a red bandanna at the wheel, and arms and legs sticking out of the back, bouncing with the dips in the street.

But the most peculiar thing she saw was something she couldn't see: Black Island. Ever since she had been a little girl, it had been the most prominent feature of Sharthington Bay.

Now, it was gone.

"She should go on the pile with the rest of 'em," the angry voice outside said.

Whisps of smoke blew past the door from somewhere to the left.

She looked back at the man sitting close and studied his face for a time. Finally, she put a name to his features.

Spanner.

Richard Spanner.

He was a doctor.

If it weren't for the ash smeared over his head, his hair would have been grey; and if it weren't for the soot on his face, his complexion would have been pink, and healthy. He was about fifty-five years old, and Lori remembered him as the man who came around at Easter and Christmas, collecting for the American Cancer Society.

He was a nice guy.

He looked tired.

She wanted to help him.

"How are we doing?" he asked, leaning forward and ignoring the grumbling voices outside.

"I'm okay," she whispered, her tongue sticking to the roof of her mouth and her dry lips pulling gently against one another when they parted.

"But how are *we* doing?" Dr. Spanner asked quickly.

The question confused her, and she hesitated before saying, "I don't know."

Dr. Spanner fidgeted in his seat, leaning forward and back and glancing at the open door twice before licking his dirty lips and saying, "But, you've got to know."

"I . . ." she said, and then fell quiet.

Another man had entered the ambulance. He was bigger than the doctor, and was wearing jeans, but no shirt. He was fat, sweaty, and looked like a blacksmith. When he stepped up into the van, the truck dipped back and he wrapped one big fist around a silver handle on the wall. For a moment, he seemed to be thinking about something and, then, apparently decided that he had come far enough.

"What'd she say?" he asked the doctor from the apparent

security of the ambulance's doorway. His voice was gruff, urgent, and directed only at Spanner, as if Lori were not present at all.

"Tell him what I said about her being the same color! Tell him she should go on the pile too!" someone shouted from behind the blacksmith, causing him to look disgusted and wave behind himself for the speaker's silence.

"Lori," Dr. Spanner whispered. "Last night you said you could see them. You told us you knew where they were."

"Last night?" Lori said, swimming through waves and feeling a nauseated sense of emptiness in her stomach.

"Yes!" Dr. Spanner said, more intently. "How are we doing?"

Last night?

She'd seen Pete die last night, she remembered, drifting with the nausea in hopes that if she didn't fight it, it would go away.

She'd seen Pete pull himself up from the Island and die in the moonlight.

It was a noble thing he had done.

I love you, Pete, she thought.

She'd seen him pull himself up from the Island, and then the sky had gone bright, and then everything went dark, and then . . .

She'd been everywhere! She'd closed her eyes and she'd seen, all at once and together, a thousand different places, through a thousand different eyes!

She'd lifted her hand to her face and seen streaks of Joshua's blood—streaks of the Beast's Blood!—running in glowing slashes down her arms and over her skin. She'd seen her own blood, dark against blue light, running in swirls down her legs from the cuts that covered her body.

"The Brain!" she remembered screaming after the Island was gone and the sky returned to its midnight darkness.

"Burn the Brain!"

She'd stumbled out of the alley behind Rages and the pale, zombie faces hovering in the street had turned to her with open mouths. They'd watched her, stared at her, shrunk back from her in a simultaneous and darkly comical wave of fright, and bedazzlement.

"Burn the Brain!" she'd screamed, over and over again, wandering through the street, her arms upraised and her steps little more than a stagger. "It's everywhere. It's there!"

A dead woman lay at her feet, her throat a swollen sack of horrible purple.

"There!" Lori had screamed, pointing down. "And there!" she added, pointing to where Black Island had been.

"Burn the Brain! Burn the Brain! Burn the Brain!"

"How are we doing?" Dr. Spanner asked again.

Lori licked her lips.

Pete was dead.

"Give me a mirror," she whispered, and Dr. Spanner's eyes grew wide.

"Please," she added, and the doctor clenched his teeth so hard that she could see the muscles working in his jaw.

"Tell me first," he said sternly, his eyes searching out the floor.

Lori sighed, and closed her eyes.

And the visions came.

She was everywhere at once, and the sensations of disjointed continuity compounded the nausea in her stomach and made her feel as if she were spinning like a top. She felt so big, so wide and so deep. She was suddenly a woman curled beneath her bed, her head cocked at a peculiar, lethal angle . . . she was a child hiding in a closet . . . a man in a bathroom . . . a boy . . . an old woman and her even older husband . . . she was a hundred different people, all dead, but all *not dead*.

"Better," she whispered, her tongue moving slowly. "There aren't as many now. Keep burning it. Burn the Brain or it'll start again."

She opened her eyes.

And both men were gone.

Next to her cot, there was a silver oxygen tank to which she was connected, and she looked at her own, oddly curved face, reflected on its steel.

They weren't going to let her have a mirror, she knew.

They weren't going to let her have a mirror, and there was a chance that they wouldn't even let her live much longer.

"She's the same color, for Christ's sake."

No mirror for Lori.

". . . the same color."

In the oxygen tank, she could see her eyes, glowing blue.

She sighed, and rested her head back, on her pillow.

Burn the Brain, she thought.

But she knew they'd never find it all in time, because she'd seen the women from Kyrik's basement, and she knew that, because of them, the fight was over.

"Hide," she'd told them in Kyrik's living room. "Hide from everyone. Just hide, out there, in the woods. Just hide!"

And they'd hidden.

They'd had hours—all night in fact—to walk, and find a place to hide.

They were out there somewhere, in a cave, God only knew where. Their throats were swollen, and Lori had seen the cave, and the trees outside the cave's mouth. But she didn't know where the hell that cave was. She couldn't possibly know.

It was time to give up, she decided.

She was Lori Sterling.

She was the girl who had out-toughed a train.

But the Thing that had crawled up from the earth last night was a lot bigger than any train she'd ever seen. Pete had given his life to kill It, but It wouldn't die. It wouldn't ever die, really. It was as much a part of the earth as worms, or water. It was as much a part of life as death. And, as hard as those men out there might try, with their shovels and their trucks, they could only clean out what they could find. They were burning what they could find. . . .

"How are we doing?" they'd asked.

"Better," she'd told them.

And "better" was the truth.

They were doing better.

But still, out there somewhere, in a cave, hidden beneath long, whispy lengths of dripping willow boughs and shadow, It was hiding . . .

She'd told It to hide.

. . . and It was waiting.

She'd told It to wait.

Somewhere, out there, there was a cave, glowing a vivid, healthy, living blue.

Lori closed her eyes, and decided to rest.

She'd earned that much.

She'd earned a rest.